ON THE BIAS

MYSTERIOUS CHARM: BOOK 6

CELIA LAKE

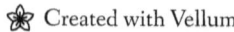

ALSO BY CELIA LAKE

The Mysterious Charm Series
Outcrossing
Goblin Fruit
Magician's Hoard
Wards of the Roses
In The Cards
On The Bias
Seven Sisters

Find a complete list of all my books at celialake.com/books.

Sign up for my newsletter to be the first to hear about future books and learn about fascinating bits of research. Happy reading!

ABOUT ON THE BIAS

Mistress Castalia Jones has built up her dressmaking business stitch by stitch. Comfortably middle-aged, she has apprentices to train, interesting clothing to design, and the freedom to make her own choices. When she overhears uncomfortable gossip about one of her best clients and his fiancee, she finds herself sharing the details with his valet, Benton.

Benton has served Lord Carillon since the Great War, not only at home in Albion, but on a variety of expeditions to distant parts of the globe. Now that his lordship is preparing to marry, Benton knows that things must change. Cassie's information leaves him determined to untangle the confusing hints she has heard. When an encounter with a difficult rooster leaves Benton in need of more direct help – and a steady hand with a needle – they begin to look at each other in a new light. But as people with different lives and commitments, nothing could possibly come of their growing friendship and trust.

~

Join Cassie and Benton in Albion of 1926 for a wardrobe full of magical dresses, three dangerous birds, and a historical costume party that sends the characters reeling.

ONE

"Mistress Castalia? It's ten to two. And you have that appointment."

Cassie had pins in her mouth as she worked on the visible layer of an elaborately pleated dress of a draping rose in a pleasant shade of dusty rose. It made it difficult to answer quickly. She had been trying to arrange the pleating to draw attention to the broad band of plum at the collar and hem, but the folds persisted in falling in the wrong places. She pulled the pins out with a frown, let the fabric loose, and reached for the pin cushion hovering by her hand. Time to leave it for now, and try again later.

"Ma'am? Do you need a hand?" The apprentice shifted nervously, as if she was completely unsure what she was supposed to do with the lack of a verbal response.

Cassie rubbed her face. "Thank you, Joselyn. Go run along and have your tea break." She'd entirely lost track of time, and that wasn't like her.

"Are you sure I can't be a help, ma'am?"

New apprentices were always a bit of a challenge. Some of them came to Cassie with some idea of how to apply magic to cloth, and mediocre sewing skills. Some had sewing skills, but only the barest idea how to use their magic, or what magic could do for them. Or there were those like Joselyn, who had a modest skill with magic and a deft but inexpert hand with a needle, but who needed rather a lot more confidence. On the whole, she preferred the last type, but the first six months were always wearing, and Joselyn was only in her second week.

"He's picking some things up." Cassie smoothed her skirts out, considering for a moment. No, she and her dress had avoided stains and tears today. There was plenty of time to tidy up.

"He, ma'am? Lord Carillon?"

The girl was fascinated. Cassie was quite sure she read the gossip papers, apprentices always did. She had, once, when that sort of thing had held more interest. Now, it just made her feel ancient, for all she was still in her late thirties.

"His valet, I'm sure Lord Carillon has better things to do than pick up clothing. "

Joselyn's shoulder twitched. "But Melitta said he'd been in here."

"That was to oversee some particular fittings." Cassie stretched and stood up. "Come on."

Joselyn followed readily enough, but still looked puzzled. "And these are different?"

"Miss Penhallow is getting a lot of new invitations, of course, people who want to meet her and see for themselves who Lord Carillon is marrying. These are - oh, an afternoon dress, that Nile green one. The evening gown, for the Healing Temple gala. And that one you liked, with the geometric embroidery. Where he and Miss Penhallow gave me more scope, as long as the dresses suit the goals. They approved the colours and the styles, of course, but everything could be fitted on the dummy."

"And you're doing the wedding gown." It wasn't quite a question.

That was on a dressmaker's dummy upstairs, slowly being built up from pieces of whisper-fine silk formed into pleats and folds to make up the bodice. Cassie nodded. "That, two dresses for other wedding events, and a number of other items." Lord Carillon was being most generous, all round.

After rather a long pause, Joselyn said, with an edge of affronted scandal, "Shouldn't it be her lady's maid who picks it up?" It had upset her sense of propriety, then. Joselyn was certain that the rigid formulae within the etiquette books she had inhaled held all the answers - certainly all the approved answers - as to who should do what among the well-off.

"I believe Miss Penhallow's lady's maid is still in training, and not overly familiar with navigating the shops yet. And Benton is quite willing."

"What's he like?" Honestly, it was like having a very energetic puppy. At least she had stopped fretting, for the moment.

"Benton? Competent. Very competent. He's been seeing to Lord Carillon for some years, I believe." She shook her head, and stopped herself before she could comment further on the man. It wasn't proper to pass on her personal concerns to her apprentice.

"Is there something wrong with that, Mistress?" Clearly she hadn't hidden her opinion quite well enough.

Cassie shook her head. "I've never quite understood those who go into service. All those years of work, and what do you have to show for it? If you work for decent folks, you get a cottage in some distant estate, and enough to keep body and soul together. If they're alive long enough to see it arranged. Maybe no children, nothing to pass along - you know a lot of those in service aren't permitted to marry, or even walk out with someone."

She heard Joselyn stop behind her on the stairs. "And you don't approve, ma'am?"

"Not much, no. That's why I have a shop, and I make clothing, and charge as well as I might. I've worked hard to build up quite a nice clientele who appreciate my skills. That's why I own the shop outright, no debts. And why I take on three apprentices at a time." There wasn't much likelihood of her marrying now, never mind children, but she would leave her own legacy, the way she chose.

"Do you think Melitta's learning a lot?" Joselyn was wistful. When Joselyn had visited the shop for three days last autumn to arrange her apprenticeship, she'd got friendly very quickly with Cassie's senior apprentice.

"I'm sure she is. You'll have your season in France, in time. And your season with the weavers, learning the different techniques. Patience, Joselyn, there's a lot to learn, and I'll make sure you learn it all well before you finish your apprenticeship." It was all part of the greater web of masters and mistresses of her art, of clothing and design. They swapped apprentices around, to let them see different needs, different clothes, different styles, different skills.

"Go on. Tea. Get out in the sun for a little, it's clear for a change. Amelia will be back this evening, and you'll want to be fresh to help her sort the fabrics out properly." She didn't want Joselyn underfoot for the pickup. She'd been honest enough, but valets discomfited her. Tying your life - waking, sleeping, meals, every breath - that tightly to someone else, someone who paid you, that made her itch. Lady's maids weren't much better, but at least they had more of a sense of women's clothing.

Beyond that, Benton himself was a particular trial, with his distant judgmental particularity. It was never anything she could quite object to outright, but he was always inclined to nitpick at her work. She was left with the impression that he felt that his service to a lord made him her better, somehow. Even when he could make no particular comment, she felt as if he were looking for the opportunity.

Joselyn bobbed her head. "Do you want me to bring anything back?"

"One of the orange scones if they have one. Or currant."

"Yes'm." There she went, blonde curls bobbing as she finally started down the street. Cassie turned away, and straightened her own dress again, picking threads from the project in the workroom off. Then she sighed and cast the charm that would get them all. Essential in her line of work, that one, whether she was using it to tidy up or gather a lost needle or pin.

She smooshed the loose ends into a small ball and dropped them in the wastebin. Then it was time to check the mirror and tuck her hair in. She leaned in, frowning; she'd have to reapply the brown dye this weekend, the grey was coming through at the roots again. She was not yet established enough that grey was an advantage. Cassie was aware she still needed to trade on new ideas and how she needed to be right up on the changes of mode.

Her body was doing well enough. Her frame had too many curves for the current fashions, but her dress was well cut, of course, and designed to flatter. She'd found a length of a sage green silk and wool mix, more than sturdy enough for a working day, but it hung well.

It would do for now. It wasn't as if Benton would care; he was not one of the society ladies she had to impress with style.

The dresses for Miss Penhallow were all ready, there in their boxes, with an envelope of swatches of the fabric to match them to shoes and accessories tacked to the inside cover of each one. Just as it should be. She had her ways of doing things, tidy and beautiful. Yes, the ribbons holding the boxes were properly tied, the cream of the box contrasting nicely with the dusty blue of the ribbon. It was not quite grey, but a pleasant neutral that allowed the other decorations to shine through.

With a sigh, she turned to settle on the sofa in the front room, spreading her skirts automatically to display the fit and cut of the cloth to best advantage. Her own apprentice mistress had drilled into her that you never knew what would draw the eye or make a sale when it came to clothing. You only knew that shoddy workmanship or any hint of dirt or grime would lose a sale, and probably a customer.

Just in time, as it turned out, because she heard the bell ring as the door opened.

TWO

MONDAY AFTERNOON

I t was Benton, precisely on time. Cassie kept her seat. She stood for the gentlefolk whose clothes she made, not their servants. She had to appreciate that he didn't keep her waiting, but something about how precisely punctual he always was made her feel as if she were failing, somehow.

She was sure he had not started his service as a footman. He was tall enough for it, perhaps five foot nine, but he wasn't nearly handsome enough for a matched pair of tall crisp footmen like some people wanted. His nose had a slight lump, like it had been broken a long time ago, and he was more solid than elegant.

His eyes were a clear blue, too sharp a colour for comfort. His hair was a mousy brown, not something with a good contrast, and his skin was worn, like he'd spent far more time in the sun than most. She wondered, not for the first time, how he'd got his job, if he'd not been a footman.

He was different from the other valets she'd met. The few others she saw, they were glad for a break in their day, inclined to flirt with her apprentices. Mr Benton, in contrast, seemed to view each appointment as a small mountain to be summited successfully, and on a tight schedule.

"Mr Benton."

She could see the almost-entirely suppressed wince at the proper title, as if he preferred not to be noticed, never mind addressed. "Mistress Castalia." His reply was precise, measured.

"The boxes are ready, and it was a pleasure to work on them. Miss Penhallow has a lovely sense of taste." And then, teasingly, she added. "And a willingness to be guided by Lord Carillon's preferences."

That got a momentary bristling, like a badger's hackles going up. That baffled her, that he should be so touchy about a compliment to his master, but clearly he was. Then he nodded once. "I will convey your compliments, Mistress. His lordship asked that I see to the bill, if you have it ready." It wasn't a question.

She'd noticed Benton rarely asked questions, everything was a statement, as if he'd been playing chess with you in his head and was a dozen moves ahead. Cassie appreciated people who were prepared to do business, but this constant challenge put her teeth on edge and made her want to flee back to her work room's peace and privacy. Of course, that was not the way to keep her business going.

Instead, Cassie inclined her head, and kept her voice pleasant. "Of course." She held out the envelope waiting on the side table to her left. That in turn obliged Benton to come closer, and he took it from her hands.

He pulled a small pocket-knife from his coat pocket, as if he used it dozens of times a day, and slit the wax seal, then glanced through the list. "His lordship will expect I've made sure that all the listed items are there."

Someone else might have shrugged and said he'd trust her. Most other people did, in fact. But Benton, blast him, would always check. Part of her always wanted to leave the boxes unfastened, to avoid several steps in this mandatory dance, but the rest of her rebelled at offering less than her best, particularly for him.

"Of course. He always does." How much was actually Lord Carillon's expectation, and how much was Benton puffing up his authority, she had no idea. Her other clients trusted her craftsmanship. For that matter, Benton wasn't even her client, just the delivery boy.

Slowly, taking her time, she stood, moving to place the boxes side by side on the long table. She undid the ribbons on the top of each box, removing each lid. "The swatches of the fabric, to match for the shoes."

Again, precisely as they always were.

Benton waited until she took a step back, to the side of the table, then he glanced at the invoice. "Day dress, Nile green, pearls, cream lace." He peered, found the proper box, and considered. "This is not Nile green."

Cassie blinked, momentarily uncertain. The dress was a pleasant yellow-green, a colour that not many people could wear well, but it would suit Miss Penhallow's blonde hair and fair skin in certain settings. With a cream shift, and a matching cream shawl and hat, the colour would stand out more, vivid and bright for the summer.

"The Nile is not this colour. The Nile is never this colour. This is the colour of poor-quality overdyed jade." He frowned for a moment. "Or possibly a muted arsenic green. We are having none of that." His voice was firm, unyielding, but not quite on the boundary with rude.

Cassie took a deep breath, counted to ten, and then for good measure from ten to one in French. She made herself smile, knowing that forcing the seeming would carry some of what she was going to say. "You are seeing it in the box, without the cream shift behind. Lord Carillon was here for the initial consultation, and approved the colour choice. It brings out Miss Penhallow's complexion very well, and it is quite fashionable this season." Muted arsenic green, indeed. As if she would.

More to the point, colour names might reflect a thing in the physical world, but it wasn't as if the colour was the river, nor claiming to be. Egyptomania made the term popular at the moment, and she admitted she liked the implied changeability. But it was, really, a somewhat more saturated celadon green, sometimes shading to a blueish green. It wasn't a colour you could pin down, even if Mr Benton vastly preferred that. He'd done it to her before, with a debate about garnet red that had stuck for months.

"It would suit the younger Miss Penhallow better. Are you certain you have not made a mistake?" The edge to his tone made him sound even more disagreeable, and she had to assume it was on purpose. He had never seemed a man to be offensive by accident.

Cassie drew herself up to her full height, not that it helped here, he was still a head taller. "Quite certain. It is a day dress, it is an appropriate colour for a day dress this season, and for wearing to the party that Miss Penhallow will wear it to. The colour was chosen for precise reasons I would not expect you to understand."

Benton's chin went up, stubborn and insistent. He was bracing himself, she could tell that. Not a boxer, she thought, but he'd spent some time doing something that made his heels dig in, and his back brace. His eyes were fixed on her, equally unyielding.

Cassie shrugged one shoulder, refusing to engage him

on the ground he'd tried to claim. "Are you questioning his lordship's decision? I have the order, in his hand, in my files, complete with the swatches of each fabric."

Those were fighting words, and they both knew it. Cassie held her breath, waiting to see what Benton did next, if he'd be sensible, or if he'd be bull-headed enough to keep pushing.

There was a long pause, then he said, "The second box. An evening dress for the Healing Temple charity auction." There was a tiny pause. "I understand you are still working on her gown for the end of summer ball." That was a much more time-consuming project, far more so than the day dresses or even routine evening gowns.

"The constellation dress, yes." She was capable of acknowledging an impasse. Now if he would do his part and drop the subject, they could get this over with. "I have kept his lordship informed of the progress for the gala gown. He approved the crystals for the work last week, and they will be applied once I receive them back from the enchanter."

They would be shimmering in a pattern of sparkling light, and would have to be applied in precise sequence. It was a matter of complexity and precision, and a moment's distraction on her part might mean a misplaced gem that could ruin the effect entirely. Cassie was looking forward to the challenge, it was the kind of thing that would not only get her name circulated among potential clients, but impress the masters and mistresses of her guild.

It was a more interesting project than the client who just wanted a massive shimmering peacock tail. In that case, the real challenge was keeping feathers in decent condition all night, not the dress design. The enchantments for the plumes were comparatively routine, and Amelia had a deft hand with them. Joselyn would not be prepared to learn

them until she settled down a bit, but she could learn how
to set out the feathers. And of course the client would not
care that she was asking for senior apprentice work so long
as it looked impressive.

Benton nodded, then indicated the second box. "The
cut on this, is it as requested?"

"The robe de style." She gestured. "You see the bodice,
the drop waist, the side panels. On some women it might
look a little frumpy, compared to flapper dress. In this
company, with many of older generations there, it will seem
more respectful. Modish but not offensively nouveau."

She considered, then added, "Robin's egg blue is fashionable. This is a slightly darker shade, due to the silk taking
up the colour particularly well, that brings out Miss Penhallow's eyes. Lord Carillon mentioned he had some jewellery
specifically in mind, I believe star sapphires?"

"His lordship's taste in gems is exquisite." Benton was
clipped and precise, and delivered the comment as if he
expected her to be ignorant on the matter. "I will be picking
up the necklace next week." He glanced at the box. "And
this is appropriately fitted for Miss Penhallow?"

"Of course. I guarantee my fittings for two weeks, and
after that I am glad to adjust the charms. He is aware of my
fees for household visits." Sizeable fees, because she hated
being dragged out to some goddess-forsaken country home
full of bats - both literal and more metaphorical. Especially
when her client mostly wanted her ego stroked. It took her
away from the sewing and designing, which she would
always rather be doing.

Benton frowned, and then continued. "The last box, a
tea dress, suitable for multiple events with different parties."

Cassie gestured. "This one here, silk, that deep lavender, with the long sleeves. As requested, there are several

shawls and an overdress to match the embroidery- you see the Egyptian-influenced design here, along the cuffs and hem. Smaller and elegant, as Miss Penhallow requested, but the colours stand out rather nicely. You will notice the longer hem, since this is for going out, we handled the tea dresses for at home wear last month." Cassie's words were clipped with stifled aggravation. If explaining each detail was necessary so he would stop arguing, well, she could and would explain every detail.

"And the shawls?"

"This smaller box here, rolled. I would not recommend unrolling them, they have been stored to avoid wrinkles. It would take me at least a quarter hour to rebox them properly." If the infuriating man would not respect her competence, perhaps he would at least consider respecting her time, or his own.

THREE

MONDAY AFTERNOON

Benton frowned. Lord Carillon favoured Mistress Castalia, and there were solid reasons for that. She and her apprentices and whoever did the piecework were skilled and attentive. One did not have to worry about poor seams or inadequate fit. She had a knack for getting hold of unusual fabrics, and of using them in ways that highlighted the wearer's best features, whatever those were. She was not the most modish dressmaker in Trellech, and certainly not in Albion, but she knew her work.

And, Benton knew, she was quiet about the requests, and did not gossip. That was worth quite a lot of money and repeat custom indeed. His lordship had been her patron for pieces for former partners, both public and more private.

Did she have to be so difficult, though? Every other artisan he dealt with on his lordship's behalf was much simpler. A review of the order, an exchange of funds, and he was out of there and onto the next task. There was always a next task. And she always had the boxes done up and tied, even though he must know by now she would insist on seeing them. Stubborn, just like she was stubborn about those ridiculous names for colours.

The supposed Nile green was only the latest in a long line of silliness. Australien, a curious ruddy sand colour. Drake's-neck green, which utterly failed to get the shimmer of the duck itself. There was even one called lusty gallant, which Mistress Castalia had sworn at some point was highly historical. It seemed very dubious to him.

Here and now, though, he could only nod. "In that case, I have the coin." He stood, coming to her desk as she sat down behind it, so she could test the coins on her scale. Any other merchant would have trusted his lordship's money, and she never did. It irked him.

Irked him enough this time that he asked, "Why do you count? You must know how it will come out."

Her fingers moved to stack the coins and weigh them, groups of five, moving them onto and off the scale briskly. She did several sets before she glanced up at him. "Some people will try to pass off fake coin." Another set, letting the coins clink lightly. "If I only tested some, people would wonder why. It is far more fair to weigh them all."

Benton frowned, but the logic was sound enough, and it did not leave him room to argue. And after all, he insisted on inspecting each item he was picking up, every time, so he had to acknowledge at least privately that an objection would be hypocritical. Instead, he retreated to the sofa and settled, waiting while she confirmed the stacks of coins.

When she was finished, she turned to drop the coins into a coin box, one of the better sort that would only release for the owner or the bank key. He also knew she would not move on to the next portion of the discussion until she was ready. She made notes in her register, and then elsewhere in the ledger, the pen nib scratching slightly across the paper.

Finally, she stood, and came around her desk again. "Does Miss Penhallow have further requests?"

Benton nodded. "His lordship hopes you can find time in your schedule for several additional items. As well as the ongoing work on the wedding dress. One to be kept private until the wedding, if you please." His voice was crisp.

"Of course. A present for the bride?"

"He wishes a velvet cloak, with mapwork upon it. A mix of locations, he has included some initial sketches, and wishes to consult on drape. Usual fees for tying up a dress-maker's dummy."

Benton could see the calculations running across Mistress Castalia's face. He wasn't sure what she was calcu-lating, precisely, but he could see the pieces being worked through. She returned to her desk, and made a few nota-tions and looked at the calendar. "I'll need to buy another dummy, if he wishes me to book it out that long."

He paused. His lordship's wishes on this matter were quite clear, and Benton was granted quite a lot of authority with the budget.

Mistress Castalia tapped the table, as if she were irri-tated with his silence. "May I see the sketches?" Her voice was clipped and precise again, though always exactingly polite.

Benton turned, drawing a portfolio out of the satchel he'd brought in. "Mistress."

She opened it, flicked through the pages, glancing at the overall design, then a "A full circle. Velvet. Sepia tones like the map, that will take some quite tricky dyework to make it look suitably organic and aged." She then considered. "Miss Penhallow's colouring would not be favoured by a true sepia."

"His lordship is open to suggestions on that front, so

long as it maintains the," the correct phrasing was difficult to find immediately, "overall scheme."

She frowned. "I will need to consult with him, and promptly. The dye is a complex question. What is his availability next week?"

Benton did not need to consult the calendar, as he had of course anticipated the likelihood of this question. "He will be in town on Tuesday or Friday, and available for an hour's appointment between two and four either day."

Mistress Castalia nodded, then tapped the sketches. "Tuesday at two, please. I will discuss the fee for the dummy with him then too."

Benton nodded. "As you wish, mistress." He then coughed. "And the others?"

She held her hand out for the list. His lordship had made a tidy summary of requirements, and she glanced down it, looking at the notes on decoration. "It has become quite difficult to get the glass beads that take those particular colour effects he likes. I will have to consult the supplier again, but may have limitations on colour. We can discuss that on Tuesday. And I'm afraid the weaver who did those Art Deco embroidery bands is not available for orders for the foreseeable future. It's a health issue of some kind. I have been exceedingly unsatisfied with the current alternatives but I will investigate the options and have samples and sketches of what is available ready."

Benton inclined his head. "I will let his lordship know. If you have alternate suggestions, Tuesday?"

She nodded, then she tapped a couple of the items on the list. "These day dresses. I thought he had said that her daytime wardrobe was more than adequate?" Mistress Castalia pursed her lips. "These seem a bit dull."

"Miss Penhallow has been invited to join several charitable committees, and wishes to make a good impression as a woman who can dress to suit the occasion." Benton kept his voice even, but he had been uncertain about that as well. It was one of those small niggling doubts that would worry him until he could identify and deal with the cause. Something about these plans had bothered him from the start.

"Which charities? I may be able to suggest some alternative ensembles. And avoid... similarity to other notable attendees."

Benton frowned. His lordship had not specifically mentioned the charities, but of course he had taken the invitation replies back, and could name them. He almost thought to suggest Mistress Castalia add that to the agenda for Tuesday, but Miss Penhallow would need one of the dresses quite soon. "The Ladies Auxiliary Society for Services to Orphans of Magical Catastrophes," he said, after a moment, "The Distaff Council on Horticultural Aid To The Needy. And the Albion Inheritance."

Mistress Castalia frowned again, and then said "So, Lady Pillon, Mistress Waterby, Dame Arcady, and their respective sets." She considered. "No, this won't do. The first dress, the smoke grey. It will clash with whatever flowers Dame Arcady picks for the Inheritance luncheon."

Benton blinked, sufficiently puzzled to find himself needing to ask. It was galling to need to, she always had an air of explaining the obvious to a fool. More than that, he prided himself on picking up cues and information without resorting to an explicit question about Dame Arcady. "Surely smoke grey is a neutral?"

"That," Mistress Castalia said, "Is a mistake."

It was no kind of answer at all. Benton raised an eyebrow, and Mistress Castalia let out a long sigh. "She will set out the hall in shades of cream, with an underlying yellow, rose, or brown tint - sepia, if you like. Against that, a pale smoke grey will look washed out. Miss Penhallow cannot wear sallow tones well, it conflicts with her hair and her skin, she needs something with a little blue underneath it."

She stood abruptly, startling him, and went to a large chest of drawers behind her desk, flicking her fingers along until she pulled out a drawer. Her movements, the sharpness of them, the unpredictability, was putting him on edge, but at least now she was focused on the cabinet.

Inside were swatches of fabric, and she pulled it out, peering at them. To his eye, they were very similar shades of a blue grey. She drew out two samples from that draw, then added a swatch of deep green-grey, like a pine forest at twilight. Then, as if it were a last minute decision, she turned to another drawer and drew out a swatch of vibrant deep blue, a hair brighter than navy. He began to see the difference.

"Please ask Miss Penhallow and Lord Carillon to let me know which of these they would prefer. I would expect to pair it with a pale grey, or possibly a white or cream. Alternately, we could look at some shades of plum or perhaps violet." She turned and added two more swatches from a different cabinet.

It was so quick and abrupt Benton felt as if he had completely lost his footing and tumbled, head over heels, even as he remained planted quite properly on his own two feet. But he nodded, bowed slightly over her hand, and simply said, "Mistress." No matter how her sudden changes and precipitous shifts disconcerted him, it would never do to show that she had put him in a position where he had to scramble to keep his thoughts sorted.

There was a long pause, then Mistress Castalia said, "I

would be interested to learn Lord Carillon's priorities in those social engagements. And Miss Penhallow's, of course." The way she spoke, it sounded very much like she knew it was his lordship's analysis that mattered here. Miss Penhallow had a fine eye, but his lordship was one the making many of the decisions. It wasn't entirely proper, and people noticing it as Mistress Castalia had made Benton ill at ease.

This at least had an easier answer. "I will let his lordship know about your inquiry, Mistress."

She opened her mouth, snapped it closed, and then said, "Two of the three have current boards whose priorities may not align with Miss Penhallow's. I am not, you understand, aware of all the eddies and currents of such groups, as a working woman."

Benton glanced up, barely avoiding a frown. Those were indeed groups for the wealthy, who could spend their days in gatherings and meetings, not working for a living. He was surprised Mistress Castalia knew as much as she did. Certainly for all his attempts to pick up gossip below-stairs in his lordship's clubs and at house parties, the gatherings of women still remained largely opaque. "Mistress." It was the only thing to say.

She waved her hand. "I will be pleased to receive Lord Carillon at two on Tuesday. We can discuss further then, and I will have a few additional ideas." She stood, almost wearily, and came back around to the table to retie the boxes.

Benton left her to it without further interruption.

FOUR

MONDAY AFTERNOON AT YTENE, LORD
CARILLON'S ESTATE IN THE NEW FOREST

"Back, then, Benton?"

Benton was carefully levitating all three boxes in through the servant's entrance, partly to make sure the boxes stayed level and wouldn't cause wrinkles, but at least as much because it kept him in practice for when the port needed to be moved without any jostling. "Yes, Mrs Mudthon. Is Mally about?"

"You will have to get used to saying Miss Stone, properly, you know."

Benton grinned, for just a moment. It was a relief to be back at Ytene, where he knew everyone, and everyone knew their role in the household. "When she's properly a lady's maid, I will." At the moment, she was still learning the art. Mally helped Miss Penhallow when she was in residence, and at the moment that was mostly for parties and particular social occasions.

The rest of Mally's time was currently taken up with a series of lessons on clothing and jewellery for every possible kind of event. She'd already known a number of cleaning magics, how to handle the delicate fabrics, and a modest amount of hair styling, but there were new things to learn there as well, to be suitable for his lordship's wife-to-be.

Mrs Mudthon waved a hand. "She's in the hall with the good light and some sewing. And Mrs Grieves wanted a word when you got in. About the dinner party."

The housekeeper was still finding her feet, though she'd been here a month now, and seemed a better fit than her predecessor. However, this would be the first formal dinner party since she'd taken over. She'd been in service for more than twenty years, but Benton realised she must be nervous, learning the ways of a new household and a notoriously untraditional one.

Benton nodded. "Please do let her know I'm back, and will come find her as soon as I've got the clothing up to Miss Penhallow's rooms."

The cook waved him off. Benton was glad to see she was in so pleasant a mood. Mrs Mudthon was normally cheerful, but the previous housekeeper had turned out to be a poor fit. Despite claiming flexibility and adaptability in her interviews, she had turned out to be one of those who wanted everything done her way. None of them needed more of the icy distance Mrs Mudthon could and would produce if she felt overly managed by anyone other than his lordship. He had been afraid Mrs Grieves would make the same sorts of errors.

Fortunately, Mrs Grieves had meant it when she said she preferred to manage with a light hand, and had quite won Mrs Mudthon over. He gathered it had been tidily done by listening thoughtfully to the kitchen needs, confirming the priorities, and asking that some of Mrs Mudthon's famous biscuits were available for her meetings with his lordship.

That brought him to the servant's hall. Mally was at a

chair by the window, with the strong light, working on a fine seam on a handkerchief, part of her training. "Mally, I've come from Mistress Castalia's. Shall I bring the boxes up so you can unpack them?"

"Thank you, please, Mr Benton." Benton liked that about her, her courtesy, and using the proper title for within the household. They would be working closely together, and quite possibly for many years to come. She set aside the sewing, tucking it tidily into her work basket before following him to the stairs.

He concentrated on bringing the boxes smoothly up the servant's stairs to the suite Miss Penhallow had taken for her visits. Of course, she generally spent the nights in his lordship's rooms, but appearances must be maintained. They rarely hosted overnight guests here at the moment, but when they did the hidden passage from her suite to his lordship's rooms was quite useful.

He set the boxes down on the long table in the sitting area. "If I might have that envelope in the top box, it has some swatches for his lordship's evaluation."

Mally nodded, untying the top box and lifting the lid to set it aside. "Oh, this is fine work, Mr Benton. And Miss Penhallow will look quite striking in them. I'll see they're all properly hung, if you'd let his lordship know?"

She let her fingers trace along the decoration on the blue dress, and Benton had to admit it was eye-catching, made of twisted ribbons in four shades of coordinating blues that twined around each other. It had an effect like waves, without the sharpness of the peaks.

Benton nodded. "Thank you." With that, he withdrew, and went back downstairs to see if Mrs Grieves was available. He knocked on her sitting room, once, just loudly enough to be heard but not so much it might wake her from a nap.

"Come." He opened the door, and found her at her table working on some of the household accounts. Her hair was up in a tidy bun, she'd removed the apron from morning work, and she looked really quite content. "Ah, Benton. Is his lordship back?"

"Not yet. He said not to expect him until half-five, he had an appointment at the Explorer's Club."

"I wanted to ask you about the menu for next week, so we can put the orders in well in advance. Mrs Mudthon mentioned that some of the guests had a few particular needs. Do you have a moment now?" She sounded uncertain.

"Ah, yes. I am not sure if you are familiar with the culinary customs of different communities? Religious ones, in this case."

She frowned, then shook her head. "Not in detail, no. My previous employers..." Her voice trailed off, and Benton smiled, because he could tell she was trying especially hard not to give offence. "My previous employers entertained within a rather narrow set of social acquaintances. Part of what attracted me to the position was the opportunity for more variety."

"There should be no pork product used in their meals, nor shellfish, nor gelatin. The couple do not eat meat - that includes poultry but not fish - and dairy in the same meal. I would suggest a vegetarian alternative for the roast, the fish can be unaltered, and you may then use butter freely and cream throughout. Mrs Mudthon does a very pleasant nut roast."

"Mrs Mudthon is aware?"

"She has had the pleasure of serving Mr and Mrs Leventhal in the past, yes. There will be no difficulty."

Mrs Grieves nodded, with some apparent relief. "I did not wish to speak on her behalf, as to the arrangements." That was quite proper.

"She will be glad to suggest several options, and his lordship has authorised whatever necessary additional expenses from the housekeeping budget."

"Oh, well, then." She considered. "Are they pleasant people?" Her tone was uncertain.

Benton nodded. "Very pleasant, Mrs Grieves, and they appreciate his lordship's interest in fine books. Mr Leventhal is a dealer in antiques including older books, and his wife assists in his work and some translation. I gather she speaks and reads half a dozen languages."

"Oh, I suppose that's the sort of thing would please his lordship, all his travels." The information seemed to settle everything in her mind, and she would clearly be on to her next needful thing immediately.

Benton was glad of an explanation that made sense to her, and more to the point that she was not taking offense at other people's customs. That would do badly here. "Do you have questions about the evening? It's rather an example of his lordship's range of connections."

"I had gathered that, Mr Benton." She paused, as if trying to figure out what to ask. He settled back, quite willing to be patient.

"Would it be a bother to tell me a bit about his lordship's social circles, Mr Benton? I would prefer not to rely on hearsay and gossip." Then she gestured. "I could see about a cup of tea, and some biscuits?"

He smiled at her. "Oh, I would be glad, and thank you."

She nodded, summoned the kitchen maid with a bell, and made her request. They sat in quiet for a minute or so - the water was usually on the boil this time of day - until the maid came back with a tray. "Scones, ma'am, freshly glazed."

These were some of Benton's favourites. Mrs Mudthon was in quite a good mood, then. She didn't normally fuss with the glaze, not unless the food was going upstairs. They took a little time to arrange things to their liking, letting the tea steep. Finally, Benton said, "You understand his lordship was the younger son, and thus a certain degree of freedom was permitted to him?"

Mrs Grieves ventured an almost teasing. "Quite a lot, I gather he's a member of the Explorer's Club in his own right several times over. Were you with him on his expeditions?"

"Yes, after the War, though he went on a number of expeditions before that, as well. I was his soldier-servant in the trenches, followed him to his later postings, then entered his service formally when I was demobbed afterwards. He preferred my service, he said. He maintained a cook-housekeeper at the Trellech house when he was in residence there. I have seen to his personal needs from 1918 to his return here to Ytene three years ago."

"And Mrs Mudthon is a family retainer from his childhood?"

Benton nodded. "Here, although we redid the kitchens before she took up a post again. She had gone to other service when his lordship's elder brother held the title and the magic. They preferred the estate in Cumbria as their primary residence and reduced the staff here significantly."

Whereas his lordship, in part, found Hawk's Breath to be tangled up with too many memories of other times. And, Benton thought, he found the fields and meadows of

Cumbria too exposed for his comfort these days, and preferred the sheltering forests around Ytene.

"And his lordship's social circles?" She had returned to that, then. Her voice was polite, but still had an unsettled note. It would be best, and kindest, to spell things out then. He was at least getting a much better sense of her priorities and values from this.

"Quite varied. You may have heard his lordship had a fondness for opera singers, and that is quite true, and musicians of all kinds." Male and female, as it were, and that was a tidier place to find a pleasant temporary pairing than many others. Also, when phrased that way, people generally assumed it was the sopranos he was interested in, not the tenors. That was sometimes a help.

"He has cultivated connections with a number of artists, and he finds many of the more modern approaches intellectually interesting. Though aesthetically speaking, his purchases tend toward the neo-Classical or at least the Arts and Crafts set, rather than modernism."

He could see the terms did not make a particular impression on her, but that was fine. They hadn't on him before he'd spent significant time with his lordship. "There will be two singers - brother and sister - at this gathering. Miss Alice Fortescue and Mr Leopold Fortescue. Both have excellent reputations as singers. Mrs Gates, from the bookshop in the village, she knows the Leventhals." She was making up the numbers. "Also in attendance, Professor Isambard Fortier, from Schola, he teaches some of the martial skills."

"French, Benton?"

He shook his head. "Oh, no, that family's been here for a long time. The Norman conquest, I think, originally, some of the earliest Third Families." Not as noble a line as his

Lordship's, the way the Great Families counted things, but venerable.

"His older brother has the lordship at Arundel, and he's a member of the Council."

"Council, my." Mrs Grieves was not sure what to make of that, he could tell. Frankly, Benton wasn't sure what he thought of it either. The Ministry was straightforward enough, but the Council acted in ways rather beyond the compass of the Lords like his lordship, with an eye to national magics that had not been anchored in a king or queen since the death of Richard III.

"Council, indeed. And, I gather, quite respected in certain Ministry circles, for an inventive approach to materia and enchantment work. His lordship is socially familiar with Lord Fortier, but he has never been invited here for a smaller gathering. The wedding, though, perhaps." Which would mean dealing with Lady Fortier, who could be exceedingly difficult, but he would not borrow that trouble just yet.

"And the Professor?"

A much easier question, that. "Professor Fortier is the younger son. He had quite a reputation as a playboy, before and just after the War."

"Such a thing." Again, he couldn't quite read her yet. He hadn't had nearly enough time to observe her, not in all the possible moods and situations that might come up. This time, he wasn't sure if she thought the stars entirely too foolish, had a fondness for them herself, or disapproved of women working when they didn't have to.

By this point, he could at least tell that Mrs Grieves wasn't sure if this was better or worse than an opera singer, or pair of them.

She did continue, though, fairly promptly, with another

question. "Is Professor Fortier inclined to be difficult? With the staff, I mean. If he was a playboy."

"Oh, goodness, no. You needn't warn the maids on his account, or the footmen. I believe his lordship is hoping to broaden the acquaintance." Which implied a certain amount of decent behaviour with the staff.

Mrs Grieves was about to ask something else. Before she could, there was a knock, and the kitchen maid. "Begging your pardon, Mrs Grieves, but Mrs Mudthon said the butcher's here with a question about the orders." It was the ordinary sort of need in a large house.

Benton stood. "I'll let you get on. I'll be upstairs in his lordship's room if I'm needed."

FIVE

WEDNESDAY THE 3RD OF JUNE IN TRELLECH

The current clients were taking their time. That was part of the service, of course. Women like them continued to come to shops like hers, rather than either having a dressmaker come to their home, or exploring the ready-to-wear options in the larger cities, so as to linger and gossip in a discreet location.

These three were all related by marriage, or nearly so. There were three brothers, two married and one about to be, all in their twenties. They were all rather similar in look, dark haired and dark eyed with sharp features, a bit like foxes drawn in india ink.

The women, though, looked nothing alike. Isalanda was blonde with what so many people called the classic English rose complexion. Aine was a redhead so pale-skinned that only striking deep colours would do. Finding clothing that would play well against their husbands was a challenge. None of the brothers were likely to pay attention to that, though at least they mostly preferred the kind of minimalist unadorned suits and robes that made it easy to create a suitable counterpoint.

Then there was the new one, who was marrying in. Mabel was a brunette in her twenties with skin that looked like she basked in the sun year round. This was Wales, so that seemed unlikely. At the moment, they were examining her summer samples, trying to decide which to have made up, and in what colours.

Cassie had been rather pleased with how the summer line had come out as a collection. Waistlines had dropped, allowing for long lines, down to a shorter skirt, and a variety of fashionable options for gathers, lace, or even frills. Not that Cassie ran to frills, but she did like the effects of a well-done bit of pleating.

She had been particularly proud of a design with a long straight fall of loose-draping silk or linen, down to a low waist, with a contrasting ribbon run through to set off the skirt. It made it easy to vary, so her clients would not risk wearing the same dress as someone else at a gathering, while being quite simple to make up quickly.

The differences in colouring had made setting out clothing for these three rather challenging, and their shapes were just as different. Aine had the fashionable shape of the flappers, which was not the crowd Cassie usually catered for, and Isalanda had strong opinions about what features to accentuate or obscure. Mabel, however, didn't have opinions, or rather, she was not being permitted to express them. That was never a good sign, either for a dress fitting or a marriage.

Cassie waved a hand for Joselyn to walk through. Having an assistant who could model made some things easier, at least. She watched, as the apprentice dutifully stepped out in a pale green tea gown, the hemline just below the knees. It skimmed past Joselyn's hips, hinting at what was beneath.

Cassie had rather liked the decoration on this, a simple pattern of embroidery in a contrasting golden yellow, angling down in a long deep V shape to below the waistline. It drew the eye, and caught the attention. "Oh, that's a rather better look on than it was on the hanger."

It was, that was why having a living model was critical to the business. "Of course, Isalanda." That was the blonde. "This shade would be a lovely one for you, complimenting your complexion. And Aine, there's a lovely rich blue that might suit you, I've a sample of the fabric here, and I've plenty to make a dress. And of course, I can do the embroidery in whatever colour you might prefer, or even inset a piece of ribbon or other decoration."

"I feel quite fatigued. A break for tea, please." Isalanda's voice was crisp and rather sharp. Bother. She was quite clear about having control over the others, and this was yet another interruption to the process of making a decision. Perhaps she was irked that Aine had been addressed out of turn.

Cassie tried not to let her frustration show, just nodding. At this rate, they would be here all day. "Of course. Joselyn, dear, run along and change out of that and then go round next door for the order. I'll just put the kettle on, mesdames." Joselyn nodded, and disappeared into the back.

"You really should have someone for the tea, Mistress Castalia." Isalanda was also the most likely to disapprove of everything.

"Oh, I always feel so harried, asking someone to run around after me. We have a woman who comes in for the heavy cleaning, of course, that's different, and the laundry goes out to specialists."

"Surely you don't cook?" Aine sounded like the idea

entirely offended her. Cassie did actually enjoy cooking. It was a pleasure to create things with her hands that didn't involve a needle, but she did it rarely during the week.

"Living in Trellech, it's easy enough. The apprentices eat at their boarding houses, and there's half a dozen restaurants near here that are all quite glad to pack things up for me. Sandwiches and such keep quite well too. It's such a blessing on busy days, not to have to worry about when a hot meal might be ready. Or burning."

The eldest of the three tsked slightly. "Not at all our thing."

Cassie was quite sure they had dozens of servants, in total, probably all horribly treated and having to pretend they were grateful for every scrap and the rare afternoon off. Cassie found it difficult enough to be patient with women like Isalanda or Aine for an afternoon, she couldn't imagine putting up with them at all hours. Surely there were other options, even if everyone couldn't run their own shops.

Cassie shook her head, then took a moment to tidy the dresses so far onto hangers and away from the sofa and tables. "Just give me a minute to get the tea going, and I'll be right back."

She ducked into the side gallery and glanced at the mirrors and illusion projections that allowed to see her if customers pried into closed drawers or attempted to make off with any of her stock. Normally she'd have one of the apprentices out there, but she was short handed again with Amelia off again overseeing the finishing of some weaving in Spitalfields. Make do must do, as her mother had said. Repeatedly.

The youngest woman was running her hands over one of the dresses on the mannequins, like she wasn't used to the cloth yet. She'd heard a rumour the woman had come from America. Somewhere outside of Albion, at least. She spoke very little, so Cassie hadn't been able to tell from the accent. This might be her introduction to these kinds of clothes, and this kind of money to spend.

The three of them fell into gossip, or at least the elder two did. Of course they were the type to ignore her presence as soon as she left the room. It was the usual sort of thing Cassie heard. People buying clothes would tend to talk about what they were buying the clothes for. She kept working on the tea, making sure not to make too much noise.

A glance in the mirror showed Mabel looking at one of the dresses, a tea dress of deeper violet with a layer of delicate silk draping over it. At first, Cassie couldn't tell if it were the dress, the fabric, or the colour that was drawing her attention, but then the way Mabel fingered the silk gave her the clue.

"No, Mabel, that won't do at all. He might be of questionable tastes, but one doesn't dare show up at something like a wedding in a dress that informal."

Mabel looked crushed but shook her head, as if about to say something. It was a pleasant dress, certainly suitable for an afternoon event, and Mabel would need something like that. Not suitable for the current expedition, though, which was a dress for Lord Carillon's wedding and a few surrounding events.

Aine draped herself against the sofa's arm and cut her off. "Do explain, Isa, you know Mabel doesn't know the difference." It was drawling, the kind of tone that sounded easy going, but Cassie could hear the cutting edge in her tone, the implied insult to Mabel.

"Oh, well. There are rumours going about regarding Lord Carillon's preferences, in bed and out of bed. And his fiancée, well, she's certainly not the sort of beauty she should be, marrying someone from that kind of family."

Mabel's voice was quiet. "Preferences?" Cassie considered. She'd thought Mabel somewhat cowed, but no, this was more like letting the others show their hands. She'd heard the youngest brother was a more decent sort. Perhaps they might make a go of it, then.

"That he prefers men, dear. You have that in America, don't you? What do you call them there?"

"It's not a thing people talk about much." Mabel's voice was a little louder. "His fiancée?"

"There was an awful scandal five or six years ago, her father and uncle and some exploration that lost a lot of money. I can't believe she can hold her head up in proper society." There was a twitch of Aine's shoulder. "Oh, she's not bad looking when she makes the effort, but it's all his money doing that, not any natural gift for it."

Isalanda snorted. "Well, we can't all be born stunning, Aine." There was the flick of a glance at Mabel, a pointed and nasty one. "Money helps some of the rest out, poor souls."

Mabel ignored it, asking, "So what's proper?"

"It's a good question, how big the wedding will be. He'll have to invite a certain number, the other Lords who hold magic in the area. That's a couple of dozen at least. Now, if he does the thing properly, it will be hundreds of people, most of the Council, if not all of them. A party all night, at least two changes of clothes. And he does have an excellent cellar. Largely inherited, but my Mortimer swears that Lord Carillon's got a fine palate. Perhaps built up in his travels, they say he went all over the place for years."

Aine laughed, the sound rather edged. "Oh, people will say all sorts of things. I heard he was rather a sot. Lost in a bottle, or something of the kind. Even that his parents sent him away, they couldn't stand for him to be in the country."

There was a shocked gasp from Isalanda. "Really, who said that?"

"Lady Beaupres. And you know her husband's a member at Bourne's and the Explorers, so he'd know more than most."

Aine shifted, an elegant arch of her body as she tucked a foot up. "Still, that's nothing too uncommon. Too many men found a bottle after the War or worse."

"Lady Beaupres suggested it was rather worse. The kind of thing that if his fiancée had any actual friends, someone would take her aside and warn her. But of course, who would."

"Lord Carillon's got friends, hasn't he?"

"Him? I hardly think so. He's the kind of man with a reputation for spending far too much time with his staff, if anything. I mean, devoted family retainers are traditional, but there's being a tad too friendly with the help, isn't there?" She considered, then added, a drop of fairness in with the nasty bitter gossip and the insinuating tone. "Though I suppose the man did lose a lot of his peers to the War one way or another. The ones you'd see together in town."

It made Cassie wonder about that, about who Lord Carillon's closer associates were. She had only heard him talk about people in pursuit of his larger plots, not where he spent his more intimate social evenings. If he did prefer the company of his staff, he certainly would not mention such a thing to her.

"You knew them?" That was Aine again.

"Oh, not at all well, I was a schoolgirl of course, watching all the handsome men in uniform. But there were stories about him, a couple of his friends. Great pavo team-mates, and mmm, pavo does do grand things for a man's... assets." She giggled, highlighting the fact she wasn't crude like some people.

Isalanda glanced at Mabel, who ducked her head and ventured a cautious, "Pavo?"

"Goodness, Mabel, you really must learn faster. Pavo is the gentlemen's bohort. The same sort of puzzles in a match, played on teams, but on horseback instead of on foot. Vastly more dashing, and there really is nothing like it for watching men in tight breeches." Cassie thought that was not the most useful explanation. It involved being knowledgeable about bohort, and she wasn't sure if Mabel had had much exposure to that, for all it was the favoured sport of the magical community in Albion.

Teams of five, yes, matched against each other and a series of ever-changing magical puzzles. She liked watching the apprentice league, herself, where the play was inventive and not generally too rough, and the puzzles often designed to reward cleverness and ingenuity rather than the force and power of the professional league. She'd only seen a pavo match a few times, though she understood Lord Carillon was indeed quite a skilled player in his younger days.

Mabel murmured something inaudible and apologetic. It didn't distract Isalanda from her larger topic.

"But he's made enemies, since he's been back." Her voice had the low drawling quality of someone laying out a bit of nastiness she'd been hoarding for the right opportunity. Or perhaps the chance to air a grudge, given how she continued. "Some of that fuss about that drink, all those people who stopped throwing such lovely parties. And some of them are not at all pleased with it, of course. I know where I'd rather be, certainly."

Cassie had heard more than a few comments about that whole mess, and how the goldwasser had drained people's magic. The Ministry had kept people from panicking, mostly by somehow ending the making of the stuff before too many people were hurt or addicted. Cassie still wondered how narrow a miss it had been.

Mabel spoke more clearly this time. "Do you know some of that set, then?" It was well-asked, Cassie thought, to draw out Isalanda like that.

"A fair number of them. Lovely people, very generous, really, and scrumptious parties. There was no harm to them, surely. I mean, most of them weren't from the old families, but the Great Families are good for some things, but so stuffy. A bunch of the crowd at the Crystal Cave, and they were such great fun."

That was one of the more exclusive after-dinner clubs in London, just on the edge of the Bloomsbury magical village. She'd had her dresses worn there, a few times, she'd seen that in some of the gossip columns, but she had thought the place entirely too sharp and full of glamour to be sensible.

Isalanda pouted, an elegant sort of pout. "And I heard recently that Lord Carillon had a hand in ruining all that. Awful man."

It rather sounded like she didn't care about who got hurt if she got her moments of bliss, or at least got to be in with the right set. Whoever she thought they were.

"But you'll take an invite to his wedding." Aine wasn't afraid to call out that bit of hypocrisy, apparently, which made Cassie like her slightly more.

Isalanda grimaced for a moment, a palpable hit, but she didn't immediately respond. Cassie thought it was about time to put an end to the gossiping. She coughed, deliberately made the teapot ring when she set it on the tray, before bringing everything back into the front room. "Here we go, all ready for a little break, and Joselyn will be back in just a minute with some cakes and sandwiches."

"Oh, yes, she hasn't been here long, has she? Wherever did you find her?" That was decidedly looking for a way to dismiss Joselyn, who was of good family and very promising.

"Three weeks or so - she's just settling in."

"And you expect to keep her?" Aine was sharp about it. "She's quite raw. Unfinished."

The woman probably thought that Joselyn did not strut well enough in the green tea dress, rather than having a meaningful critique of the substance of her work. "Oh, yes. She's already shown quite a bit of talent picking things up. We have a longer apprenticeship than some, three to five years after our other schooling, to accumulate the projects to demonstrate the varied skills the Guild requires." Cassie began to pour the tea out. "Joselyn has a fine neat hand in plain sewing, and quite an eye for colour and design already. I'm confident she'll succeed if she works hard."

Aine shrugged, one of those decorous dismissive shrugs. "Well if one has to work for a living, I suppose working with nice clothing would be better than most things."

Cassie bit her tongue to avoid commenting. The tiny even stitches, the rush jobs, the perfect fitting, all came at a price, not that these kinds of women would think about that.

Benton opened the door, cautiously. It was open, the lights were lit. It was dim and gloomy outside, and the contrast was jarring. At the same time, he felt like he were intruding. "Mistress Castalia?"

"Back room." Just the two words, and rather sharp. This was new, and he was sure he didn't like it.

He carefully closed the door behind him, then paused. He wasn't sure who she was expecting. Not him, surely. He'd merely mentioned that he would bring the payment by sometime in the next few days. His lordship had made his decisions, the payment was for the new materials.

Making his way to the other end of the hallway to the back fitting rooms, he coughed. "Mistress Castalia? It's Benton, Lord Carillon's man."

She was standing in front of a dressmaker's dummy. She turned, tucking pins automatically into the folds of a pocket of her apron. She turned, as he came into the back room, as if caught out at something, but he couldn't imagine what.

He cleared his throat. "His lordship sent along the payment for the new fabric. Is this a bad time?"

Mistress Castalia shook her head. "No, of course not. Oh, did it start raining again? You look rather damp." It sounded rather automatic, if kinder than he had anticipated.

Benton hadn't noticed. He'd had several errands, and his lordship was good enough to make sure the charms and protections against rain were redone regularly on his hat and cloak. Not like in the War, when the damp and mud got everywhere.

He paused long enough that she continued. "You must let me make you a cup of tea, while you warm up. Do have a seat here, I'll be back in a minute." This was even more confusing than her telling him to come into the back room. She had never offered tea before.

If he didn't know better, he'd think she wanted to talk to him about something, but he had to admit a cup of tea would be welcome, even from her. He glanced around and spotted a sofa with two padded benches to either side, and settled cautiously there. It seemed of sturdy fabric that wouldn't take damage from the damp.

He had not been into the fitting room before, either. There was a curtained alcove for someone to change, a clothes rack where items could be hung, and a dressmaker's dummy tucked into the back corner. Stairs against the back wall, almost hidden behind a large draping curtain, led upstairs to some sort of second level.

Everything was quite tidy, except for where she'd been working, where there were little scraps of thread, and a few longer loose threads. He remembered from his mother's sewing that those were basting threads, removed once something had been properly hemmed.

Benton listened, as she disappeared into the side hallway, but he didn't hear a kettle sing. Instead there were the little taps and noises of someone setting out tea cups and saucers and perhaps a plate of biscuits, the gurgle of pouring tea.

After only a minute or so, Mistress Castalia brought a tray out, setting it on a small table. "I'll be mother, shall I?" she said, and asked, "How do you prefer your tea?"

"One sugar, please."

She nodded, dropping a lump in the cup and pouring the tea without comment, then handing it over to him before doing the same to her own cup. He stirred three times, precisely, as he always did. Under his breath, he murmured the little charm his mother had taught him as a child, for health and luck, the one that must have kept him safe this far.

He looked up to find her watching him, rather intently, her own cup held halfway to her lips. She set it down with a quite audible rattle, the kind of service he'd never approve of.

"I do have the coins, Mistress," he said, after a moment.

"Is that all you think about?" It came out sharply, enough that he blinked at her. She had lulled him enough with the tea, perhaps, that her sudden turn into hostility was startling rather than the familiar thing he had guarded against since their second encounter, years ago, when he had realised she did not care for people in service.

"His lordship asked I bring it round."

"And is that - how you order your day?" Her voice had that edge to it again. It seemed rather a waste of energy to him, disapproving of other people's lives.

Benton paused, taking a breath. In his younger days, as a hallboy, he'd been known to get into fights for that sort of thing. Age - well, age and the War - had settled him, and the adventures with his lordship after the War had taught him flexibility and patience. Or at least more of both than he'd started with.

"His lordship has wide-ranging needs. It is my pleasure to see that they're handled sensibly."

Something in the answer wasn't quite what she expected. It was mildly satisfying to put her off her game so visibly after the way she had left him wrongfooted. "Sensibly?"

"In an order that makes sense without wasted effort or coin. Too many valets and house stewards make more work for themselves - and the rest of the household staff - by failing to plan ahead. I've never wanted to be that sort."

She waved a hand. "Sensibly." She rolled it around for a moment. "And so a sensible man like yourself is servant to one who needs that sense?"

Benton could not tell for the life of him if that was meant to be praise or insult or both, and precisely where the insult was intended. He was fairly sure there was meant to be an insult in there somewhere. He took a long sip of his tea, then set it down, the handle precisely angled.

"I am quite happy in my position, Mistress Castalia." He paused then said, a bit more firmly, "I know it is the modern thing to question the tradition of service, especially long-standing service such as mine. I know there are other options, and I choose to stay where I am."

Mistress Castalia looked him up and down, then snorted. "And whatever I said, you'd have an argument for it, wouldn't you?"

He shrugged, permitting himself the minute twitch of a shoulder. "Why should I argue? You would not be convinced by it. Easier to teach a pig to sing."

The expression on her face was worth the comment. He did not think she would refuse to do the work they'd arranged. He had more than enough practice in his lord-ship's service reading the bodies of everyone from titled lords and ladies to dockworkers and porters. He'd had to learn how to avoid a fight, which had long been his first instinct when something went wrong. That hadn't served since the War, and certainly wouldn't do now.

"Did you mean an insult, there?" Her voice was tighter.

"No more than you meant one a few moments ago." He kept his voice even, deliberate. His lordship would not thank him for getting this wrong. Good dressmakers were hard to find.

That was the proper response, because she paused, took a breath, and nodded. "Your loyalty does you credit." It was a bit grudging, but it was true, and not everyone would acknowledge it.

They sat in silence for a minute, until she poured more tea into her cup. She raised an eyebrow in question, and he nodded, and she poured for him as well. "I did have some-thing to bring to his attention. Or yours, I suppose."

Benton inclined his head, the slow measured nod that encouraged just a hint of intimacy and trust. "Mistress?"

"I heard some unpleasant gossip, yesterday. About Lord Carillon."

Benton paused, holding still. Some people, saying that, would do their best to lure him into some indiscretion. Some were fishing. Some would seek to take a snippet of information and use it to their advantage. A few would stoop to clumsy, gangling blackmail attempts. So undigni-fied. Instead of enquiring, he just said, "There is always a lot of gossip out there, about anyone with a title, I've found."

He considered which bit of gossip this might be. There were the old rumours about his lordship's enjoyment of both men and women, or his fondness for men of a certain artistic bent. He'd thought that had cooled, since their return to Albion. Certainly his lordship had gone to some substantial effort to be discreet about such things.

The engagement had brought up a lot of unpleasantness about Miss Penhallow's father and uncle, people wanting to blame her for the failure of the expedition, which was ridiculous. There had been some rumours more recently about what happened to end the goldwasser parties. In the last few weeks, he'd begun to suspect someone had realised his lordship had had more than a trivial role in that. It was nothing he could pin down, just that nagging sense.

Mistress Castalia shook her head. "This was something different. I hear the usual range regularly. Women will say all sorts of things when they're half undressed, with their sisters or friends."

"Which were these?" Benton kept his voice easy.

"Sisters-in-law." She paused, then said, "Lord Carillon, there are people who do not like him very much."

"That is also common." He kept his voice even, waiting to see where she went with this. He could see half a dozen paths, and he didn't know which one she was on. Venturing an opinion in advance of more information might give things away about his lordship, and that would not do at all.

She frowned at him. "I am trying to explain."

"I know his lordship has enemies. He is a man who tries to improve the world, those who wish to push others down do not find it agreeable." He kept his voice even, steady, seeing what she'd do with this. Or if she had any information other than gossip. He had thought idle gossip would be beneath her.

"By all Arachne's threads, man, I am trying to do you a

favour." She had shot up in her chair, standing, leaning, for just a moment before she drew back, without sitting down.

Benton swallowed, feeling the old fears rise in him for a moment. He could almost hear someone shouting at him, when he was a child, then again during the War. All the memories it stirred up surged for a moment. It made him remember, far too vividly, the times one adult or another had torn into him for something he hadn't understood and was doing wrong. He made himself reach calmly for his tea cup. He blessed the long years of practice that meant he did so smoothly, with no unwanted rattling.

"Pardon, mistress. Do go on?" Falling back on the formal words, the setpiece phrases, would give him time to settle, even as he maintained the careful appearance of poise. Her temper would cost him later, he'd be no good for detailed focus until he'd got time to himself to soothe his nerves.

She glared at him, in silence. Then she stomped off toward one end of the room. She stood there, looking down the hall toward the front room, for a long pause, nearly a minute. He held his teacup, carefully, in his hand, sure that any noise or movement might set her off. Again.

It was not something any woman in service would have permitted herself, not past the age of fourteen or fifteen. There was no space in a great house for that kind of tantrum, and he had always found that profoundly sooth-ing, that they all had the same standards and expectations.

Though, for all the flare of anger, he supposed he had to grant that she had kept herself in good control. Apart from the stamping, she had not slammed anything around, or struck out. Small favours, then.

Finally, she turned back. "You are utterly infuriating. But I do not know if there's anything in it. I find I rather like

Miss Penhallow, and Lord Carillon is certainly good for business. If I did not tell you, I would feel guilty if something happened."

Benton simply inclined his head, waiting. She was talking it out, she would come to some decision, he could then make his own choices. Prodding her further seemed quite likely to produce another unpredictable result, and he couldn't afford that today.

Mistress Castalia took another long breath, and came and sat down, perching on her bench. "Two sisters-in-law, being quite catty to the young woman who is marrying in. One mentioned that there was a lot of gossip about Lord Carillon, and if someone were kind, they'd take Miss Penhallow aside and tell her, but who would. That last is a quote, mind."

He could not place the women immediately, but with a little research, he would be able to identify them, or his lordship would. He did not need her to tell him their names. Benton nodded. "I have found Miss Penhallow most thoughtful in her choices, and I do not think the comments of anyone, including her sister, could turn her from his lordship."

Mistress Castalia nodded. "There was some of the usual nasty gossip. Preferences for men, for other women, that he'd fallen into a bottle. You know the sorts of things, I'm sure. They've been in the gossip papers often enough. Don't servants gossip?"

"Not the ones of quality, Mistress, no, but that does not mean we do not listen." No new gossip then, precisely, just old gossip getting dredged up. People gossiped about those they saw as above them, or different than them, or who had things they didn't. Gossiping about people who had less was not nearly as enjoyable, apparently. His lordship had money and status, people would gossip about that. And he had strong opinions and acted on them, which led to more gossip.

A tiny quirk of a smile broke her seriousness for a moment, before she sobered. "The more complex gossip was about something with a drink, and parties, and Lord Carillon being the one to interfere, somehow? It was clear he'd made some enemies. I don't know, perhaps they intended to use his relationship and wedding to make some trouble."

"Was some specific plan mentioned?" Benton leaned forward now. The fact the gossip was that clear was indeed new. It combined rather oddly with the resurgence of the old rumours about his lordship's flexibility in intimate matters.

"No, nothing like that. If there were, I'd tell you."

"And the source, reliable in that sort of gossip?"

"Reasonably well informed, I think." Mistress Castalia paused, then said, "I won't tell you her name, but she mentioned Lady Beaupres, about some of the more personal gossip. The drunkenness, in particular."

Benton nodded, then ventured, "Lady Beaupres hoped his lordship would settle on her eldest daughter. Not at all to his lordship's taste."

Mistress Castalia tilted her head. "In what way?" Her temper had faded, and she sounded curious now, intrigued.

"His lordship has quite varied tastes in many areas, appearance, interests, and so on. But he does prefer his close associates to have some interests, and to have relatives who are not abysmal to be around. Alas, he never got close enough due to the latter to have any confidence of the former."

He was rewarded by seeing her blink, then smile, again quite briefly. "Oh. So, will you tell him?"

"I will inform his lordship that the usual sources remain themselves, and see if the details add anything new to his plans. What else I tell him, that depends. He relies on me to see to see to some things, while he focuses on his own projects." Then, because he was grateful, he added, "Thank you for having a care for his interests."

She went still for a moment. "That matters to you?"

"Of course, mistress." He then cleared his throat. "You must have other tasks for your afternoon. Thank you for the tea, and your kindness, but I do have my own errands to see to. Please let us know when you'll be ready for Miss Penhallow's next fitting."

Mistress Castalia half-rose from her bench. "I, yes, of course." She seemed more than a little flustered, and Benton judged it best to make a smooth escape. An entirely honest one, he did have a number of visits left in his afternoon. But she did not seem like the sort to be comfortable in the aftermath of even the most impersonal intimacy.

He handed over the payment, and she was sufficiently off-kilter that she simply said, "I'm sure it's fine, I'll let you know if there's a problem with it."

SEVEN

Amelia, Cassie's second apprentice, was back from her work with weavers in Spitalfields, seeing to the final details of some fussy weaving for magical work robes that had to look good as well as fill their function. It was a good deal louder with her in the shop. Not precisely in volume, Amelia's voice was carefully modulated. But there were rather more words being said than the past few days.

"Come here, Joselyn, see how the pins go here? That makes it easier when you come to make adjustments. Just one of those little tricks."

Cassie, in the front room and working on her account book, overheard the murmurs of Joselyn's response, too quiet for her to make out the words.

They went on, back and forth for a good twenty minutes, before Joselyn came into the front room, carrying a cup of tea. "Tea, Mistress? Amelia said it was time for a break."

Cassie couldn't help smiling. "Amelia's very precise

about her time. And a number of other things. How are you getting on?"

Joselyn glanced at the back room, and then paused, and they both heard the door to the tiny back garden open. "That'll be Amelia going to talk to that nice apprentice from the button maker at the gate. She must have missed him," Cassie said. Buttons were a more skilled trade in the magical community, since they were often crafted to hold specific charms and enchantments or protect against them. The young man had good prospects.

"You don't mind, mistress?" She held out a plate with three scones on it, the nice orange glazed ones from the shop next door that Cassie particularly liked.

Cassie shook her head, setting her paperwork aside and taking the cup. "Oh, and a scone, grand." She considered. There was a pacing to the lectures you gave apprentices, she had found, and it was about time for this one to Joselyn. "An apprenticeship is about many things, and that includes learning how you want to be as an adult. That's why there are so many social options, for apprentices with different people, for you to meet and get to know each other."

Joselyn perched cautiously on the sofa and nodded, attentive.

"However, that shouldn't interfere with your apprenticeship. You are still here to learn the art of dressmaking, and to develop your own style. Especially early in your apprenticeship, I don't want you getting distracted or getting your heart broken. Heartbreak is good for poets and artists, and not at all good for dressmakers. Tears stain silk and satin and a dozen other fabrics, after all, and if you can't see the needle properly, you run a chance of stabbing yourself. Well, more frequently than otherwise." She finished it with a grin.

"Oh." Cassie let Joselyn think that through. "What do you prefer I do, Mistress?"

"For now, focus on your learning, you have a lot to get used to. New place to live, all sorts of new tasks. If Amelia or Melitta want to take you to one of the apprentice gatherings, you go right along, they're scheduled not to interfere much with your duties. Or if you want to go on your own, once you get a sense of how they go. But I'd rather not see you considering pairing off for a good year or three."

Joselyn nodded slowly. "Have you ever - pardon, Mistress. That's not a thing I should ask."

Cassie snorted. "No, you shouldn't." Then she sobered. "The War wasn't kind to a lot of us, even the ones who didn't die. The two men I thought I might - want to make a life with, maybe, they both died. We weren't close yet, nothing like engaged, just flirting at apprentice dances and picnics and over the back fence. We were still all establishing ourselves."

Joselyn looked distraught. "Oh, oh, I'm sorry, Mistress."

Cassie waved a hand. "It happened to a lot of us. So many young men." She shook her head. "And then during the War, my Mistress - I was one of the last of her apprentices - got ill, and I took over the shop, and just kept going. Most of her others had married or retired for other reasons by then, or had their own places all established."

"Is it hard, setting up a place?"

"As you get along, we'll talk more about that. There are plenty of options. Some people just take on a small number of clients. Some have a shop, like this. Some work in bigger fashion houses, especially if they're, say, good at technique but don't want to do design, or the other way around. Or keep their own books." She sent piecework out to half a

dozen women, did the design work, oversaw her apprentices, and did everything else.

"And you?"

"I don't mind the books, and I like the design work. Not
the most modish thing, but taking it and doing something
interesting with it. Practical, often, for people who are..."
Cassie considered how to phrase that. "People who have
other things in their lives than looking well-dressed. A lot of
designers feel pockets, even the magically hidden ones, spoil
the line. Or that every tiny faddish thing should get equal
time. I'd rather make clothes that look good on the person
who will wear them, and do what they need to do."

"Is that why you like Miss Penhallow?"

Cassie laughed. "Oh, yes. Mind, Lord Carillon had me
doing clothes for a few of his previous lovers. Partly because
I wouldn't turn my nose up at it like some people. When he
started, I couldn't afford to be too choosy. Taking him on
meant I could turn down a few people who were rather
awful to their mistresses, and I'd much rather his custom.
And now he wants to make sure his fiancée is well dressed
for what she's taking on. That's a pleasant challenge,
helping her create a style that carries through the different
things she's doing."

Joselyn nods. "But you want them to go together? The
things you're making for her?"

Cassie nodded. "Exactly. I like to pick a palette of
colours. Not necessarily just a few colours, but things that
fit together while also suiting the setting they'll be worn in.
Evening gowns are more elaborate and generally more saturated colours, and afternoon tea gowns are more muted."

"That Nile green one, yes?"

"Exactly. And the robin's egg blue."

"How do you decide on the colours? I mean, don't people have opinions?"

"Some of them do. Some of them are right about their opinions, and some of them are terribly misguided, but if they're paying, you can't always argue too much. I like draping people with a fabric, and letting them see it. The intelligent ones, they'll figure out what looks good if you let them see it. It's important to consider the light, too. Did you wonder why I have that booth in the back?"

"I did, Mistress. It's all tucked under the balcony to the workroom."

"That space lets me adjust the light. Charm lights are different than gas, or than electric, if someone is going some-where that has them. And outside, of course, is entirely different. Some colours will look fantastic under one light, and far too harsh or garish under another, and some will do well in all three. For someone who'll only ever be seen under charm lights, it's easy, but for the others, you want something like that booth to test."

Joselyn frowned, then nodded. "And that's part of having it be all your shop. You have to think about things like that, and do the upkeep on it."

"Exactly. Most people don't understand that, but your mother does charm lighting, of course it would make sense." She caught Joselyn glancing at the last scone, and said, "Take it, I'm not that hungry."

Apprentices were always starving, it was one of the laws of the universe, even in a dressmaker's. Joselyn snuck the scone onto her plate and broke it apart. She was quiet for a good minute before asking, "How do you get to be really good at it? How do -"

Cassie tilted her head. "Most people worry about that earlier or later. Before they apprentice, or at the tail end."

Joselyn shrugged. "Never followed anyone else's sense of time, Mistress." She flushed. It was true enough. Cassie had caught her daydreaming or taking too long on things more than once. Other times Joselyn had been done with a task long before she expected, and done it well.

"I think you'll do fine. We'll see how you get on, and go from there. Is there a part you're worried about?"

"Dealing with people, mistress. I mean, I saw you with those three women, the sisters-in-law? And then you were different, when that Mr Benton was leaving. Lord Carillon's man."

Cassie frowned. "You saw that?"

Joselyn ducked her chin, visibly embarrassed. "He was coming out when I came in? And I looked into the back room, and you don't normally entertain people there?"

Time for a quick evaluation, then. Joselyn was young, just starting her apprenticeship. Amelia had a knack for matching the weaving and the final design. Melitta had a decided gift for securing delicate glass beads in place, and the design that laid them out. But she rather thought Joselyn might be the best balanced, the most able to set style and manage her own shop.

"You remember the three of them? The married ones said a few things while you were getting the tea things that - I thought Lord Carillon should hear about."

Joselyn frowned. "But you told me about the confidentiality of the work, that people would talk."

"I did. And I do believe that. It's not our place to gossip - or even hint at - problems in marriages, or possible divorces, or pregnancies, or dozens of other things. But in this case, the gossip was directly about Lord Carillon. And as I said, I value his patronage, and I like Miss Penhallow."

Joselyn frowned again. "And that makes it all right?"

"It means that it is something I handle carefully. Benton is his trusted valet. Whatever I think of being in service, I am quite clear about his loyalty. And about his ability to decide what he needs to know."

It was only when saying it that it felt real to her. She'd felt like she needed to tell Benton, she'd been too bothered by the gossip, a nagging pressure under her skin. Most talk of that kind just flowed around her, and this was different. Even if she couldn't figure out why that thread had changed colour on her, she could respect it and find it a place in the needlework. She knew she wouldn't be able to live with herself if she hadn't told Mr Benton, even if she couldn't explain why.

"If you say so, mistress." Joselyn was dubious, and Cassie couldn't blame her. It wasn't logical, but there you were. People weren't, sometimes. Even her.

EIGHT

The dinner party itself had gone quite well, at least in terms of food and service. Benton found these occasions quite trying, as a formal dinner service was neither one of his particular strengths, nor one of the skills his lordship employed him for. It was one reason he would be quite pleased if they could find a butler who suited the household's needs. Then he could hand the formalities over lock, stock, and barrel.

The Leventhals had, as his lordship expected, been charming and visibly delighted at the opportunity to examine the tapestry restoration in progress. They had even come early for the chance to do so. Mistress Pride, wife of his lordship's head stableman, was restoring them as her apprenticeship project, and the work was coming along well. She'd been pleased to explain the work involved.

Mrs Leventhal had been quite thoughtful about particular colour choices, mentioning that a number of her extended family had been in silk trade in various ways. Benton was quite sure his lordship would be following up on that promptly.

The other guests turned up precisely on time, commenting favourably on the charmed lights along the trellised path from the portal, and the range of cocktails available. Benton had not, of course, been entirely privy to his lordship's plans for this particular evening. There certainly were plans, since it mixed some people his lordship liked, and two couples of less certain status.

The glancing comments he'd heard from the Willacys had been mixed. Benton thought Dorinda Willacy had gone to Schola, but not her husband, who was a Dunwich man. That meant he knew some of the trade magics, but he wasn't from one of the older trading families, not with that name. He'd married up, likely, and it didn't agree with him. This was not his first formal dinner party with strangers, but he was visibly uncomfortable with the range of tableware and kept trying to get in the staff's way. Worse, he kept everyone on edge, making the kind of comments that would give insult in half a dozen ways.

Torcan Willacy had made his fortune in munitions during the War, Benton thought, which made him a curious guest, since his lordship usually avoided such. But there had that been that conversation with Miss Fortescue about her current season's performances at the Trellech Opera House, and perhaps why he had been invited. Benton felt certain his lordship had some particular reason, regardless.

The FitzDonalds were more puzzling, to him. He thought they had been overly quiet at supper. His lordship's guests tended to the less boisterous side of things, as a whole, but they usually were agreeable about making conversation. These two, however, had been almost abrupt with discomfort. Benton couldn't figure out why they'd been invited, but there must be some reason.

The conversation had been strained, the few times he

had come in for various tasks. His lordship was clearly up to something, but Benton could not sort out precisely what. Nor, for that matter, how successful his lordship felt the evening to be. It had been good fortune or good planning - likely both - that no one had felt like taking up Mr Willacy's insults. The professors had, instead, played it like a game, between them, redirecting the conversation to safer topics over and over again. He supposed that working with students at Schola, in sometimes politically-charged times, would make them adepts at that particular sport.

"Mr Benton?"

"Yes, Mally?" He paused in counting the silver back to look up.

"Pardon, but I - am not sure if something is my proper place." She had the nervous look, like when she'd first come to the house, as if everything she was doing was wrong. She was a sensible young woman with a fine sense of what needed doing, after all. If she was unsure, he wanted to sort things out promptly for her.

"Why don't you go make a cup of tea for us both. I'll finish this up, and then we can sit and talk it through."

She bobbed with the half curtsey he was still trying to train out of her, and disappeared. He finished counting the forks back into the tray, ran his finger over the metal one last time, and then closed and locked the silver case, pocketing the key.

Mally was waiting with two cups of tea when he got to the small staff room. It was quiet this time of night, since it was kept for staff who needed a private word, or dealing with the accounts. Benton settled in the chair on his side of the table, and then said, "You've had a busy evening, but I presume Miss Penhallow has retired for the night?"

Mally smiled. "Yes, Mr Benton, quite content. She was

most pleased with the repair to her bedside table, and asked me especially to thank you for seeing to it so promptly. And she said she did not expect to need me for a bit in the morning."

Benton nodded. They both knew without saying that Miss Penhallow would be found in his lordship's bed, if anyone went looking there, rather than her own. She would retreat to her own room only once she was ready to face the world. It had been some weeks since she'd been able to stay overnight for one reason and another. Benton quite expected he'd be summoned no earlier than half-ten. "Then we've a little time. Do tell me what concerned you, Mally?"

"It was the FitzDonalds." She paused. "Pardon, do you know if his - his lordship is close to them? Cares for them?" She had the anxious note in her voice, and she was leaning forward, her fingers momentarily fussing with her skirts.

"His lordship has not previously extended an invitation, nor am I more than passingly familiar with the name."

"Oh. Oh. Good. I think."

"Were they known to your previous employers?" Benton decidedly disapproved of Mally's previous house. They had been up to their necks in making and distributing the goldwasser, not caring who they hurt with it. More than that, they had run the house badly by all accounts. They had treated their staff poorly, neglected the training that would keep the staff healthy and well-occupied, and had no idea how many customs they had trod upon that existed for good reasons.

Well, and he perhaps still held a grudge they had refused to permit him to accompany his lordship to the party that allowed his lordship to untangle the whole unpleasant mess. Benton remained certain that if he had been allowed to stay, it would have been much better for his lordship. And it would make figuring out the source of the new gossip about his lordship's role in the matter much easier.

She hesitated. "I think I've heard the name, Mr Benton, but I can't remember where, or what." Her fingers moved, scrunching up her dress nervously. "Maybe they were guests? But I don't think I ever saw them, not enough to know for sure."

"Did something happen tonight, then?" He would need to draw her out, then. "Something in particular?"

"Miss Penhallow asked Jory to fetch me, Mrs Fitz-Donald had a slight problem with her dress. Her husband came out with her, and they were talking, in the side room. She was, she was quite upset with him, for not warning her when she pressed him to accept the invitation that it might include the Leventhals."

"Ah." Benton paused. "The Leventhals are Jewish. You may be aware, Mally, that many people are, one might say, dismissive of them as a group. There is a lot of unpleasant history there."

Mally considered. "Oh." And then, "They seemed very kind." She sounded both baffled and uncertain what her role was here.

"His lordship finds them both quite well-informed and interesting conversation partners. I expect they will continue to be welcome guests here for some time to come."

"Oh." Mally glanced up at him, visibly trying to read him better.. "You hear all sorts of stories, Mr Benton. Well, I suppose it's easier for you, you've travelled. got to know all sorts of people."

Benton nodded. "I have, yes, and enjoyed it. But Albion has many sorts of people, it is just that we keep to our own circles rather intensely, don't we? Where we live, and what we do. If we have never met someone of a certain type, they seem mysterious to us." He paused, and added, "I heard Mrs Leventhal compliment Miss Penhallow on how well her hair was done, by-the-by. She is not, she does not fuss with such things herself, but she knew quality when she saw it. And she had the kindness to offer the compliment."

That got a smile from Mally, who still appreciated the praise and needed the support to her confidence. "Thank you, Mr Benton, I am pleased to know that."

He nodded, and said, "You had something else, though, didn't you?"

"Sir." Mally gathered her thoughts. "Mr FitzDonald said that he couldn't see why they'd accepted the invitation, given the company they knew his lordship might keep and how cross Mrs Fitzdonald was about it. And his wife, she was very precise about it being something of a favour to Mrs Willacy? I didn't understand that at all. And said that there was something about a project Mr Willacy didn't want his lordship interfering with, not a matter of her husband's concern. He mentioned something about her female friends, but not any names."

Benton frowned. "Curious. I don't suppose they made any mention of what."

"No, sir. I would tell you if they had. His lordship, Miss Penhallow, they've been nothing but kind to me. And you and the rest of the staff here. It's so much better than my previous place, I'd never..." Her voice trailed off.

"There, Mally. We're glad to have you, and you're doing a fine job. Thank you for bringing this to me, I'll make sure his lordship is aware."

Mally nodded, then said, hesitantly. "They mentioned the rumours about his lordship. His - um. Preferences. Whether he was looking at Mr Fortescue that way."

That rumour was certainly coming up quite frequently of late, and with no particular reason for it that Benton knew. "Mr Fortescue is not quite to his lordship's tastes in anything but music, as it turns out. For several reasons. But his lordship does find him entertaining and good company. And his sister more so, she has a charming knack for conversation."

Mally bobbed her head again, then said hesitantly, "Should I tell Miss Penhallow any of it?"

"If she asks you a question, answer it as honestly as you can. The question of what to say if they don't ask...." Benton paused. "That's a far trickier problem."

"May I ask how you handle it, sir? It seems to me that would be the proper guide in this house."

Benton smiled, and nodded. Mally had a fine hand with a compliment as well, when she thought it would be welcome. "If it is something that seems to relate to his lordship's plans and goals, then I tell him, as fairly as I am able. I define relevant somewhat broadly, you understand, including the plans he has not articulated in my presence."

"Ah." Mally considered. "They didn't say anything like that. Nothing direct about Miss Penhallow. They didn't care for her, but that's no surprise."

Benton nodded, then something caught at his memory. "Do you happen to know if Mrs FitzDonald is a member of any of the groups where Miss Penhallow has invitations in the coming weeks?"

Mally nodded. "Mrs FitzDonald is a chairwoman for one of the committees for the Albion Inheritance. I wondered if that was why she was invited."

Benton nodded, then paused. Admitting ignorance was not his preference, but this distaff side of the society calendar was still largely a mystery to him. "Do you know anything about what they do? I am afraid it has not come up in his lordship's diary before."

"It's some sort of social group, for the Great Families, you know, the ones who can trace their families way back. My previous household, they weren't, they didn't qualify, of course. If I understood right, Miss Penhallow qualifies for membership on her mother's side. But I don't know much more than that. They do some charitable work, but there are other events as well."

"I presume his lordship has some reason for pursuing the opportunity, then."

"So I should tell Miss Penhallow, perhaps, that it seemed like the Willacys or the FitzDonalds had goals of their own. And that they seemed discomforted by the rest of the guest list, but I didn't hear anything specific?"

"I am quite sure she'd appreciate that. Did you get a chance to hear the singing?"

"Oh, yes." Mally's eyes lit up. "Miss Fortescue has such a lovely voice, and her brother is so handsome. Does he - what does he normally sing?"

"Opera, as a rule, the dashing hero. But he can some-times be coaxed into more informal music, as he was tonight, after the Willacys and FitzDonalds left. I did like the one where Miss Fortescue played, with that syncopation to it?"

"Do you know much about music, Mr Benton?" There was a wistful note to her voice, and Benton realised he would have to gently discourage her. Not only was she rather young for him, it was not appropriate for there to be too much personal intimacy between the likes of them. He had seen often enough what happened when a relationship between staff ended badly. He would continue to fail to notice the more personal, then, the hints she would like more with him, and keep it to suitable topics.

"Only what I've picked up on travels with his lordship, whose tastes are quite eclectic and varied." He paused, considering how to phrase it properly. "I find seeing people enjoy making it more interesting than the music itself. Seeing them do a thing they have practiced for many years, but in the moment, creating something new."

Mally considered. "Isn't that good service? For us? When we do the thing just right, and it flows?"

Benton smiled. "It is. And that's a fine way to put it." He finished his tea, setting the cup down silently. "You've had a long day, even if you can have an easy morning tomorrow. You should go up and take your rest."

"Yes, Mr Benton. Do let me know if I can be a help in the morning." With that, she cleared the cups onto the tray and took them back to the kitchen, then he heard her footsteps go up the back stairs to her room.

NINE

"I think you're right about the dye colours."

Cassie smiled. Of course she was right, this was her chosen work, and she was very good at it. She reached out to adjust the drape of the mocked up cloak fabric, in a wool of a similar weight to the velvet they had planned. She set the charmwork on the base of the dressmaker's dummy to spin slowly, and stepped back. "As I said, sepia will not suit Miss Penhallow at all. Perhaps if she were still adventuring, and out in the sun, but not as she is at the moment."

Lord Carillon leaned back, considering, watching the dummy slowly spin with his eyes half-closed and his head tilted in thought. "I suppose not. You can do the design?"

Cassie nodded. "I've done a few similar things - a smaller map, but the same technique. Here." She brought out an album of her custom work, with both her watercolour sketches and photographs of the final work along with swatches of the fabric. "This is the one I mentioned to Mr Benton when you had the idea."

He reached for it, taking his time looking through it.

"That's along the right line, yes, but you're thinking blue-greys and deep greys, rather than the browns and sepia."

She nodded. "And some metallic thread for the embroidery work to highlight the cities, little radiating lines, and something similar for the rivers. There's a technique that will allow me to brush a similar effect on the ocean. Rather 'wine dark sea' in the original meaning, the glimmer, not the colour."

"You know Homer?" He looked up.

"It's common in some design houses to have someone reading aloud - or it was before the radio was quite so available. The mistress who trained me had someone reading most of the time we were working, an aunt whose hands were no longer steady enough for small stitches. Classics, on the whole, though of course in translation."

Lord Carillon tilted his head. "I admit, I'd never considered literary training essential to your profession. But I suppose you'd need to be conversant, what with people going to costume parties and such. Or having themed balls."

"It does make those substantially easier to discuss, yes. I read rather widely, considering. Classical references, folk tales, and of course the current news."

"Ah, I suppose that would affect your business. Who's on their way up, and might commission something, who's on their way down and might need to be reminded about their bills..."

"Lord Carillon!" She should sound scandalised, and couldn't quite bring herself to do it properly, she knew perfectly well he was teasing.

He grinned at her, letting the formal pose drop. He glanced around, checking, and she offered, "The apprentices are out at the moment."

"Thank you for mentioning a thing or two to Benton. I

know you've rather a lot to balance, and Miss Penhallow's scarcely your only client. I would not like to put you in a difficult position with others."

She considered, then shook her head. "You've been quite good to me over the years, and Miss Penhallow is a pleasure to dress and work with. You are not my only client, no, but you are a steady one, and will continue to be, I hope. I found I felt," she hesitated only briefly, "Uncomfortable at the idea of not letting you know."

He leaned forward, regarding her. "Benton was quite prompt about telling me, of course."

"He seems most loyal." Cassie wasn't sure what else to say there. The truth, of course, was likely safe here, even if that same loyalty made her uncomfortable.

His lordship nodded. "Extremely. And you're not sure what you think about that, I believe." His tone had an edge to it now, like he'd got a puzzle in his teeth.

"I hope I've not given offence, your lordship?" It came out of her mouth, before she could stop herself. She hated that her distaste were this obvious, too, even to someone as observant as she knew Lord Carillon to be.

Lord Carillon waved a hand. "You have been entirely appropriate with him. But I noticed a certain distance." Benton had been sent off on other errands this afternoon. Cassie was suddenly certain that was no accident.

"I prefer making my own way in the world." Cassie paused, trying to figure out something that was truthful but also not insulting. "I don't understand why someone would choose to be in service, if they had other options. Clearly Mr Benton is competent, organised, thoughtful, and entirely capable of a number of other positions and opportunities."

It earned her a broad smile. "And I am exceedingly

fortunate to have his assistance rather than someone rather less competent," he agreed. "His reasons are his own. I've not pressed him on that topic, other than making it clear at intervals that I would be lost without him. Mind you, I've also made it clear I would be glad to set him up in some alternate employment if he preferred."

The tone in his voice, something wistful, made her wonder again about the gossip that he and Benton were more intimate than lord and his valet. But she didn't think it was that, precisely, or at least not just that.

Cassie frowned and decided to be brave enough to venture, "May I ask what his answer is? If it is something you are willing to share, your lordship?"

There was another flashing grin, a flip of his hand. "He gives me one of those looks, and says something along the lines of 'I am quite content, sir.' And then he goes off and does something noticeably impeccable. As opposed to his usual quieter excellence."

Cassie nodded, considering. Knowing that Lord Carillon had offered him his freedom, as it were, and that Benton wouldn't take it, made her think better of both of them, somehow. She returned to the earlier point rather than linger on it further. "I am glad he thought it worth informing you, your lordship."

He watched her for a long moment, then said. "If there are other things of the kind you are willing to pass along, I appreciate it. But I equally understand the importance of keeping the confidences of other clients."

She nodded, and was saved from a longer reply by Joselyn coming in with the tea tray, and Amelia following with a package of folded silk. "It was ready, Mistress. Should I unwrap it?"

Cassie nodded. "Your lordship had said there would be

a few other social events. May I ask the - focus of the interest in the Albion Inheritance? What kind of impression Miss Penhallow would prefer to make?"

"Lizzie would prefer to do other things, but it is one of the preeminent associations for women of social stature and long ancestry," said Lord Carillon. "And as such we have decided she should make an effort. If they do not take to her, well, we will have some additional information." He seemed very at ease with either prospect.

"In that case, are we aiming at something to their tastes, or something to Miss Penhallow's tastes, and seeing what they make of that?"

"I would be most interested in an illustration of the differences. Is this something we should get Lizzie in for? It would need to be another day, she's got a bit of a project at the moment elsewhere." His tone suggested it was rather an involved project that required significant planning. Perhaps something like the goldwasser had been, if he'd been as involved as the gossip suggested.

"I might explain it to you, and you could discuss with her, and she could stop in?" Cassie offered, thoughtfully. "Joselyn, if you'd bring out the two dummies in the back, that I set up this morning, and Amelia, if you'd set up those lengths for draping?" The two young women bustled off, taking the small neat steps of the well-bred.

The dummies were brought out, one shrouded in a swath of muslin. Cassie stood again, gesturing. "These are both samples, you understand, show models, not to anyone's specific measurements. There are sticking charms, a few places."

"You do a set of those, I understand. To illustrate cut and colour range, without making things up specially."

Cassie nodded. "Exactly. This is a similar cut to the

others I've made. Flattering on Miss Penhallow, but not so modish as to upset the older ladies with more conservative ideas. Though it does help if they can at least move into the Edwardian era, not the Victorian."

"I do like my lady's ankles rather too much to hide them entirely behind folds of cloth. Along with other portions of her, naturally."

Cassie couldn't help snorting. "Your admiration of her form is a tad obvious, Lord Carillon, so you're aware."

He grinned and mock-saluted her, waving a couple of fingers near his temple. "So. Our alternatives."

She gestured to one of the dummies, displaying its mockup. "If you wish her to be suitable with little anyone could complain about, I would suggest something along these lines. A deeper blue, not quite navy, but somewhere deeper than cobalt. Sedate, decorous. Perhaps a string of pearls, or a single notable pendant. Cream and the dark fabric, you understand, the contrast?"

"You had mentioned something about the colours at the event."

"Dame Arkady prefers shades of brown or sepia with cream. An evocation of the old texts and history, might be a way to think of it, parchment and faded oak gall ink. The deep blue will contrast nicely, without competing, and will do better than that smoke grey that was suggested."

She was unclear if it had been Lord Carillon, Benton, the lady's maid, or Miss Penhallow who'd had that idea. Whoever it was, they should be talked out of it. "At other times, I might suggest a purer white, but that would clash with Dame Arkady's choices."

He leaned forward. "Ah, I think I see the problem. And the parchment and sepia shades would not flatter my Lizzie, no." His voice was quite fond.

Cassie nodded. "So that is the more conservative choice. Unexceptional, easy to vary with a different shawl or some such." She then moved to the other dummy, pulling the muslin cover off. It revealed an emerald green silk dress with a drop waist and a broad band of decorative art deco ribbon across the hem and waist in a bouquet of colours like sun through a stained glass window.

She was most gratified to hear Lord Carillon whistle sharply between his teeth, and she didn't bother to repress the grin on her face. With most others she might have, but he'd enjoy her reactions, she knew that about him. "This is a dress that makes a statement. That is undeniably modern, and is having none of the historical foolishness."

"Rather not, no." He considers. "It is a stunning dress. I will have to think whether it suits the goals of the event, but would you make it up for Lizzie? The decorations, you'll want to adjust them to match her figure precisely, I know." Clever man, to know that just taking it wouldn't do, and would spoil the line. "We will find some use for it, even if that is her wearing it about the house for my admiration." Then, grinning, he added. "Mind, it deserves a larger audience, and I will do my best to find it one if we have to invent an entire new charitable arm to do so."

Cassie smiled back at him. "Both, then?"

He nodded, and she went off for her order book to make note of all the details. That would keep them all pleasantly busy, and with interesting enough work. The blue dress would be a good project for Joselyn to work on, with close supervision, which was all to the better.

TEN

"Thank you, Benton."

It came quietly, as his lordship was making his final personal preparations for bed. Benton turned from where he'd been pulling the blankets back. No need for the charm that made the water bottle warm tonight, it was a pleasant early summer evening.

"Sir?"

"Seeing to everything. The clothes for tomorrow, thank you for remembering I had the early hack scheduled."

"I am quite aware, sir, how much your day is improved by it."

Lord Carillon laughed. "There is that. Which improves your day, I'm sure."

Benton did not reply to that. It was beneath his dignity, and certainly beneath his lordship's. "Breakfast at seven, and Gossip will be ready for you at half-seven." She was his lordship's preferred mare for a morning ride at the moment.

His lordship nodded, then came padding over, nudged his slippers off, and his robe, letting Benton take it as he shrugged out of it. He got into bed, then said, "I'll have a few errands for you day after tomorrow. Trellech and London."

"Sir." Not unexpected, at all.

"Miss Penhallow's approval for two gowns, and there's a book at that auction. I trust you to act in my stead. I've got another matter of business."

Investigation, then. "May I inquire which project, sir? So I can have the proper clothes ready?"

His lordship snorted. "I knew you'd ask. You always do." He was quite contented. "War profiteers with a dangerous eye for new sales."

"Are you certain they won't know what you're after, sir?" It made him more certain that his lordship had been up to something with the dinner party.

"Oh, this isn't me attempting to sneak. This is me being invited as myself, and being amiable and seeing what gossip I can catch."

"Is it the kind of amiable where you'll be escorting Miss Penhallow?"

"Alas, no, she has a spot of work to attend to herself. But I will meet her afterwards. She tells me if you provide a purple flower or handkerchief or whatever other accent you choose, that will do nicely. Not a cravat, she understands you will not stretch to that."

"Purple, sir, not lavender?"

"Purple. Roman purple, Jovian, even. You know the shade."

"Naturally, sir. I will see to it. And your afternoon plans? Who are they with?"

"The Willacys will be there. Possibly also the Fitz-Donalds."

"Ah, sir." Benton went and hung the dressing gown, and

set the slippers tidily on the rug that would keep them lightly warmed through the night.

"You expected something else?" His lordship was sitting up in bed, leaning his elbows on his knees, and looking quite amused.

"It is quite common for you, sir, to have three or more plots at once. I was not certain this one connected with the supper last Saturday."

His lordship laughed, and said, easily, "The wedding planning is worth at least two plots, as it turns out. And the stables are another."

"I am quite confident in your capacity for additional plots, sir. After all, this is nothing compared to Nepal, or that trip to Brazil."

"You have a point, Benton. And nothing at all compared to the tail end of the War."

Benton turned. "I certainly hope not, sir. That placed entirely too much strain on you, sir, no matter how necessary it might have been. It made it quite difficult to provide sufficient quality of service." He would never criticise his lordship directly, of course, but pointing out such difficulties was proper service and attention to detail.

Mind, his lordship's move to Intelligence work, and his insistence on bringing Benton with him out of the trenches, had likely saved both their lives. It made it fiendishly difficult to complain about the strain of that work too much.

"I remain, as always, most attentive to your standards, Benton." There was a long pause, then a "This isn't too much for you? Seeing to the staff?" There was the faintest note of uncertainty in his lordship's voice.

"Of course not, sir. It's been a pleasure to see to the proper staffing of the house. Mrs Grieves is settling in very well."

His lordship nodded. "Still. Properly we'd have a butler." It was not like his lordship to worry about this sort of thing out loud.

"Sir, I hope the service has met your standards. I would rather handle things myself than have a butler who does not suit." Benton was not sure how to make this more clear than he already had, but this repeated return to the question worried him.

"Oh, quite, quite. Just. One has to check." He waved it off, then, as an unfortunately unresolved concern, and shifted, as abruptly as ever. "What about the other arrangements?" Ah, there was his sharp attention to detail.

Benton paused, considering. He had had an unpleasant visit with the staffing service that afternoon, but had not had a chance to bring it up until now, his lordship having been out all evening.

"Out with it, Benton." His lordship, of course, did not miss a thing.

"They had some concerns, sir, about, there's gossip, sir. About Miss Penhallow, about some of her father's creditors making noises. About whether the wedding will go through."

"Is there." It was low and flat. Hiding things from his lordship was not a solution, but Benton hated that note in his voice.

"They had not heard anything particularly concrete, sir, but they did ask if you would increase the deposit."

"How much?"

"Fifty percent within the week, the full amount payable within the month. They are willing to have it held in escrow in case there are concerns about the service provided."

"What are the terms for that?"

"The Scali are quite glad to provide the service as part

of their stewardship of your holdings, sir. I checked this afternoon."

"If the Scali are acceptable to the staffing service, we will do that." He paused. "I suppose that means they didn't have a recommendation for a butler. If they're that dubious about me."

"No one they cared to recommend at the moment, sir. They said they might in a few months." A few months would mean after the wedding, of course, and at least remove that detestable cause for gossip.

His lordship frowned. "I dislike the fact it is making difficulty for you. Is there truly no one you've found through other sources who might do?"

"Sir, there have been a few options, but the initial interviews were not promising." Benton considered, then said, "I wondered if one of them might actually be there at the behest of some other employer."

"Espionage, then, or sabotage? However did you spot that, Benton?"

"He inquired into the habits of the household a little too much and entirely too soon. There are standards, sir, for an initial discussion, before one even sees the houses. And when I inquired as to his references, well, sir, not everyone has your gift of remembering their cover story."

That phrasing at least made his lordship laugh. "Well, most people are amateurs in the game, thankfully, or that part of my life would be rather more difficult." Again, he frowned, teasing out another line to follow. "Did you find any possible connections?"

"A family close to the Willacys were one of his previous employers I could trace, sir. But it seemed, honestly, a bit subtle for them, from my observations so far."

"Quite. Mr Willacy has not struck me as a subtle man,

overall. Though I suppose there might be reason he'd extend himself."

"Reason, sir?"

"Their eldest son was a few years younger than I am, and he was killed rather horribly early in the War. And there have been some rumours about the younger son. They're quite protective of him, they pulled rather a lot of strings, I believe, to keep him away from the front. Begged for favours, I suspect, they may have trouble repaying."

"And Mr Willacy himself has industrial interests not to your taste." Benton added, after a moment, "Or mine, of course, sir."

"Poison gas is a horrific thing. When I think what it did to too many good men." He shook his head. "Speaking of, do find a time for the Leftons to come for the evening, just an intimate dinner. You'll need to coordinate with Kate's duty schedule."

Benton nodded. "I will see what can be arranged, sir. A weeknight would do, then?"

"Oh, yes, if it suits them and is not a bother for the household." His lordship tapped his fingers. "That doesn't solve the problem of a butler. I suppose there's still the option of training someone up to our standards. If we can find someone inclined."

"I shall keep an ear out, sir, for anyone who might potentially suit." Benton made a note to go talk further with the Servant's Guild.

His lordship nodded again, then said, "And the other staff? They're doing well?"

"Very well, sir. I will convey your appreciation to Mrs Grieves."

Lord Carillon snorted. "Seeing as how I am not complaining about their service." He looked rather pensive for a moment. "Do you miss the old times, Benton? The adventures? It's rather different now."

Benton considered. "I was pleased to be able to travel so widely with you, sir, and see to your needs. But I am also glad to be back in Albion, and take up a different kind of challenge. Setting things up so you can take up your responsibilities, entertain properly, and so forth."

"You don't find it boring?"

"Sir, some households might be, but yours is unlikely to become such a place."

That earned him a laugh. "And you like Lizzie, and the changes that will bring?" His tone had taken on that earnest, slightly nervous edge again, as it often did when he made this particular query.

"It is not my place to like or dislike, sir." As his lordship was entirely aware. But there was that fleeting look of uncertainty again. Benton paused, then said carefully, "I look forward to the challenge, sir, and Miss Penhallow has been nothing but considerate with the staff and her expectations. I look forward to ensuring she receives the same standard of service."

His lordship nodded. "Well. Good night, then, Benton."

ELEVEN

"The coin, Mistress."

Her attention was caught more by the angle of his face than his expression, at first. It was a grey and gloomy day out, rather abysmal weather for May. The lights in the shop were dim, since she was closed for fittings. Every bit of savings mattered.

"Is something the matter, Mr Benton?"

That was a decided twitch of his shoulder, quite unlike his usual solid patience.

"Tea, Mr Benton?"

He shook his head, a minute jerk. She was about to say something when there was a crack of thunder, and it began to downpour, rattling the glass in the windows.

"You can't go out in that. Let me make a pot, come up to the workroom, we can keep an eye out for when it stops." She considered the rush of water. "Or slows, at least."

Benton looked trapped for moment, but apparently even he could not bring himself to face that kind of drenching rain if it were not absolutely necessary. "Mistress."

"Back, up the stairs, through the door at the top, any comfortable chair."

She heard him obey, if slowly, the creak of his footsteps on the stairs up to the workroom. By the time she followed him with the tray, he had perched on one of the arm chairs, and was looking intently at the dressmaker forms that lined the back of the large room.

"No food or drink past that line, not that I expect that will be a problem." She gestured at the bright blue line on the wood floor.

He nodded, glancing at the tray. "Very generous, mistress. It is not a problem?"

"The apprentices are out for the day, I was intending to catch up on my accounts. Nothing that can't wait. You were the last person I was expecting to stop by." She paused, pouring the tea, remembering how he took it, and handing it over. "Please do use that little table, there."

"This," his voice was cautious. "This space seems more comfortable."

"I don't often let clients up here. It's a working space, not for show. Fabrics in the wardrobes there, trim and decorations in those cabinets." She was proud of the long series of repurposed apothecary cabinets, each marked with a sample of the beads or ribbon or trim that were stored inside on the label. It made for a showy sort of display, appealing to the eye.

He considered. "But you do the sewing up here?"

Cassie nodded, and gestured to four sewing machines, on desks shadowed by the eaves at the moment. "Most of it, yes. There's a little dumbwaiter over there to bring them up and down safely. But the light is better up here - well, when it's not pouring, though we have charm lights, too. And there's much more space, and less worry about a client stepping on a pin or sequin or bead."

They sat in silence, sipping their tea, for a good three minutes, before she ventured a cautious, "You seem a little troubled, Mr Benton. I hope Miss Penhallow and Lord Carillon are well?"

He shook his head. "Nothing like that, they both enjoy excellent health, thank you." It came out sounding rather more priggish than he usually did.

"I'm glad to hear that." Pressing was not going to do her any good, she could tell.

They sat in more silence, until finally he said, his voice quiet, "May I ask if you have heard further gossip about his lordship? Or Miss Penhallow."

She considered. "If I had, I would let you know. Nothing new. Is there some reason to be concerned?"

He shook his head, sharply enough that the teacup jerked slightly in his hand. "Thank you, no."

This was continuing rather difficult. "How are other plans proceeding for the wedding?"

Benton frowned. "Slowly. More slowly than I would prefer." And then there was a burst of mild frustration. "I have arranged expeditions into uncharted wilderness with decidedly less difficulty."

"Expeditions?" She'd heard stories about these expeditions, but never much in the way of details.

"You know, I believe, that his lordship has quite a reputation as an explorer? In his younger years, he pioneered new routes in the Amazon, bringing samples of various plants and beasts for scientific evaluation. We travelled together through Nepal and areas of Arunachal Pradesh."

Cassie blinked at the latter name, and he offered, "Very northern India and part of the area that has at times been

Tibet." The latter came out quite clipped. Perhaps he thought her ignorant, and she tried not to bristle outwardly at that.

"I've never had the opportunity to travel." It seemed the only possible thing to say. "Is it difficult to arrange a trip like that?"

"His lordship relied on me absolutely to hire men and buy sufficient in the way of supplies. Food, equipment, a Healer used to the area and familiar with the local customs, diseases, and plants. A translator, often."

"That seems, well, yes, that seems more complex than a wedding. Even his lordship's wedding."

It earned her a brief smile, and a nod, acknowledging the implied compliment. Then he said "Alas, it does not seem to be the actual case."

"Are you worrying over something in particular? If I can be any help, I would be glad to listen. In confidence, of course. I do have some experience of society arrangements."

There was a long pause, then Benton set down his cup, precisely in the centre of the saucer, and folded his hands, as if he were deciding on something. "There is some unpleasant gossip. About his lordship, about Miss Penhallow, about whether the wedding will proceed as planned."

"I had no idea there was any question about such serious matters as that." She took a moment to come up with a judicious phrasing. "I assume it is all entirely ridiculous gossip?"

Benton shrugged, that minute jerk of his shoulder that he permitted himself. "Some of the gossip is - not new. Rumours of his lordship's preferences for interesting tenors, that one is quite old, and had in fact been rather quiescent until recently. Some nastiness about Miss Penhallow's father and uncle, whether she will now make good the losses of their expedition. You mentioned you read the gossip papers."

"That seems quite unfair." She didn't specify which part. Then she added, out of a desire for honesty, "The rumours about the tenors, I ignore that sort of thing." It made her consider Benton's voice. She felt he might be more baritone than tenor but that didn't mean much against the rumours about Benton and Lord Carillon in private.

Benton looked up, his face in shadows from the way the light fell. "Gossip does not attend to fairness." It seemed like some precept handed down over the ages.

"If you said some of the gossip is older, that implies some is newer."

"His lordship has his projects, and he enjoys being cat among the pigeons. He is known not to care for those who make their living in munitions. Not the factory workers, they find jobs where they must, but the people who design and grow rich on such things."

"Is that a problem, still? It was the war to end all wars, surely."

Again, that little twitch of the shoulder. "There are rumours of several kinds."

She reached for her tea, for the last bit in her cup, draining it. "Is there - some way I might be of assistance? Passing on anything I hear?"

He said, "I do not think so in this case," then, slowly, added, "I wish I had some way to find out more."

"In what sense, Mr Benton?"

"I am - in many circles, people know me as his lordship's man. Loyal, unyielding, incorruptible. There are times it has meant I could not provide his lordship with adequate service."

There was something in how he said it, despite all it

implied about him shaping himself to someone else's life, even down to the gossip, that made her heart break. He wished to do this thing, and could not, that was as clear as the sign on her shop.

"And yet you wonder how to explore the gossip?"

Benton looked up, and nodded once. "Precisely. I do not think that is something you could help with."

Cassie set her cup down. "Where would you like to explore?"

Benton paused. "His lordship and Miss Penhallow have certain areas covered, I believe. Perhaps lower class gatherings. Servants who do not know me."

"Working men?" Cassie did indeed have an idea, though it was almost ridiculous to think that Benton, primly dressed and proper, could pull it off.

"Something like that. If there is agitation among factory workers, or people bringing supplies in, or servants of those who are well off. But the servants would know me, or be likely to. And the others, I am not of them. Of their kind."

He sounded almost sorry about it.

"I don't know much about where you come from, Mr Benton." She said it hesitantly. He might take it as insult, or dash away into the downpour, or do something even worse.

There was that little straightening of his shoulders, then he said, "I grew up on the home farm. I was in service from the time I was thirteen. As a hall boy, then a footman, before going to fight."

"Was that with Lord Carillon's family?"

"No, a cadet line of an aristocratic family in Kent. Quite a large household staff at the time, everyone with particularly defined roles."

"Old-fashioned service, then." She couldn't stop her voice from sounding a bit tight.

"You don't approve, Mistress?" She realised, then, that he was asking questions, that something had shifted, that meant he was no longer insisting on pretending he already knew everything. He must indeed be worried, to ask her, of all people.

She shrugged, minutely. "I come from a working class family. Making our own way. We were very lucky. I did well enough on my exams, they let me go to Alethorpe, and that changed everything. It meant I could learn the sewing magics there, the things that make clothing, and then someone, one of my teachers there, she arranged the apprenticeship. I only finished paying it off last year."

He blinked. "Paying it off?"

Cassie shrugged. "People who take apprentices can set their own fees or standards. Sometimes it's fairly modest. Sometimes it's not." It was why she had three apprentices, despite the amount of time and effort they took, it had been the fastest way to build the business. She pressed on, explaining. "Sometimes it depends on favours and families. My brother apprenticed with someone who had a son who wanted to apprentice to my uncle. A swap."

Benton nodded. "A large family, then?"

"Smaller than it used to be." She paused, hating how this always took the conversation into an awful silence. "My brother died in the War. The other young man, too."

Benton left a moment of respectful silence, then spoke quietly. "My sympathies, mistress."

Cassie nodded. There was nothing one could say, really, other than fall into awful platitudes that only made things worse. She picked up her tea cup again, and returned, rather resolutely, to the original topic. "If you want an introduction to working men, if you could - bring yourself to dress and act the part, I might have an option."

Benton frowned. "Why?" It came out rather more bluntly than his usual.

Cassie shrugged. "I don't approve of your choice of employment. But your loyalty, your commitment, those are admirable things. And I do, as I have said, appreciate your employer."

"May I ask what you had in mind?"

"Could you be a betting man? And if so, how do you feel about a cock fight?"

TWELVE

FRIDAY AFTERNOON

Benton blinked at her once more. "Cock fight?" Once again, she had done something entirely and unsettlingly unanticipated.

Cassie leaned back, watching him. "Cock fights. Men. Roosters. Nasty things, but it's a good place to meet people of a certain type. And if you lose, you can commiserate with people over a beer afterwards."

Benton frowned. "I do not," He turned it over in his mind, now cautious. "When I was in the army, that kind of thing ended badly." Also, it was illegal.

"What was it like when you were younger, then?"

Benton shifted, uncomfortably. "I had a bit of a temper when I was younger. By the time I went into the Army, I had learned to have more control. But that meant not doing things where I might be tempted."

"What sort of things would tempt you?" She was leaning forward, interested. "You seem very well controlled these days."

He lifted his chin. "Being in service, under a good man,

that has been a great help. Knowing what is expected of me."

The early years of his service had been gruelling, and sometimes unkind, but these days he appreciated the discipline he'd had to learn. Being told exactly what was expected, and what would be seen as excellent. The butler training him to keep his temper, to have an even keel, to be pleasant to work with, even if he didn't care for someone. Not things she'd had to learn, or at least not in the same ways. He was clear about that.

It wasn't the answer she was expecting, because she tilted her head and blinked at him. "You're an interesting puzzle, Mr Benton." Her tone was unfamiliar, one he had not heard from her before.

He shrugged slightly to cover his confusion. "I am as my life made me."

That puzzled her more; she opened her mouth and closed it again with a slight snap. "How did you end up as his lordship's soldier-servant?"

That was at least an easier conversation, though Benton paused to gather his thoughts. "My parents had been in service, before they married. I was the second oldest, and it was decided better for me to go into service than some other occupation. I became a hallboy as I said. They taught me the necessary tasks." He hesitated for a moment, then added, "My family thought the structure of a great house would be good for me. They were right."

"Did you go to school before that?" He expected her to ask about the structure, and was both relieved and confused that she hadn't.

"Only the village school, but there was tutoring for the staff on the estate. Reading, writing, mathematics, enough in the way of charms and stillroom magics for the cooking and cleaning and lights and all." He paused. "Diction, posture, presentation, if one wished to be considered for more public opportunities, as a footman, perhaps some day valet or butler."

She nodded. "Actually, I'm not clear on what a hallboy does."

"Before the War, a large country house might have dozens of indoor staff. One begins in the less skilled positions and moves up." Benton paused, organizing his thoughts into precise rows. "It depends on the household. I polished shoes, set table in the servants hall, helped with trays for the children and senior household staff. Nothing public. Carried things up and downstairs."

"And you were how old? Thirteen, you said?"

"When I started." He adjusted his position just slightly, a subtle thing, to keep from getting stiff. "We were on rotation, one day in four, we fed the charms in the kitchen, and had a lighter work day. I liked those. It was polishing the plate and doing reading and writing assignments."

Cassie frowned. "Feeding the charms. Oh, like the oven and stove?"

"And the cold room. A great house has a cold room instead of just a cabinet. All big things, they take a lot of magic to run them."

"That must have." Cassie considered, as if she were trying to decide whether to admit to something. "The couple I do in my flat, they leave me feeling tired for an hour or so but I only have to do them every week or two."

Benton shrugged. "That's why it was the young men. The hall boy, the boot boy, a stableboy or two, a junior footman. And we'd feed the stove and oven first thing, and have our breakfast. Then the cold room and the charms to keep pests away and the laundry after that."

Cassie nodded. "What did it feel like to you?"

"Water pouring." It spilled from him before he could say otherwise. "A stream." He couldn't help glancing up at the torrents of rain pouring down the skylights on the roof.

She caught the glance, and laughed. "Not quite like that, but even, flowing?"

He nodded. "It felt easy to me." He'd learned early on it didn't feel like that to other people, even most people. When he'd tried to talk about it, ask about it, there had been awkward silences and changes of topic he had stumbled with. His lordship had treated it differently, an easy gladness that Benton could offer that service as well. Benton had gathered, from little tidbits his lordship had dropped into conversation, that Benton's magic was rather stronger than the norm, but that simply made it harder to talk about. Being arrogant wouldn't do.

"Do you use much charmwork otherwise?" Her voice was curious now, and her fingers had shifted to fiddle with a tassel on the shawl flung over the back of her chair.

"Some. Mostly for hand cleaning - spots on a shirt, or boots, or so on. We're still hiring on staff at Ytene, and training them. His lordship's cook has strong opinions. I've picked up other things, over the years, to serve his lordship's needs." Not that he would explain those. His lordship's needs were rather too complex and revealing to discuss, in that regard.

Cassie laughed. "So how did you go from being a hallboy to a valet?" She was seeming oddly easy with him, now, for some reason, and it was rather difficult not to believe that she would turn on him again without warning.

Benton shrugged again, slightly, trying not to let his worries show. "I had risen to second footman, before the War, and then I was called up. I was not tall enough, you understand, to have much hope of first footman. And I was not sure what I would do, only the War changed everything."

"Not tall enough?"

Benton leaned forward. "Footmen are often paid for their height and their handsomeness. And I have not much hope of the latter either. But I was clever enough, and excellent at keeping track of the details, and those were a help."

"Tsk, Mr Benton. You have an interesting face." There was a note in her voice that he couldn't make any sense of, like she was teasing, but she had no reason to be teasing him.

"That is rarely a compliment, Mistress Castalia." He kept his voice even, wanting her to consider their respective positions.

She blinked, as if she wasn't sure where the conversation had twisted on her. "I mean it sincerely. You are attentive, thoughtful, intelligent, perceptive."

"These are," he said, pausing for the right words, "Not the things many prefer in their servants. They prefer we not draw attention. Nor is it a thing about my face."

Cassie waved a hand, dismissing the latter point entirely. "Someone does, clearly."

"His lordship is exceptional on a number of fronts." Benton paused, realising he had never explained this to anyone. No one had ever asked. "I was sent to the front, and assigned to his lordship's unit. His previous soldier-servant had been invalided out, they found out I had been in service, and assigned me to him. A temporary thing, everyone said. I think they felt I wasn't good enough for him."

"Only that wasn't what happened?"

Benton shook his head. "His lordship was pleased with

my service. Perhaps that I always provided hot water to wash and shave in, regardless of conditions. Warming water has always been one of my better skills, magically, and one his lordship particularly values."

He glanced up, and Cassie was grinning at him. "Oh, how clever of you. Did you know that?"

Benton shrugged again. "I knew what made me feel better, Mistress. His lordship's preferences and mine run closely alongside each other when it comes to the daily comforts."

Cassie got an impish look in her eye. "And in the more private ones?"

Benton straightened, grimacing. "I do not comment on his lordship's private pleasures." Now he knew she must have got hold of some of the gossip about him catering to his lordship's particular pleasures in private, and that would not do at all.

She put up both hands in a gesture of regret, palms toward him. "Pax. Just. Your entire life is wrapped around his. Do you get any time to yourself?"

Benton frowned, and almost wanted to leave, but no, the rain was still bucketing down. Instead, he reached for his tea cup, took a deliberate sip, and set it down before he said, "I am content as I am."

It earned him a frown, but she nodded, and simply said, "More tea?" When he nodded, she poured. Once both cups were refilled and the sugar added, she said, "I was the child in the corner sewing dresses for dolls. Mine and everyone else's."

"It is a useful talent, Mistress." It came out rather bare, but it was true enough.

"I was very glad when Alethorpe took me. And then when my teacher found the apprenticeship for me. Otherwise I would have, I don't know." She waved a hand. "Been a seamstress for someone else, I suppose. None of the design work."

"I am not particularly familiar with Alethorpe. His lordship is a Schola man, of course, and I have had the pleasure of visiting the island with him a few times."

"Well, for one thing, Alethorpe is not on an island. It is up in Norfolk, on good solid land. Tucked into a hollow, there's the school, in a large old hall and set of boarding houses, and then a small village to provide necessities."

"It was established after the Pact, was it not?" Benton considered the fragments of history he'd heard.

"Yes, to replace a school in London that served the same focus. We didn't do much with history itself, mind you. I gather Schola is different. I was on good terms with those in my boarding house, but not so close we spend much time together now. I learned the things I needed to learn, to set myself up eventually, to be, oh, I know how to explain it." She gestured broadly. "The Greeks talked about a parthenos, a woman who was not bound to someone else's choices. I always rather liked that."

"No history, but the classics?"

Something in that made Cassie giggle, and then completely collapse into roaring laughter. Benton blinked, completely unsure what he could have said to cause that reaction.

It took a good minute for her to regain her composure, but she finally told him. "Lord Carillon asked much the same thing. It is common to have a reader when the sewing work is done. The classics in translation are a common choice, as they help with various costume party needs."

Benton blinked, then said, carefully. "Thank you, mistress. It seems quite different, yes, but practical."

She seemed about to say something else, but at that point, there was a break in the sound of the rain, and she looked up. "You should take advantage before it starts again."

Benton nodded. "My thanks for the hospitality, mistress. And the conversation. Please don't trouble yourself, I can find my way out."

"Even if I overstepped?"

He shrugged. "Most people don't apologise." That said, he stood and nodded once, before making his way down the stairs and out of the shop.

THIRTEEN

FRIDAY EVENING

"You're looking thoughtful?"

Cassie looked up. She'd stabbed herself in the fingers with her needle five times inside half an hour, a sure sign she was distracted and should stop working. Finally she had given up and gone down to the Crafter's Circle, one of the pubs that catered to the crafting guilds in Trellech. Decent lighting, unlike most pubs, designed for people who brought their handwork with them. And they were good about keeping the well-polished dark wood of the tables clean.

In this case, she had found a table well positioned to have a bit of privacy, but make it easy for her to spot people as they came in. She'd been hoping to catch Greer.

She waved a hand, which had a bit of knitting on the needle, and led to several looping curls of indigo blue yarn going everywhere. Greer gestured at the bench opposite, and Cassie nodded. "Sit, sit. Round on me, if you like."

Greer grinned, and ordered a pint as the pubkeeper's wife went by. "So. What're you thinking about?" She was irrepressible, the kind of person who didn't want to run her own shop because it would be far too much work. She had, however, turned out to be a wonder at dyeing fabrics consistently.

Thus, besides being a friend, she was a very useful person to know in Cassie's line of work. More importantly, at the moment, she had a vast number of cousins, many of whom were less lawfully inclined than she was.

"If you knew someone who wanted to get working class gossip. Workman's gossip. What would he need to do to fit in at a cock fight?"

Greer peered at her rather suspiciously. "That's a specific sort of question." She paused, then added, "And a dangerous one."

"You did ask." She glanced down, and set her needles clicking again. It was simple knitting, meant to be a pair of wristlets to keep her hands warm when it got round to winter again.

"Not the sort of answer I expected. What brought this on?"

Cassie considered her answer carefully, not wanting to share other people's secrets. "There's a nasty bit of gossip, and I know a man interested in tracking down what's going on. His usual sources aren't much help, and getting in with people who are less inclined to legality might be handy. I thought of some of your cousins."

Greer waved her hand. "Now, I'm sure you're not saying anything against Anghus or Bruce or Douglas or Nick or Brown Thomas."

"Nor Roy or Kenny or Keith. Or Euan. How's Euan doing, by the by?" Euan had had a particularly bad War.

Greer waved a hand. "Trying to settle down and not into a bottle. Failing at it less than he used to. We're hopeful. I'll let him know you were asking."

Cassie nodded, then continued. "Anyway. Don't need anything terribly awful, but a different sort of person."

"And regular gambling wouldn't do it?"

Cassie shook her head. "I don't think so. It's - it's posh gossip, this. But the man I know wants to find out if there's a darker current underneath. People actually planning to hire out trouble."

Greer leaned her elbows on the table. "Cock fighting. Drovers, carters, crafters, or servants?"

Again, she considered what to say, how much to give away. "It's a servant wants to pick up some gossip, hear what people are talking about, and he thinks he'll be recognised."

"Aim for the crafters, then. The other two will spot someone out of place fast as you can say soldi. And if they spot him standing out, they'll think he's a Guardsman." Lucia paused. "Will he look like he is? Sassenach or something else?"

"English. Very English. Entirely upright sort. Veteran, no injuries I'm aware of, so nothing too noticeable. Is there a way we could get him in?"

"If he's below stairs, surely he'd have his own contacts?"

"Valet, so." Cassie wriggled her hand. "You know I don't understand all of how that works, but that's a problem, right?"

Two of Greer's sisters were in service, they'd been round and round about this for years. She frowned, then said "Could he pass for man on hard times, looking for a bit of a gamble? A family debt, something like that?"

Cassie considered. "Loyal as the day is long, so he might be able to play that right, with a little planning."

"Clearly, telling him to be less upright's not the thing.

That sort never can pull it off. It'll stick out, even if it's Anghus or Roy with him."

"That's who you're thinking?"

Greer's shoulder twitched. "They've got a regular thing some Friday nights no one ever talks about. If it's not cock fighting, it's something else that will do."

"Oh, would you? Sometime in the next week or two, maybe?"

Greer looked at her, eyes gleaming. "What's in it for us?"

"Pah."

"Fair's fair. It'll take a bit of setting up. Borrowing some clothes. Introduction of someone. Servant from London, maybe? Explain a bit of why it's not someone they know?"

"That might do."

"What does this person look like?"

"Oh, five nine, give or take? Tall enough for a footman, but he broke his nose somewhere along the way. Not sharp looking, anymore."

"Thirties? Twenties?"

"Must be thirties. Veteran, like I said, and he was a grown man before he went fighting."

"Hmmm. Loud noises a problem?"

Cassie had to stop and consider that. She wasn't sure. "I don't know. I suppose I could ask."

"Not a good place for someone who can't deal with the noise, a cock fight. Or hold his drink. I suppose you don't know about that either."

"He's done a fair bit of travel, in some rough places. I think he can probably manage?"

"Oh, iron stomach? That might come in handy, actually. How broad in the shoulders?"

Cassie found that one easier, she couldn't help sizing

people for clothing. Even men. "That much, give or take a little." She held her hands out. "I suspect he'd be cautious of his hands, a pair of gloves might be a thing."

"Fair enough. Right. I'll see if I can sort out a cap, the right sort of clothes, some gloves, and boots. If I can get them, can he pay me for them?"

"I think that will be fine. If it's not too dear."

"That sort of clothes aren't." Greer was immensely practical.

Cassie let out a breath, and leaned back. They were just discussing details now. "So, what kind of favour do you want?"

Greer shrugged. "I'd rather you owe me one. Nothing illegal, per se. Our conversation isn't. What your friend gets up to is his business."

"He's not..." Cassie stopped. "Well. Friend's not the word I'd use?"

"Is he handsome? No, you said not handsome enough for a footman." Cassie inhaled, surprised by her sudden desire to protest.

Thankfully, the beer came then, finally, a pint tucked down in front of Greer, and a second pint for Cassie. She picked it up, drinking a bit to stall on saying anything, but that only lasted so long. Finally, the silence got too loud, and she said, "He's not the sort of man I usually talk to at all."

"Well, anyone who's met you for five minutes knows what you think of being in service."

Cassie winced. "I'm not that bad. Am I?"

"It is one of your more repeated opinions." Greer wasn't giving any leeway.

"He, he knows that about me." She let out a breath. She'd been too harsh on him, she knew that. Whatever she thought about service, what he was doing had some value in it. And he cared about doing the thing properly, which she had a growing, if grudging, respect for.

"How did you meet him, anyway?"

"His - the person he's valet to. Related errands, payment for dresses for his chosen partner, that sort of thing."

"Are they your particularly showy dresses?" Greer was looking for the advantage to her, of course, she had an eye for business.

"Oh, a couple of them. Still in progress. And a present for her that's the reason I was asking you about those blue and slate grey dyes."

"For the velvet, I remember. Did that come out like you were hoping, in the tests?"

"It has, yes. I'll have the final diagrams for you in a week or so. Mapping them out so they lay right and a bit of map isn't somewhere terribly unflattering is rather more complex than you'd think. And yet he also insists the map be useful."

"You went for the full circle, didn't you?"

"I did. Thankfully, she's never had any desire to go to Antarctica."

Greer laughed at this, rather loudly, and took another long drink of her beer. "Oh, that would be a challenge, wouldn't it? Well, I suppose that works well enough. You bring it along as soon as you can, I want plenty of time to get the shading right."

Cassie grinned back. "Of course. And I've got a commission for the Healing Temple ball I want to check with you. Layered colour effects, with some magical effects on some layers, light, sparkle, that sort of thing."

That took them in a much more comfortable direction, thankfully, and held them until Cassie paid their tab. Waving goodbye outside in the street, she took herself off to the small flat above the store and her well-earned bed.

FOURTEEN

TUESDAY THE 23RD OF JUNE, YTENE

The third time Benton rattled the tea cup as he put it down, Lord Carillon looked up. "Benton?" They had been sitting after Benton got his lordship ready for bed, talking over various household matters, and his lordship had insisted Benton join him in the tea. Benton had long since learned not to argue.

It was a question rather than a scolding, but Benton still felt it hit, as solid as a buffet on the arm.

"Pardon, sir." Unfortunately, that didn't smooth anything over.

"You are not yourself, Benton. I do know the signs." His lordship did tend to notice things, and it was both a gift and a terrible annoyance sometimes.

Benton took a deep breath, and then said "Would it be a difficulty, sir, if I were away from the house on Friday evening?"

Another man, a weaker man who didn't live for his service, might have grinned at the expression on Lord Carillon's face in that moment. "An evening out, Benton? You may certainly have permission. I had thought, well, Lizzie asked if I'd come for a Thursday to Monday. Out at her family place, see it in the glory of summer and all that."

His lordship was blushing. Goodness. "I will have plenty to do, sir, and I am sure the sea air would be good for you. And for Miss Penhallow. Should I see to arranging a hamper, so she does not need to spend too much time in the kitchen?"

Lord Carillon settled back in his chair. "If it would not be a difficulty for Mrs Mudthon, that would be a kindness." Which meant of course that Benton would arrange it promptly, they both knew that. And that it would have Miss Penhallow's preferred delicacies, and the fussy biscuits, and half a dozen other treats.

"And the younger Miss Penhallow?"

"Visiting friends, I gather. Someone she had known during her time away." She had spent a decade or so off in sanitaria for her health. He supposed it was good she had friends from there to visit, several ways around.

"I am glad she has the opportunity, sir. I will let the staff know."

There was a long pause, and his lordship was working around to asking something. Benton turned to adjust a few things on the dressing table, tidying a few items into their proper places. He heard a quiet, "Is it a chance for the staff to rest a little, when we're not here?"

Oh, his lordship had no idea how things worked, and why should he? He'd not been in charge of a fully staffed household for long. And Benton did his best to keep the minutiae from his lordship's attention. His lordship had other things to be doing.

"When you are not in residence, sir, it is a good time for the staff to do some of the heavier cleaning. The floors and the polishing, and so on."

"So you are saying that if I went away for a week every season, everyone would be polishing the marble and shining the wood, and rubbing that lovely furniture polish on things. The one that smells like honey and lemon?"

"Yes, sir." Benton couldn't help a slight smile. "I gather historically that was part of the reason for nobles to travel from estate to estate."

"Huh." Lord Carillon turned around to peer at him, over the arm of the sofa he had been stretched out on. "Would it make things easier, we could, well, I suppose if we go to Trellech, that's work for them there. Or Cumbria."

"We are very pleased to have you in residence here, sir, and I am quite certain I speak for the entire staff. And I won't answer for Mrs Mudthon's happiness if you aren't here regularly to sneak biscuits while they're cooling."

It was the perfect answer, and his lordship's expression shifted from worry he was failing at something to glee, with a "Well, then. Can't disappoint Mrs Mudthon. Perish the thought."

His lordship leaned back slightly, as if sorting through matters in his head, and then continued, "Go arrange what you need to arrange. I'll be taking the portal Thursday after breakfast, and back Monday evening for supper. I'm sure you'll have plenty to keep you busy, but you should certainly take the evening on Friday. Let the other staff know they may have an extra half day in there, schedules to be arranged with Mrs Grieves or yourself."

Benton made the slight bow. "Thank you, sir."

He found Mally first, sewing by the good light charms in her mistress's rooms. "Mally, his lordship has granted an extra half-day between Thursday and Monday, he is away to see Miss Penhallow."

"Oh, thank you, Mr Benton." She bit her lip, then

looked up at him. "Is there, do you think I could, the portal?" Her voice was uncertain. "I know it's not for regular use."

"It is not for regular use because his lordship does not want people coming through the courtyard at all hours. Did you want to see your mother?"

"Yes please, sir, if it's not a bother. I could do my lessons, and then go through the portal, and come back next time it was convenient?"

There was something exceedingly earnest about Mally. She was so grateful for the opportunities she had in this household, how much she wanted to do well by her mistress and by his lordship. He approved, but he would be glad when she settled into the role a bit more.

"I will ask his lordship in the morning, but I am sure we can arrange something suitable. Your mother worries, doesn't she?" It must be nice to have that as a person one could visit. He remembered when it had been.

"Oh, yes, Mr Benton. She's ever so pleased at all the things I'm learning. She likes to see the new stitches I've mastered, and the book of hairstyles I've been putting together. All the little details. Nothing private about Miss Penhallow, of course, or his lordship, but a little about the larger parties, the things that are in the newspapers, about people's dresses and all."

"That's entirely proper, Mally. It's right to be cautious with what we say outside the household." This was the kind of thought he wanted to encourage, not rote obedience, but thinking how others might piece together what someone said, even to their mother.

"People are very loyal here. Not like my last place."

Benton had to smile at that. "Your last place didn't treat you in a way that encouraged loyalty. And if you'd been loyal to them, you'd never have found your way here, would you? You were very helpful to his lordship and Miss Penhallow, in their investigation. His lordship rewards loyalty and from all I've seen, Miss Penhallow is cut from the same cloth."

Mally ducked her head. "I just, I think about how quickly I went to them, there, and I feel ashamed, if that's the word."

"You knew something was wrong, and you were asked to do more things that were wrong. And unsafe for you. We do things differently here." She knew that, but reinforcing it wouldn't hurt.

Mally nodded. "I appreciate your - your reassurance, Mr Benton. Your example." Then she blushed, rather dark, and he nodded, not commenting further, just murmuring, "I'll be downstairs talking to the senior staff for a few minutes, if you have questions. Have a good night, Mally."

With that he went off, winding through the back stairs down to the kitchen in the basement before going off to find Mrs Grieves. He found her with Mrs Mudthon, having a cup of tea in the housekeeper's parlour.

"Mrs Grieves, Mrs Mudthon." He inclined his head to both of them, and was not surprised when they waved him in.

"Tea, Mr Benton?" That was Mrs Grieves.

"If there's some still in the pot, please."

He waited while she poured. "One sugar?" When he nodded, she dropped it in, and handed the cup over. "Is his lordship settled for the night?"

"Yes." Benton wasn't sure how to bring this up. They'd ask questions, he was sure of it. At the same time, they needed to know and promptly. "He will be staying with Miss Penhallow, Thursday after breakfast to Monday afternoon. I asked if I might have an evening for a personal project. He was kind enough to grant the entire staff an extra half day while he was gone, scheduling at your discretion, Mrs Grieves, for the female staff."

"And yours for the male?"

Benton nodded. "I will let the men know at breakfast tomorrow. Anyone I should caution about behaviour?"

Mrs Grieves considered. "I think not, but better not to let Jory and Nell have the same night. They're still - well. They might be a tad foolish, yet." Nell was the under housemaid, and Jory was third footman. They'd started around the same time, and tended to focus on each other, to the exclusion of other staff, which was no good. His lordship did not forbid personal relationships between his staff, like many houses did, but skimping on the work or excluding other staff was not something Benton would tolerate.

"Of course. That's easily enough managed."

Mrs Mudthon was less easily managed, since the thing she said was "Which evening were you to be away?"

"Friday, Mrs Mudthon. I have an invitation to a social event. Something that might serve his lordship's goals in the long-term."

"That's scarcely a night off for yourself, Mr Benton."

"I am not at all sure what I would do with a night entirely for my own. It's been a quite long time since I had that freedom."

Both women tsked at him slightly, and then Mrs Grieves ventured a "Not even to see family?"

"My surviving family are in service, ma'am. We do not generally have the opportunity. We write, of course. They are glad I am back in the country, so the letters arrive promptly."

That got them distracted, at least, onto asking about

some of his travels that Mrs Grieves hadn't heard yet. Those travels had provided him with dozens of stories safe to tell older settled women. By the time they were done with their tea, it was time for Benton to excuse himself, so he could be up to talk to the grooms in the morning.

FIFTEEN

"Y ou sure he'll be here?"

Greer was not a patient woman. She was sitting on the couch in the front room, swinging one leg back and forth from the knee.

"Quite sure. Or he'd have sent a note. He's not late." She knew he would be here when he'd said. Tonight, she was finding that certainty more than a little soothing.

"Anghus and Roy won't wait past half-seven."

"And it's not yet half-six. Ah, there, I see someone on the steps."

There was the sharp knock she'd begun to associate with Benton, and Cassie hurried to open the door and let him in. For once on one of his visits, it was not raining. He had a leather satchel over his shoulder.

"B..." She paused. "I'm afraid I never asked your first name."

The question rather startled him. "Oh." He took his hat off, tucking it under his arm and offering a hand to Greer. "Thomas Benton, Mis..." He glanced at the necklace she wore with a guild token. "Mistress."

"Greer, I'm Greer. No last names tonight, it's safer where you're going. Can you manage that? I know it's a stretch."

Cassie cleared her throat. "Greer's sisters are in service. She understands the habits? We've got the clothes for you."

Greer waved a hand. "Go change, yeah? You'll want a few to get used to the way they fit."

Cassie could see that this was more than a little over-whelming to Mr Benton. He nodded, and said "May I change somewhere, Mistress?" with a slight precise bow to Cassie. She gestured. "The changing room at the back, the one that's empty."

As soon as he'd disappeared down the hall toward the back, out of immediate sight and sound, Greer hissed. "You said he wasn't handsome."

Cassie blinked several times. "Not handsome like a footman!"

"That jawline, mmm. And I have suspicions about the shoulders. Lovely posture, and oh, that voice. Not the accent he started with at all, I'm sure."

"He mentioned something about diction lessons, the first place he was in service."

"Oh, that would do it. One of the proper old houses, before the War, they took care with that kind of thing. Not like half the places nowadays. Too many of them don't have an idea what to do with staff, how to train them up into new duties, from below stairs to valets and lady's maids and so on." Greer looked off after him. "Fought in the War?"

"That's how he came into Lord Carillon's service."

"Pity that. That's a fine man, there, and a good-hearted one. Not enough of those left walking the earth." Greer was purring now, with an entirely lascivious glint in her eye.

Cassie hissed. "Greer, stop." She had no idea why she

was scolding Greer, it wasn't like Greer would listen to her. Something in Cassie's stomach felt small and tight and uncomfortable.

"You, Cassie, love, need to unbend. You could have a lovely fling, I bet, if you could persuade him."

Cassie turned away, and said "I'm not like that, Greer, you know that." Greer had plenty of flings, and Cassie couldn't bring herself to that kind of casual affection.

Her friend just laughed, and then they both heard footsteps coming back. There was something different about them, and Cassie could not pin it down immediately. When Benton reappeared, he was wearing boots instead of shoes, he must have brought those with him. Dark gray wool trousers with a few well-placed darns, and she could see a faded white shirt at collar and wrist. He had a suitably faded black jumper over it against the chill of the evening rather than a jacket or coat, no tie, and a soft cap on his head.

It wasn't just the clothing that was startling, it was the posture that went with it. A veteran's uprightness, but suddenly shabby and worn. She could see a moth hole or two in the sweater, badly mended, and it made her fingers twitch to fix it properly.

Greer chortled. "Oh, that's a fine thing. Veteran, down on your luck, then?"

"I gathered..." There was a pause, and a wholesale shift in the shape of his face, the set of his jaw, like a dog shaking water out of his coat. "Aye, I am, and hoping for a turn of the wheel to pick me up again." The whole accent changed, the vowels shifting, the entire timbre and rhythm of his speech. Normally he was precise, clipped, the kind of polish he must have worked so hard for, if that was how he started.

Cassie couldn't do anything but blink, and then realised

her mouth had dropped open and closed it with a sharp clack of her teeth.

Greer looked him up and down. "You might just manage, at that. Goodness. I didn't think you'd pull this off."

He glanced at her, and said, "Man knows his roots, Greer." Curious, how the r dropped out, but there was a space, where it ought to fit. She'd never heard anyone pronounce Greer's name like that, and it was clearly right for the role, because Greer took a step back. Then she nodded once, precisely.

"Right. See you down the corner in ten minutes. Come up to me, tell me you're glad to see me, something that sets off our going off together, and we'll be rolling from there. We're to a pub, down near the carters. I'll introduce you to Anghus and Roy, and they'll take you to where you're going." She looked him up and down. "Are you Thomas like that, or Tommy or Tom? Do you have a nickname?"

There was a tiny pause, and Benton said "Tam."

"Tam." She took one last look at him, and stood in a rush of skirts and fabric, striding to the door. Cassie couldn't quite read her response, whether Greer was more or less interested in him now.

When it closed behind her with a little ring of the bell, Cassie said, "Are you sure about this?"

He spread his hands. "I will do the needful thing, Mistress." The clipped voice, the proper accent, sounded suddenly entirely different, not the same man at all.

She took a step back, not sure what to make of him now. A man who could change like that, like the flip of a coin, suddenly she wasn't sure she knew him. "Is this too much for you?" Something in her wanted to press, wanted to get to the bottom of the wrongness she felt.

"I'll make do. I've made do all my life to now, plenty of

practice." He sounded intent on his goal, and she found it made her like him more, especially when he put it like her mother had. It made her want to reassure him, to tell him it would work out. Frankly, it startled her how it made her want to go with him, or see him after he was done, or something.

She saw, though, that pressing him further was making him more uncomfortable, and took a deep breath, trying to settle herself. "Do you have a story about how you met Anghus and Roy?"

Benton nodded. "We sorted that in notes. Friends of a friend. That part's true enough, actually, served with someone they knew well, he's since died." He brushed past that so quickly she almost missed the flash of grief. "Made free with the connection, in hopes I could win a bit of money."

"And you've coin? Do you need change, or a loan for it, or something of the kind?"

That got her a dignified. "I make quite a good salary, mistress, and rarely spend it." It was nearly scolding in tone, and she realised she was fussing over this rather a lot.

"Is there anything I can do?"

"Go back to your loft, mistress, and the sewing. This will work, or it won't, and there's not much you can do at this point to make it one or t'other." He was slipping back into the accent for the evening. "Thank you for passing on the gossip, and thank you for arranging things with Greer." He glanced off toward the door. "She's very determined, isn't she?"

"That is a way to put it. You will let me know how it goes?" She wondered if he realised Greer found him quite appealingly fit. Or what he'd do if he knew.

"When I have the opportunity, mistress. I expect to be

quite busy on the estate the next few days." He had drawn that sense of reserve around him again, even though it was at odds with the clothes. "I'll be by next I have errands to pick up my clothes. They're folded up for you to keep, thank you, in the satchel."

There wasn't anything she could say to that, so she simply nodded. "I'll make some tea and go to the workroom. Let yourself out, the door will lock behind you." It seemed kindest to let him gather himself.

There was a single nod from him, precise and sharp, and she turned, walking through the small hallway to the tea kettle and hob. She glanced up at the mirror that let her watch the front room, watching as he shifted, shrugging his shoulders, then rolling them.

He took a couple of steps one way, a couple another. As she watched, he let something shift in his right knee that suggested an old injury he usually outstubborned. That seemed to satisfy him, and he made his way to the door in that slight uneven stride. She had not noticed even a hint of it before, but it certainly seemed genuine enough, and he did not seem the sort of man who would manufacture such a thing.

She counted the ticks of the clock on the shelf beside her for a full minute. Only then did she go and look out the window. It was still light out, and the crowds were moderate for a summer evening, but she couldn't see him down the street. Or Greer.

SIXTEEN

FRIDAY EVENING AT A RURAL BARN

Benton was doing his best to keep his footing in the crowded and loud barn. There was a ring set up, wooden walls four foot high, around the octagonal fighting ring, with benches rising on four of the sides. The others were space for the men holding struggling cocks, and further along for the exchange of bets. They were deep into the second round of fighting now, and Benton was trying to look anywhere but the centre of the ring. People were shouting, the roosters were crowing, and he could barely hear himself think.

Anghus, a big brawny man, more ginger than brown in his hair, clapped him on the shoulder, and pointed. "That man there, he's the one you're wanting. Introduce you in the break."

Benton kept his voice low. "Who's he, then?"

"Goes by Frankie. Knows near everyone, runs a bit of everything. Above board and not, depending. Fair enough man, if you play fair with him." There was a scuffle to one side of the ring, as one of the roosters got free, his handler scurrying after him even while he was shaking a hand that was dripping blood from a fierce pecking. A cry went up from the crowd, the sound of people baying for blood.

Anghus patted his shoulder, and said "No taste for it?" in his ear.

Benton shook his head. "Had enough blood in the War."

Another man might have asked why Benton was here, then. Anghus just shrugged, and leaned over to Roy, snagging some of the roasted nuts from a twist of paper. Then he let out a roar himself at the birds in the ring.

Twenty seconds later, it was all over, both cocks in the ring down. Their handlers swooped in, with a crowd of others, and Anghus nudged him. "Now's our chance. This way." He stood, shouldering aside someone standing in the aisle, and Benton followed him, keeping close behind him. Anghus waved at several people, clapped half a dozen on the shoulders, and shouted something incomprehensible across the space at someone who was waving at him.

They came to a halt by Frankie, and Anghus waited only a moment before leaping into the conversation. "Frankie, mate, got a friend of m'cousin's here, Tam, Tam's needing someone knows somewhat about a thing."

Benton found Frankie eyeing him, a sort of cautious neutrality in his gaze. One eye was a bright vibrant blue, nearly as blue as his lordship's, and the other had a scar running across it, a cloudy space on the eye itself.

"Aye. What's it, then, Tam?"

Benton had thought about this all week. The comment his lordship had made during the goldwasser investigation had stung, that Benton was too forthright, sober, and impeccably honest to be convincing in subterfuge. His lordship was not wrong, precisely, so Benton had given considerable time to figuring out how to present himself.

"Owe a debt, to a lord has been kind t'my family." He let himself fall into the accents of his childhood. "Need to know if there's any jobs going to make things rough for Lord Carillon, out New Forest way."

It clearly wasn't what Frankie had expected, the man rocked back on his heels with a speculative sound.

"Just information you're wanting, then? Not someone to take the job?" It was as if he were checking. It might just be that information was one kind of cost, and damage was another, but he wondered what Frankie's limits were. Asking for information as a stranger was tricky, but not near as tricky as asking for harm to be done.

"The information, ye... yeah." He stopped himself from the crisp hiss of the s.

"It'll cost you. What're you good for?" Frankie tossed it off easily, like he said this a dozen times a night.

Benton shrugged, the right amount of casual in it. "Bum knee, can't carry things too well up and down anymore. Some magic skills. Read and write fair 'nough, someone needs help with records or paperwork."

Frankie flicked his fingers. "Not the usual sort of thing. Need folk, job's a bit on the rough side. To look the other way. You work?"

"Below stairs, sir. House in London. Not pretty 'nough for a footman, most men wouldn't have me to valet. General man, see to the household. Small house, sir, elderly couple, not much opportunity there."

"They have kids?"

"Did. Don't anymore. Got a nephew lives with them." Benton kept his voice flat. He knew well enough that if he hinted that way, there might be an inquiry about houses to burgle, or something else of the kind.

"Don't have much to offer then, do you?" There was a

call from nearer the ring, and Frankie said, "How do I get hold of you?"

"Message to the veteran's club drop boxes, Trellech or London. Or Anghus here, can get hold 'f me."

"Don't want your posh folks hearing from me?"

"They'd not understand. Might be turning me out, and where would I be then?"

"Frankie, hey, Frankie, got a minute." The voice came from behind Frankie to the left, toward the bookmakers.

Frankie waved a hand. "Check in after the next set. Three rounds tonight, paired matches. Think about what you can do."

Benton knew a dismissal when he heard one, and he heard Roy behind him. "Oy, Tam. Buy a man some more nuts, yeah?"

The next pair of fights went as badly for the cocks as was expected. There was screeching and blood and the rattle of people cheering. Benton did the minimum needed, watching the people instead. Observing how they inter-acted was a way to block out some of the noise, or at least keep his wits about him.

This trainer was leaning forward, hopeful. Perhaps he was glad that a rival wouldn't be competing against his bird. That one was chewing his nails, as if more were riding on the match than usual. He let his eyes shift around the crowd, let himself be drawn to unusual noises or movements that stood out.

When the next break started, he bumped Anghus with his shoulder, and said "Going to check with Frankie, ta. If I don't see you later, check with your cousin, yeah?"

Anghus nodded, and leaned over to say something in Roy's ear, and Roy nodded too. The background noise had got louder, behind him. It sounded like people had picked up some other sort of card game or match that had the crowd around the table cheering for one or another of the players.

He made his way down the rough wooden steps, around the edges of a knot of people gathered about an older woman who was gesturing wildly with her hands. It was not something he needed to be concerned about, so he noted them and moved on.

He was most of the way over toward Frankie when there was a sudden commotion behind him. He turned, automatically, and before he realised what was going on, there was a buffeting of wings and the crow of a rooster.

Benton threw his arms up, and there was a heavy weight hitting them, full of feathers and scratches and something sharp clacking near his face. He moved instinctively, tugging the weight downwards, trying to remember the way he'd learned on the home farm as a child. What he'd learned much more recently, in his lordship's service, had him rather turned about for a moment before he managed to get the bird under control.

He felt the stabbing pain along his rib a moment before he heard the "Oy, that's mine, he is, give him over." Another voice, a little closer, said, "Settle, Mike, he's the one caught your nasty thing."

Two men came over, Mike stomping and frowning with black hair and a moustache, the other red haired and more amiable. Mike said again, "Give him over," and held out a large burlap sack between his hands.

There was no graceful way to hand over an angry and dangerous rooster, not and maintain any dignity. Benton did what he could, gaining another half dozen scratches for his troubles. Light ones, mostly, along his hands, but one that tore the sweater and shirt under it to the skin, a second sharper sudden pain, near the first.

The man stomped off, the rooster struggling against him. The other man who'd come over shrugged. "Mike's like that. You all right, mate?"

Benton wasn't, but he wasn't going to admit it. That show of weakness could be fatal, he knew that all too well. "Few scratches." he grunted. "Nothing much." He kept it short, he could feel the accent slipping, for all it was the one he'd been born to. The man who could fight through pain spoke differently.

It got him a shrug, a clap on the shoulder. "Ta, man. Nasty thing."

Benton couldn't help but agree, but he nodded, and then looked around to figure out if there was a way to extract himself. Go somewhere he could sort things out. He could feel something sticky from the side, where he'd felt the pain, and could only hope it wasn't obvious. Or that none of these men, the roughest and most dangerous, were as much like sharks as they wanted to be.

"Oy, Tam." That was Frankie.

Benton turned, nodded.

"Mike's bloody fixed on that bird. And there's good money riding on it winning. My money." There was a strong threat in there.

"Bird got loose, figured best to get it under control."

"You know roosters?" Frankie was leaning back a little. Less of a threat. Good. Something in there seemed to have caught his interest.

"Worked on the home farm, where my parents were, when I was little. Picked up enough." There was a line here. Not bragging, but giving enough thread to give Frankie something to work with.

"You good with other birds? Livestock?"

That got a shrug. "Out of practice. Not so many oxen or pigs or roosters in London, aye?"

Frankie snorted. "True. Help us move some stock. Need an extra set of hands. If it goes well, might have some news for you."

Benton chewed on that. It wouldn't do to be too eager. "And if you can't get the news?"

Frankie laughed, and jostled his arm. "Information, or I'll pay you same as the others. Maybe pass you along to someone else, if I can. Fair?"

It was fair enough, so Benton nodded. "When?"

"Next Thursday. Meet at sunset, pub near here, the Fallen Star."

Benton nodded. "Sunset. Fallen Star. Anyone to look for?"

"Me." He gestured. "Jackie, that's the man with Mike."

Benton nodded. "Fine, sir." And then a "Ought to get home, or they'll be asking me where I was."

Frankie laughed. "Can't have that, can we. People getting curious. Thursday next."

Benton nodded, and then Frankie turned away and he could slip out into the dark, onto the road, back to the portal.

SEVENTEEN

LATE FRIDAY EVENING AT YTENE

Benton got back to Ytene very late. There'd been a slow walk to the portal in the village where the cock fighting had been, and he'd had to take the portal back to London, Southwark, to keep up his story, before he could take one back to Ytene. There had been a wait at Southwark, some sort of performance, he thought, rather than a sporting event. By the time he was standing on the paved courtyard at Ytene, he could barely keep himself upright, and it was past eleven.

He nodded once at the groom on duty, fully aware that there'd be gossip in the morning. His lordship was known for having odd errands, but rarely ones that would have Benton coming in this late at night. Or wearing decidedly working class gear.

The kitchen staff had gone to bed, at least. He made it up the back stairs to his room tucked back near his lordship's rooms. Deeply grateful his lordship wasn't in residence, he closed the door and took advantage of the fact his door had a lock. Hearing it click into place, he turned, moving to the pitcher of water the housemaid had left earlier that evening, pouring it out in the matching basin.

He cupped his hands around the basin, willing himself to warm it. It did. He had to remind himself that he wasn't nearly so badly off as he'd been in the trenches. He was well fed, he'd slept in a comfortable bed last night and would again shortly. No one was actively trying to kill him, not even the rooster.

Even so, it took a minute for the water to warm to something satisfactory. Only when he felt it was truly where he wanted did he set the basin down, and begin to undress, moving gingerly. The cock had clearly got him, somewhere along his side, it hurt to lift his arm now.

He got the jumper off with difficulty, only to see a long tear down the left side, all the places the yarn had been shredded. The edges were stiff, and it was only after he touched it he realised it was blood. Mostly dry now, and invisible on the black jumper.

That worried him, and what he saw when he got the button up shirt off was worse. There was a fair bit of blood, and he let out a grunt as he began to dab it. It was in a bloody awful position, too, he couldn't get a good angle on it, he could only work by touch and pain. Finally, though, he thought he'd got it. He could pour the red-tinged water out the window, the plants below wouldn't mind.

Benton took a breath, and went to the expedition trunk at the end of his bed. He hadn't had the heart to put it in storage in the box room after his lordship claimed his title and stayed in Albion. Now he was grateful, because it held quite a good first aid box, with plenty of gauze and salve. He rubbed some of the wound salve onto the cut, wincing as it smarted, then managed to awkwardly arrange the gauze over it. It didn't rustle or bulge too badly, he didn't think it would show under his usual coat and vest.

He was, though, deeply grateful that this was Friday, and his lordship wouldn't be back until Monday. It was their way for Benton to get on with his work, he wasn't a man who needed to be told every detail, just as his lordship didn't need to hear every piece of what he did. But this, unhealed, he'd be asked about, and he wasn't sure how he'd explain it.

It felt fragile, not just the injury itself, though that was bad enough. But the way he'd got it, being at an illegal cock-fight, chasing a fragment of gossip. He thought his lordship might disapprove. Maybe not. But he was in no hurry to test the outcome, at least not without something to show for it. His lordship did appreciate results.

Nothing for it, he could only go to bed and rest up. He paused, then rummaged in the drawer of his dresser for the pain tablets for the ache he could feel more clearly now. Then he got into bed, closed his eyes, shifting awkwardly to find a comfortable position, and then he was out.

He woke hoping for a bath, to get the scents of the fields and the smoke and tobacco out of his hair, but it was not to be. There was an insistent knock on his door at seven in the morning, just as he was getting out of bed. "Mr Benton? Gam's got a problem with one of the horses, got hurt, sir. Mr Pride's got the horse, but can you come see to Gam, please, decide if he needs a Healer?" One of the other stable lads.

Benton rubbed his face. "How badly hurt?"

"Something in his leg, sir. He's sitting down."

"Run and tell them I'll be down in a couple of minutes. Don't move him more than you have to. See if someone in the kitchen can make a pot of tea and maybe some scones to go round. No food or drink for Gam until I look at him."

There was a "Sir, yes, sir." and steps receding back down the stairs. Benton levered himself up, grimacing as he moved. That cut had seized up, and badly, but there was nothing for it now. He added a wrap to support it, the technique he'd learned when one of the men he'd served with had a broken rib. It was awkward to do on himself, but needs must. That done, and a clean shirt and suit on, he went off to see to the chaos in the stable.

The chaos was considerable, as it turned out. Benton arrived in the stable yard to find three mares being walked around slowly in circles, well separated. One of the stallions - the shiny copper one - was neighing and banging against the stall he'd been shut in.

"What happened, then?"

"Gam was taking Smithy off to the far pasture, and he got loose, got into the mares. Got kicked hard, in the thigh, and you know more about that kind of injury than I do. I didn't want to call in a Healer without checking." Rufus ran his hand through his hair. "And someone's got to tell his lordship, and that's not pleasant news first thing in the morning."

"Let us see to Gam, then. How are the horses?"

"Smithy's edgy as anything. I'll have a word in his ear to settle him down. Wanted him to walk off a bit of the spark while I saw to Gam. The mares got worked up, we're walking them cool so they don't get into trouble eating when they're under stress."

Benton nodded. "Right, Gam, here. How're you feeling?" He bent down and regretted it immediately, a stitch forming in his side.

"Bloody awful. He kicked me." It was gruff, for all the man was maybe twenty-two. Benton considered how to go at this.

"That's what I heard. Where did you get kicked, then? Can you show me where?"

Gam gestured at the middle of his thigh.

"Ah, that's a nasty place for a kick. Solid kick or glancing? How does it feel?"

That got him a sour look, but Gam gave it some thought. "Square on. Aching. Throbbing. Not sharp, dull. Real - real much." It was grudging, Gam wasn't the sort who'd admit to pain, Benton thought, but the way he was talking and breathing, it hurt a fair bit.

He nodded, and said "Right. We're going to have you stay right here, leg up, and get a Healer in. Just to make sure."

Rufus was immediately at his side. "Who's best to go?"

Benton frowned. He probably should, but he wasn't up for two trips through the portal, the wrenching that sometimes happened, or waiting around for a Healer. Also a Healer might notice he wasn't doing as well himself as he should be.

He had to make a decision. "Let me get one of the house staff to go. You see to the horses, make sure someone stays with Gam. A cup of black tea's probably fine, but no other food until the healer's checked. Some of the potions react badly with different things."

Rufus nodded, and started giving the half dozen stable-hands milling around specific directions. Some to see to the horses and the morning chores, some to keep walking the mares, and one to sit with Gam while he went to calm Smithy. Benton pushed himself upright, and then made his way back through the kitchen. He paused to ask the kitchen maid to get tea for the stable staff, and maybe some scones, before going in search of Mally.

Mally was in the staff hall, working on sewing again in

the morning light. "Pardon, Mally. Would you be able to take the portal through to the Temple of Healing in Trellech, and ask one of the healers to come attend? A kicking injury with one of the horses. As soon as someone can, it was a nasty kick. I don't think it did the worst damage, but I know it's hard to tell, a thing like that."

She bobbed up, setting her sewing in the basket. "Of course, Mr Benton. Let me tuck this away and get my hat. Is there anything else they'll want from me?"

"There's a large desk at the temple, they'll ask what you need. You give his Lordship's name, and the portal sigils, you know those. I'll have a sealed slip, authority to request healer's aid for staff, by the time you've got your things."

Mally dipped, a reflexive half-curtsy. "Right generous he is, Mr Benton. Be right back."

Dreadfully informal, but Mally was good-hearted, and they were both lucky to be working for someone who thought ahead to his staff's needs. Or at least put his seal to a permission slip when Benton had suggested it when they set up the estate.

EIGHTEEN

MONDAY THE 29TH OF JUNE, TRELLECH

Cassie kept jumping every time she heard something rattle the door. For a wonder, it wasn't raining, but the wind was quite strong. She rarely scheduled appointments on Mondays, but she'd let Benton know first thing that the dresses for Miss Penhallow were ready. She was hoping that might bring him out.

That was a true thing, but only because she'd spent most of Sunday working on them to give herself something to do. She gave the apprentices the day off, generally, and this week they'd all been out and about. She'd sent them off today, as well, to see to various errands that would keep them busy until it was time for supper at their boarding house.

Thankfully, that meant they hadn't seen her waiting up on Friday in case there was news from someone. Or that she'd been up in the workroom until midnight sewing on Saturday night and again on Sunday when she couldn't manage to sleep. Now it was after lunch, and she had lost her second wind and was regretting her past choices.

Cassie had been working on attaching beaded lace trim

to a dress, getting it ready for a client. This was easy work, at least, just needing little precise stitches to secure the lace in the right place. The dress itself had come out well, a dusty rose with pleating on the short sleeves to draw attention upwards to the face. It would do well for the client, a woman in her late twenties, hoping to marry and showing off a flourish of the romantic, but not wanting to look like a bright young thing.

She yawned loudly, covering her face with her hand, and then jumped, when she heard a knock on the door and the bell. She hurried over, tugging her hair behind her ear and out of her face, opening the door to Benton. "Come in, come in."

It was only when she looked up at his face that she frowned. Benton was usually implacable, competent, and in control. There wasn't anything obviously changed, but she could see he was holding himself differently. Stiffly, but not with his usual poise. Just enough for her to notice, at least after a moment's reflection.

"Tea?" Tea was the only thing she could think of.

He nodded, frowning slightly.

"Come back, do. Upstairs, or we can sit down here in the back room?" She was babbling, she realised.

Benton made a slight gesture with his hand, then shrugged with the other shoulder. "As pleases you, mistress. And I had to come to town for another errand, it was not far out of my way to come here."

"Oh. Well. Tea, then."

He went and settled in one of the chairs. She bustled around in the tea nook, getting things ready and setting up a small three-tier stand with scones and a small pot of jam and some marzipan.

Benton blinked when she brought it out. "You didn't need to fuss, Mistress."

"Look, do call me Cassie. Since we're plotting at things together."

He looked pained. "If you insist." Not that he used her name, she noticed.

"How did it go on Friday?" She settled down in her chair, almost missing the minuscule wince.

"I am meeting certain gentlemen on Thursday evening, when I may hear something to my advantage."

It made her laugh, the way he'd switched back into his quite proper clipped accent. "More of the plot, then?"

He nodded a little stiffly.

"Were Anghus and Roy difficult?"

"Well, Roy was very possessive of his roasted nuts." He sounded much more amused by Roy than anything else, which meant he hadn't pressed the issue. "Anghus introduced me to someone who knows the right sort of people. He was watching me, rather closely."

"Because of how you behaved?"

Benton shrugged, again, that half-shrug. "I know how that sort of thing goes. I'm an outsider. Anghus and Roy knew a fair number of people, but they weren't locals, not where we were. Border Scots, am I right? And Greer as well?"

Cassie nodded. "The whole family's from up along there." she agreed. "I don't know them all, just, oh, a dozen of them. Which is about a fifth of the immediate family in Greer's generation."

"How did you come to meet Greer, then?"

"Apprenticeship. She was a couple of years behind, apprenticing to someone my mistress worked with regularly.

They're dyers, not dressmakers, but of course we rely on each other's work quite a lot." She waved a hand up at the workshop. "That map-based cloak, for Miss Penhallow, I think his lordship means it as a wedding gift? She's helped me with the dye."

Benton inclined his head. "His lordship mentioned something of the kind, yes. And Greer is good at what she does?"

"One of the best, though I don't flatter her that much to her face. She's got a deft touch with the fragile colours, the ones that can go all murky or dark or blotchy. And she has an excellent eye for colour, striking things that go beautifully together. She's part of why I've made the name I have for setting fashion, not just matching it. Trusting her eye."

Benton looked away for a moment. "Are you friends, then?"

Cassie shrugged. "As much as I am with anyone. There's another half dozen people, mostly women, I get a drink at the pub with regularly. Perhaps go to a concert or a play, for a bit of company. Five of us not married, three are." She wondered why he was asking so much about Greer. Her interest had been rather obvious, was he interested in Greer?

"Is there..." He stopped suddenly. "Pardon, Mistress, that's prying."

"I did tell you to call me Cassie. And I'm quite capable of telling you to mind your own beeswax if you ask something too nosy."

He snorted. "Well, is there a reason you didn't marry? Though I suppose the War's a common reason."

"I was fond of two apprentices, my age. Neither of them came back. Buried in France, so I can't even go look dolefully at their graves." She shook her head, not looking at him as he spoke next.

"Would you? You don't seem the kind to mourn forever." His voice was kind, much kinder than she expected, as if he were truly sorry for what she'd lost.

Cassie looked up, peering at him. "What makes you say that?"

Benton made that curious half-shrug again. "You've made a complete life, here. Your shop, your space, your control of who you welcome and who you do not." He reached for his tea cup again. "I've seen enough widows to know that for some of them, there's always a space beside them. For the man who used to be there, the pace of his conversation, the way he moved his hands."

Cassie blinked. It was a form of poetry she hadn't expected of him, and a remarkable intimacy, considering. "Observing his lordship, or something else?"

"The people chasing after his lordship, people in the village I come from. And I have, my position requires a certain amount of patiently waiting for other people to do things. It allows one to devote time to watching others come and go, how they interact when they don't believe you're looking. Or when they don't think that a servant is worth paying attention to."

Cassie was delightfully distracted by that. "Oh, of course they do that to you too. They do it to me all the time. It's amazing what people will say in my dressing room, even though I'm only a curtain's width away."

Benton nodded. "As, well, what got us started on the investigation. Women talking away, not thinking that what you hear might matter."

Cassie grimaced. "Quite. They've not been back, but I

can't find it in myself to be too upset by that. I prefer a nicer class of patron."

He tilted his head at that, then peered at her. "You mean that, don't you. It's not about social class for you. How curious."

"Oh, I'm quite pleased to have a few people with titles or money. Preferably both. As is my accounts book. But I like doing interesting work, for people who want more than the newest fad, willing to collaborate on finding the right things for their needs. The more of that work I can get, the better."

Benton considered. "It must be challenging, to build a business like that."

Cassie grinned suddenly. "Very. I went through a lot of cheese sandwiches. Stale bread, too. But it's satisfying to have it be my own work. And now things are stable, I stand a good chance of keeping it that way for a long time to come."

"That is your goal, then?"

"Several more decades of this, yes, then handing the business along to someone else. Oh, there will be something like pret-a-porter for magical types soon enough, maybe with some limited charms that go into the hems and the seams. But I think there will always be a market for custom work, for altering for the best fit, for accessories that are one of a kind. And of course, charms for different effects, drawing the most flattering light, making one more graceful, or all the things that make a complex gown easier to wear."

Benton nodded, leaned forward, and then winced suddenly.

"Are you all right?"

He tried to brush it off, but then he winced again, and

he was turning a rather distressing colour, flushed and visibly in pain.

"Does something hurt?"

That earned her a most dubious glare.

"Something does. What have you done to yourself?"

"Ah, um." He grimaced. "There was a difficult rooster."

NINETEEN

MONDAY AFTERNOON

"How was it difficult?" Cassie leaned forward, watching him closely, and now she could definitely see the signs of pain.

"It - got my side." It cost him a great deal to admit that, she thought, but at least she had an idea what to do with this.

"Have you cleaned it out properly? Dressed it?"

"Best I could, Friday night. It is in an awkward place."

"You look like you're starting an infection. Or worse. You know there's an old wives tale about them having poison. Did it have the cutting spurs they use on?"

Benton frowned, then said, "I - no?"

"That's probably why the infection. Dirt all over. Right. Take your coat and shirt off. I'm locking up so no one will come in." She could only hope that he wouldn't take the notion to go all mulish on her again and refuse to let her see.

The look on his face would be delightful to recall later. She was quite sure he hadn't had a woman tell him what to do like that since before the War. She waved a hand.

"Come on. Jacket and shirt off. I'll get the kit, but I can't work on something I can't reach."

He looked like he wanted to argue, but then he made the pained face again. "If - "

"I insist. Come on." That said, she went off to the front room, locking the door and turning the sign around. She looped back through to get the sizeable chest she kept tucked in the back hallway, bringing it out with a bit of effort, and setting it down.

Only then did she realise that Benton had indeed followed her instructions. He was working on the last few buttons of a nicely pressed crisp white shirt, revealing a broad chest, lightly haired. He had a tracework of scarring across one shoulder, but she thought that injury had not been too bad. It almost had a beauty to it, an intriguing symmetry she wanted to recreate in thread.

She felt him looking at her, and she ducked her head. "Pardon. Ah. Yes. Let me look at it. I suppose you didn't do anything sensible like seeing a Healer."

"I would scarcely draw attention to an illegal cock fight when I am hoping to get information from them still." Benton sounded almost offended she'd think he would let down the side like that.

Cassie looked at him, summoning her best apprentice-master look. "I'm sure Lord Carillon wouldn't want you hurting or worse."

Benton's face turned icy, severe. "Take a look, mistress, since you insist." Clearly, she had once again pressed a little too far, presuming upon that relationship in all its baffling touchiness. On the other hand, this was necessary.

Cassie nodded, and when he lifted his arm, she peeled back the gauze and tape, and then winced. "This is, I should get a Healer."

She felt his tone, the chill of it. "How bad is it?"

"There are definite signs of infection. And it looks like," she frowned. "Like you'd torn the wound open."

He flicked the fingers of his other hand. "Suggestions?" It came out gruffly, an order, not a request.

Cassie sucked in a breath, and said. "I'm handy with a needle and thread. Obviously. I could clean it out thoroughly, sew it closed. But if it doesn't work, you'll have to see a Healer tomorrow or Wednesday at the latest. Any hint of a fever, for example."

There was a long silence, then he said, "Do it," then there was a grudging "Please. And then tape it up again."

She let out a long breath. "I - I know one of the charms to numb it for a few minutes. And I've got a potion to clean it out properly. But you'll have to be careful after that."

He just grunted. "Do what you need."

"Can you sit like that for a few minutes, or would you rather be on your side?"

Benton grimaced again. "Perhaps better on the couch." It was grudging, but she knew she'd find it difficult to admit weakness. He must feel the same. Cassie helped him move over to the sofa, laying down a blanket first, and then figuring out how he could position himself, the swollen line of the cut quite visible.

She brought a lamp over, positioning it for the best light, then set up a small table, with everything to hand. First she set out the potion bottle, to clean everything out. Silk thread and the sharpest finest needle she could find. Freshly laundered silk handkerchief to dab the potion in the wound.

She paused and then carefully brushed her fingers along the tail end of the thread, concentrating hard, until she felt the needle and the silk thread join into one. That would be the smallest hole and the least damage in the sewing.

Finally, she closed her eyes, and spoke. "Right. Charm to numb everything first, to give it time to settle. Then I'll sterilise as much as I can, and then we'll do this." She paused, and ventured a "I can give you a bit of nice medicinal brandy after."

He didn't smile, but he nodded, entirely stoic. Cassie had to pause, half-close her eyes, to remember the chant she'd learned working in the hospitals, helping the proper nurses, in the midst of the War. Then she remembered the woman who'd taught it to her, the lilt of her voice. She settled into it, repeating it five times before carefully poking an area of redness with one finger. "How's that?"

Benton didn't jump, didn't flinch. That was quite promising, yes. "I'll be back in a minute." From there it was scrubbing her hands with the carbolic soap she kept for working with certain kinds of fabrics, before they were fully cleaned up from the dye process. She came back, letting her hands dry in the air, then settled down on the stool she'd set up, picking up the potion, and soaking the handkerchief in it. Finally, she took a deep breath and began using it to soak the wound, dabbing and poking.

The glance or two she got at Benton's face showed him half-biting his lip, insistently holding still. The slashing cut couldn't be comfortable, but his position was even less so, awkwardly propped on the sofa as he was. There was nothing for it but to keep going, and so she did, with all the stubborn determination she could muster.

Soak the injury, let the potion get into all the crevices as much as it could. Dab around the edges, anywhere there seemed to be the slightest scrape. Only then, when the edges were raw and bleeding slightly again, did she reach to soak a clean handkerchief. She drew the needle and thread along it, and then made one last rinse of her hands.

The charm was holding, she could see that, but Benton clearly felt this was something different, the way he grunted as the needle first went in.

"Does it hurt?" She had to check.

He didn't move. "It feels odd." It was a disgruntled noise, ill at ease, but determined. The best way through was to keep going, that much was clear. That is what she did, keeping the light shining clearly as she pieced together his skin as carefully as she'd sew pieces of fine gauze together, thread by delicate thread.

It took her a good ten minutes. When she sat back, finally, her hands shaking, she saw he was no longer conscious. It was enough to panic her, but he'd shown no signs of pain.

Not wanting to jostle him, she shifted slightly on her stool, and then just sat, waiting and watching. Time passed, enough that the colour of the light began to shift, as it came through the windows. She'd heard the bells outside ring for three before he moved again, reaching with his good hand to rub his face, and then wince. "I - pardon, Mistress."

She shook her head. "We're all set. It's a hair after three."

Benton made such a face, all frustrated deference gone to agitation. "I must be back for his lordship, promptly." He pushed himself upright, and winced again, as that moved everything, and she said hurriedly, "I didn't tape you up. Let me do that. Can you change it tomorrow morning, if I do."

"I'll manage." It was grudging again. "If you could tape it up."

She nodded, and bent her head, focusing on the tape and gauze, making a smooth layer over the stitches and wound. "Take the bottle with you - just dab it on, with the cleanest silk. Let me give you a couple of pieces. Silk's better, cotton sheds more fibres, that's the last thing you want when you're cleaning it out. If you have other cuts, do it to them too, but always a clean cloth."

He didn't argue, so she pulled away, moving to package up a small box with the bottle, the handkerchiefs. "The dress you came for, it's in the front room, all wrapped. It doesn't need special handling, nothing too delicate. Do you need to check the inventory?"

It was automatic, assuming he'd fuss about it, but he flushed briefly. "I think that is not necessary. Today."

That made her smile, the tiny grace he was granting. She handed over the smaller package, waiting for him to finish buttoning his shirt and slip on his suit jacket. "The charm should wear off fully in half an hour, if it hasn't already. Be careful, I made the stitches as even as I could, but if you do something that pulls on them..."

She was babbling, that was no good. He paused, looking her up and down, and then said, evenly. "I appreciate your efforts, Mi... " he began, then he stopped, and said, most precisely, "Cassie."

That done, he went promptly off to the front room. He gathered the box for the dress she had finished under his good arm, and went out the door before she could say anything else.

TWENTY

Benton found the next few days difficult in more ways than he liked. The wound in his side seemed to be healing better, and he applied the bottle Cassie had given him twice a day, carefully bandaging it up each time. It hurt less each time he did, even though that whole side of him was stiff - and coming up in ridiculously purple bruises, to boot.

It was no bother seeing to his lordship, who had come back to Ytene in a ridiculously good mood. Another man might have been singing in the streets, tipsy on champagne. His lordship settled into the library, plotting some present or project or trip of some kind. He stayed there for Tuesday, and most of Wednesday. He almost didn't notice when Benton asked for the time on Thursday to see to a matter on his behalf, and merely waved him off with a "Quite capable of undressing myself. Do bring over that catalogue from the auction next week, would you?"

Benton thought about whether he should fill his lordship in on the plans, but at the moment he was grasping at clouds and mist. There was nothing solid to report, and he rather thought his lordship was thoroughly busy with his own projects. That was normal, often. His lordship asked if he had questions, but they both went off on their own trajectories.

Thursday found Benton changing into working class clothes again, then going off to find the portal to the location he'd been told about. He turned up right on time, when Frankie was beginning to gather a handful of men out back of the Fallen Star, which was a somewhat disreputable looking pub. Frankie nodded at him, and said "This here is Tam," without introducing any of the others.

There was a little sorting out of who was good with what. From snippets of conversation, Benton realised they were in for a spot of rustling. Some sort of fowl, he thought, though he wasn't entirely sure, no one stopped to explain anything. It was a jumble of names and references.

After ten minutes, everyone got up and climbed into a nearby wagon, sitting on the hay. His side had healed enough that it wasn't agonising going over the ruts in the road. He was sure, though, this was not what Cassie had meant by taking care of the injury.

They pulled up after twenty minutes in a field running along the river, and Frankie grunted. "Right, all. Out."

Benton paused, near the back of the wagon, and Frankie said, "Haven't you figured it out yet? Marking and taking a few swans. Know someone will pay right good money for them. Won't hurt 'em, much. But needs people not afraid of the beaks."

That was not entirely what he'd expected. Treason, under the Old Laws, before the Pact, and not exactly law abiding now. Which made it a good reason for him not to get caught. "Am I working with someone?"

"Oy, Lance. Take Tam with you." Lance was an older man, grizzled, with ginger hair where it wasn't going a muddy grey. He grunted and Benton took that as all the welcome he was going to get. Lance turned, picking up a pile of fabric from a heap near the back of the wagon, and tossing it to Benton. It turned out to be a somewhat grubby canvas sack and a couple of lengths of burlap.

"You done this before?"

"Better with chickens. Catch them, wrap them up?" Benton suggested.

"Aye." Another grunt, another nod. "You go first."

Benton sucked a breath in between his teeth, and looked around. There were two swans, there, on the edge of the river, and he could see several other pairs up and down the river, with other sets of men getting closer. Wishing there were something like the Horseman's Word for swans, he swallowed and knew there was nothing for it but to act swiftly and decisively.

He managed to get close enough to make a proper lunge, getting the swan behind the head a moment before mighty wings began beating against his hips and thighs. His foot broke through grass on the river bank and he went into the water to his knee. He'd expected Lance to help, but he heard sounds of an outraged swan behind him. Lance must have gone for the mate to the one wriggling in his hands, trying to bite him.

It yanked one way, then the other, and Benton felt the stitch in his much-abused side. He struggled, nearly topping over with the thrashing of the swan under his hands. It was soft and strong, all at once, the softest thing he'd ever felt, despite the swan's attempts to snap at him. He finally managed to sink to his knees on the solid ground, pinning the swan's wings against its body. Then he got it under him, and got both hands on the neck, to keep it from twisting around and pecking him.

Someone tossed a burlap sack to him, and a length of rope, and Benton managed to work both around the swan, keeping the wings in place. "Bring it up to the wagon, yeah? There's cages, Hull's putting them together." Another wagon had pulled up, Benton could see, and there was a row of cages going up in it, enough for half a dozen pairs.

Benton grunted, and spent another minute wrestling the swan into position so he could tug it under his good arm, and hold the head. Getting up from the ground sent a shooting pain through his rib cage again, but he soldiered on, stubborn, until he was next in line with the swan.

"Here." It was taken from him, nudged into a cage, its mate tossed in behind and the cage sealed up. As the last of the swans were rounded up, Frankie came over and clapped him on the shoulder. "Stand you a beer, and pay you in talk. Aye?"

Benton nodded. "Back at that pub?"

Frankie grunted, spitting to the side. "Aye. Ten minutes, we'll be done. Bringing in the last two now. Want to get out before anyone spots us. Swans go one way, we go the other."

There was nothing to say to that, so Benton nodded, moved a few steps away, and waited until everyone was gathered. Someone threw blankets over the cages, and they must have had some kind of silencing magic woven in, because while they weren't much as blankets, the noise stopped immediately. A gesture from Frankie sent all of them scrambling into the other wagon. The road back was rougher than the way in, and Benton tucked his arms around his chest, as if his fingers were cold. Bracing helped some, but not nearly enough.

It was only once they were settled in the pub and Frankie had ordered him a pint that he began to relax just slightly. The other men formed a loose group in the back, but Frankie gestured at a table in the far corner.

"Nice evening's work."

Benton nodded.

"Ask you again?"

Benton shrugged. "Hard for me to get free, yeah? I won't talk, don't know more than nicknames, and I'm not stupid. But - not for me, most of this. Bit old in my bones, city boy more than I thought."

Frankie laughed at that, throwing his head back. "Your face, when you had to go into the water. You drying off?"

Benton shrugged with his good shoulder. "Enough. Old shoes, at least. Not stupid, yeah? Knew we'd likely be mucking around somewhere, if you'd taken a shine to me from the rooster."

"Fair enough. And you've done your part. We were shorthanded, and it's best to take them in pairs. So. I owe you a bit of payment."

Benton spread his hands. "Information, aye."

"How'd one like you come to owe Lord Carillon a debt, then?"

He'd expected something like it. "Lot of debts in the War. Saved a man's life."

Frankie tapped his fingers on the table, a rough vibration at each stroke. "Know someone who's chauffeur to a fine lady. Good with machines, he is. Heard a bit of gossip. Said I could give you his name. He owes me a favour, so you tell me if he doesn't come through."

Benton inclined his head. "And this clears it?"

"Enough. He doesn't have much else to offer."

"And he'll tell me something useful?"

Frankie nodded again. "I've heard a fair few rumours about Lord C. Ups and downs. Charms a lot of them, but there's quite a few don't like that lady of his, the one he's marrying. And I've heard a few nasty things. Nothing solid, just - rumblings. Fairly recent. Don't know the way toffs do things, but if it were my sort, I'd be saying someone was looking for a bit of revenge. If I were him, I'd be watching my back. That kind of thing." He flicked his fingers. "You know how it is, you feel the watcher, looking?"

Benton stopped and took a breath to quiet the automatic desire to leap to his lordship's defence. "Anyone in particular?"

"Bunch of the nobs who do those fancy parties. Women's societies, all the tiny tea sandwiches and all. Feels like that sort, not our sort, doing honest work. My wife's a catering cook, does some of them events."

"Hard work, that, doing it for a crowd."

Unexpectedly, Frankie smiled. "Ah, she's a good one, Bess, she'll be glad I met someone agrees she's right. You married?"

"Service." Benton pointed out. "Not a thing they smile on."

"Ah, that's a bloody shame. Right woman, there's a fine thing."

Benton was bemused by this side of Frankie, but he just nodded. "So. How do I talk to this driver of yours?"

Frankie slid a piece of paper over. "Lady goes into Trellech on Friday afternoons for tea, he can meet you. He parks by the north gate, and fetches her a carriage, there's a pub for carters there. Show up around three, ask for David. Put a bit of red on your hat, a ribbon or something, if you can, he said."

"Right. Ta. For the beer and the work and the news."

Frankie shrugged. "You need more work, you look me up. Don't mind finding work for a steady man who knows how things work." With that, he stood up, and went to join the others. Benton followed, staying for twenty minutes, before excusing himself to get the portal back to Ytene.

"Do I need to sew you up again?"

The words were out of her mouth before she realised what she was saying, how that tone of half-insulted worry would come across to him.

He waved a hand, and said "No." Then he paused and actually thought about it. "I don't think so."

It was half past twelve. As soon as she'd seen him outside, seen the way he was standing, she'd sent the apprentices off for lunch and on several errands that should take them until at least two. Then she'd turned the sign on the door to read "Closed".

"I have an appointment at two," she said. "Tea?"

He nodded, and somehow the acquiescence was more troubling to her than the lines of exhaustion in his face.

"Did Lord Carillon see you this morning?"

That got a definite wince. "Of course, Mi - Cassie."

"And he didn't tell you to go back to bed?"

Benton drew himself up, stiffly, then winced. "He would not do such a thing. It would," He paused, choosing his words carefully, all of a sudden. "It would be a deep insult. To imply I could not manage my duties."

"What happens when you get sick?"

"If it might harm his lordship, stay in bed. If it is merely challenging, I handle tasks as needed. His lordship is kind enough to ensure there are a number of potions to deal with most common complaints, or at least speed them along."

"Did you take them?"

"I did, yes. So that it wouldn't affect my service."

"Does he know?"

Benton had been trying not to think about that. His lordship had been rather overtly distracted this week, but there had been a look, Wednesday evening, which Benton had not argued with. He had instead gone to his room without comment. Talking about it would not have helped, it would distract his lordship when he had the scent of his own quarry. And Benton would mend. He had before. "I have not told him, no."

"I do not understand you. I swear, I do not understand how anyone could..."

She turned to see Benton leaning against the sofa, looking almost amused. "You don't. If you bring me tea, and one of those scones, I can try and explain." And then a slightly pained noise and an additional, "And if you had a hot water bottle, I would not refuse it."

The tone as he said the last, the tentative offer they both knew it was, made her snort. She went off to make all those things happen. It took precious minutes, but she supposed he could tell her something in the time they had left.

Ten minutes later, he had tea, scones, some slices of quiche she'd been saving for supper, and a hot water bottle tucked up against his side. With an added soothing charm on it, for good measure. She liked the way he was relaxing with it.

"What did you learn?" She might as well start with the most straightforward of the questions.

"There's a man I'm meeting around three at a pub on the edge of the city. I need a bit of red for my hat - ribbon or a scrap of fabric. If you can oblige? I didn't have time to find something this morning."

Cassie nodded, her mind flicking away to think of something suitable, before she caught herself. "What did you have to do?"

"A spot of treason."

She couldn't help gasping. "Treason?" He seemed very calm about it.

"All the swans in England belong to the King. We scooped up a dozen from a river. The Thames, I assume."

Cassie whistled. "And how do you feel about that?"

"Well, he's not a magical king, is he? And they're swans. It's not the worst thing I've done in service to his lordship."

Cassie frowned at that. "Does it bother you?"

"Being bothered is a habit I can't afford. They weren't hurt, they were being taken somewhere." He sounded tired, as if worrying about being bothered were entirely beyond him.

That first, oh, that bothered her, made her realise the gaps between them, all over again, but it wasn't a thing she could argue with. Not as they were. "And were you hurt?"

"Wrestling a swan was not easy on the stitches. But it didn't open anything up. I applied the potion and wrapped it. It aches but will mend." He shrugged with his good shoulder, but she noticed he moved the hot water bottle a little closer.

"Let me know when you need another." Again, it came

out sharper than she'd meant. "And this man you're meeting, he may know something useful?"

"I am not terribly hopeful. Frankie didn't think much of what he had on offer, other than that he is good with automobiles. But he may have gossip we can put to good use."

Cassie tapped her fingers on her teacup. "And the rest of it? Any news?"

Benton shook his head. "I think his lordship is enmeshed in other matters, but I am not sure precisely what. And of course he has spent time with Miss Penhallow."

Cassie leaned back. "May I ask what you think of it?"

"A personal question, isn't it?" For a moment, she thought she'd overstepped again, but his tone wasn't quite as forbidding as it seemed at first. Certainly he was smiling slightly, not frowning.

"We have moved on to - something more personal, yes? I have used one of my better fine needles on your skin."

"I do not believe Madam Foster's Guide to Etiquette lists that as a permissible stage in acquaintanceship." His voice was even, almost flat. "But she did not cover a number of other eventualities in my life so far, so I suppose I must forge my own way." It came out with a sort of world-weary faint amusement.

It made Cassie smile, then wave her hand. He was actually unbending enough to tell her jokes, now, and she liked that, that he trusted her that far. "Miss Penhallow?"

"She is clever enough to match his lordship." He paused, considering whether to say something. Cassie couldn't tell what, but she was beginning to be able to spot that look, that kind of pause.

Benton continued, slowly. "His lordship had a difficult War. And our adventures afterwards, they left him with a certain wanderlust. Before his brother and father died, that might have been fine. But when he had to take up the duties as Lord, I was concerned he would never be comfortable in one place long enough to see to the relevant magics. The ones that keep the fields green and the harvests plenty."

Cassie frowned. "Is that, is that still a thing?" She was cautious, unsure if she was about to give offence.

"Enough places, yes." Benton leaned back and he was smiling now. "His lordship takes it seriously. Oh, someone in his position could be gone for some of the rituals, if he has done them three years in a row. But it is good to balance those out. And different places have their own requirements. The New Forest cares about the first of May, and harvest. And a few minor dates for when the mares and stallions are turned out for the season, that kind of thing."

Cassie considered. "So he won't travel now?"

"Not as often. Not as far. Not until he has an heir, certainly, preferably a spare as well. But Miss Penhallow grew up travelling with her father and uncle. She missed it, I am quite sure. And his lordship is looking forward to their honeymoon, planning a trip to places remote enough to be interesting, but near enough to not be too long or dangerous a trip."

"And you have experience. Rather a lot of experience." She thought back to what he'd glossed over previously. "What was it like travelling with Lord Carillon?"

That earned her a very thoughtful look. "Rather different than being in Albion." He took a moment to sip his tea. "We were often the only two people in a dozen miles who spoke English. Or most of the Romance languages. And then there were the quite real challenges of the expeditions. Arranging supplies and guides and transportation."

"Do you speak the languages of those places?" That couldn't be right.

"Oh, not all of them. Though I can muddle through in a dozen now, for buying basic supplies and finding someone who speaks a language one of us knows." He set his teacup down. "I miss it. The challenge of it. Figuring out how to get from place to place. Seeing to his lordship's needs here, even with arranging a suitable household and staff, that is not the same thing at all."

Cassie frowned. "They're both far more complicated than anything I've done."

Benton snorted. "Mistress Castalia, you have earned your mastery in your art form. You have all manner of designs and embellishments in your head, and do not forget I have seen your workroom upstairs. That is a kind of organisation I do not know, the same way."

She protested, "But it's all fabric, and thread."

"And who is the one who was adamant that Nile green was a particular shade of cloth? Even if it does bear little resemblance to the actual Nile." How strange for him to return to that moment, really, given how out of sorts it had left both of them at the time. His tone made it clear he considered it something of a joke between them, though.

Cassie had to laugh, had to take it the way he clearly meant it. "Well. I yield for the moment. But what is the difference between an expedition and a household?"

It was a question that made him think, and he held out his cup for more tea. Only once she had filled it again and added a lump of sugar did he sip and finally speak. "The challenge of the expedition is the unknown. If one is going where few Europeans have gone before, there are all sorts of needs that must be brought with you. Food, safe water, sufficient shelter. Healing supplies. And then of course whatever equipment is required for the location. Protection from wild animals."

"And there are fewer of those in the New Forest?"

Benton laughed, something that surprised both of them. "Generally not as lethal. Though there are botolons." He pauses for a moment. "His lordship is, thankfully, not among those for whom the touch of a ginsy is lethal."

"How do you find that out?"

Benton's tone became very dry. "Touch one and not die. A year ago, that was."

Cassie was about to say something else, when she glanced at the time, and said "Oh, goodness. And you still need something red."

"You have an appointment, of course." Benton stood, then awkwardly held out the now tepid water bottle. "May I clear the tray for you?"

The thought of his precise, tidy movements in her back hall made her shiver. Something in that was immensely intimate, and uncomfortably appealing. "No, thank you, that's fine. Do you have some... there's a cafe next door or one across the street," she offered. "Until your meeting."

She turned, going over to the small case of ribbons she kept handy, rifling through one of the small drawers. She drew out a three inch scrap of bright red ribbon. She folded it, charmed it in place, then reached for one more piece, darker, mounting it in the centre. "For your hat." She could have done something simpler, but he deserved more than the most trivial solution.

He bowed slightly, and then took his hat, inserting it precisely where it would stay in place. "I will have a wander down the street, I think. His lordship expressed some interest in the new shops going in up that way." He didn't comment on the ribbon at all, beyond that bow, and it left her rather frustrated, not knowing what he thought.

Cassie nodded, picking up the tray, then feeling horribly awkward. "We didn't really talk about the next steps."

"After I see a man in a pub. And see to his lordship's needs. It may be a few days."

There was nothing she could do but nod. Her curiosity was much less of a priority than most things in Benton's life.

"What did you learn?"

It had been a week, and Benton had not been able to get away until then. Now he was in the back of Cassie's shop, after she closed for the day. His lordship was safely off for another few days at Miss Penhallow's family home. He was not sure if that was his lordship giving him more room to manoeuvre, or his lordship enjoying his pleasures in simple living. Likely both.

"Your apprentices?" He was curious where they'd got to, not wanting to have people overhear this. They were at least up in the workroom, where they were less likely to be disturbed without warning.

"Gone for the evening. There's a bohort tournament for the Guild teams tomorrow, and a supper dance afterwards. They are all up in their rooms fussing over dresses, as they should be. Possibly also hats, though I admit millinery is not one of my better creative gifts or an easy one to teach."

"The bit of ribbon you gave me worked nicely." It had, too. He could remember the man glancing around the room and spotting him immediately.

Cassie smiled, and said, "So your contact found you?" She shook her head. "I feel like we're in a novel."

"The question is, is it a well-plotted novel, or is it one of those chaotic ones where all the clues are hidden until the final exposition?"

Cassie waved a hand. "I hope the former. Does that mean we have to call everyone together in a drawing room at some point?"

"I rather hope not. Good service is invisible, thank you." Despite that, he was amused.

"So what did he tell you?"

"First, he made sure I was the person Frankie had sent. I allowed as how I was, and that this would clear him with Frankie if he was honest with me."

"You added that bit." Cassie was leaning forward, though she nudged the plate of scones a bit closer.

"I endeavour to provide his lordship with exceptional service." He'd have sounded entirely too prim, only he was smiling. So was Cassie. He realised with a start she was beginning to learn to read him, that she made sense of his admittedly dry sense of humour.

"What did you learn?"

"David - that's the chauffeur - drives for an older woman, well up in the ranks of Albion's Inheritance. And she is good friends with several families his lordship has been curious about."

"Is that the reason Miss Penhallow's going to the gathering?" She sounded curious, beyond the bare requirement of keeping the conversation going.

"It is part of the reason, yes." Benton frowned, thinking through what had been said. "She has some plan in mind, certainly. Beyond the usual expansion of connections before the wedding."

"It seems an awful lot of gossip." Cassie sounded entirely dubious of the whole situation, and he couldn't blame her at all. It was murky and complicated, and he knew he was seeing only fragments of what was going on. "I admit, I find some of it baffling. There was that piece about - what was it, jewels that turned out to be paste?"

Benton snorted. "You should know better than most that the distaff side is often more comprehensive than the sword side."

"That is quite archaic language. Women have been carrying swords quite a long time. And for that matter, a number of the master spinners and weavers are men."

"That's introducing logic. Certain turns of phrase defy rationality. Besides, a number of people in question are rather antiques themselves."

Cassie laughed, freely. "Oh, rather, yes. Fashion shows that quite well. The arguments some people have about waistlines and hemlines and bobbing their hair. Not that I think bobbing hair is magically sensible, there is actually rather a lot of practical lore about magic resting in the hair."

Benton leaned back. "It depends on the particular protections and connections one wishes to maintain. His lordship cut his short after..." He did not like to remember the time immediately after his lordship inherited. He took a breath. "I do have two questions for you. What do you know about someone named Wallington Aylett? The name came up."

Cassie frowned at that. "I've heard the name."

"He has connections to alchemical research of the sort that his lordship particularly disapproves of."

"Munitions?"

"Poison gases, in specific. His lordship lost friends to it. One of his friends lost his sight to it, and many of the other men in his command. And his lordship is right when he says it is a perversion of magic, born of cowardice and cruelty."

"Very strong opinions, then." Cassie's voice became quiet. "Did you ever," She didn't know how to finish that sentence.

"Not - close enough to do damage. But I was in hospital when they brought men in. It was..." Benton had to stop. "War is awful. Trench warfare triply so. Being gassed was something so far beyond that. It was not, the damage could appear days or weeks after a battle. For some time, they did not know that was the case, men would go back to fight, and wake screaming."

Cassie shivered. "Oh." And then she asked, carefully. "So Lord Carillon would quite like to stop this. I do know a little bit about Wallington Aylett. Not directly, but I have heard a bit."

Benton nodded. "Whatever you can share would be a help. The man became rather reclusive after the end of the War, from what I can find out nobody has seen him for nearly two years."

"He has a reputation as being quite an inventive alchemist. I know there's a potion or two he's designed for healing work. Something, some process that was hard on fullers or tanners. Something in the ingredients they use for it, that made people sick. And he came up with something that helps. I think it was before the War, though. The War changed a lot of people."

"That is commendable, I suppose." Benton frowns. "I, no, let me think. I will need to do some research. Perhaps his lordship's library will have what I need."

"What are you thinking of?"

He waved a hand. "A passing thought. Alchemists." Then he considered and added, "I will let you know if you

can help." It felt both odd and proper to make the sugges-
tion. The way Cassie lit up when he did, that felt even more
strange. "Anything else?"

She stood, moving to pace in the empty space between
the chairs and the dressmaker's dummies. "It's nagging at
the edge of my mind, a loose thread, those are so annoying."
It sounded like what he felt sometimes, the sense that something needed attention, an item out of place that put him on
guard.

Benton watched her, stepping across the space, four
steps and a turn, four steps and a turn, several times.
Finally, she turned back and said, "I remember hearing he
was connected with some sort of dye. A byproduct of other
research, though he's developed a few others. Some plant
not particularly known for its dye properties, but I can't
remember. It was when my Mistress was ill, I was - well.
Distracted."

"Do you remember the colour or the plant? Could you
ask Greer?" Benton leaned forward.

"You're worried." Cassie wasn't questioning him, but
looking rather startled.

"I am. Do you have those moments, where you know
something is important, but you have no idea why?" He had
never said this, this clearly, to anyone else, for all he knew
his lordship knew and valued this about him.

"Occasionally. I admit mine are usually very prosaic.
Or, you know, a glimpse of someone in a particular kind of
frock."

The image amused him for a brief flash. "This is one of
those. A moment where the light is brighter. A loose thread,
though that is not quite the idiom I'd use." Benton turned
his hand over. "You have the same sense I do, I think. If
about different things. When something feels off." He

realised, with a start, that he trusted her, liked her, wanted to sort this out with her. More than they already were.

"And that bothers you. Something small, and about your, about Lord Carillon."

"You were about to say something else?"

Cassie shrugged. "It seems wrong to refer to him as your employer, even if that is true. It's something else."

Benton nodded. "I gather most employees do not see their employer in the bath. Or after any number of questionable choices." He waited a beat, and added, "Though those are few and far between for his lordship."

Cassie reached for her tea, fidgeting slightly. He knew the look of it, that she was trying to figure out what to say and how to say it. "The - when you were picking things up, before. You mentioned, you expressed your commitment to Lord Carillon. Would it be presuming if I asked why you stay with him?"

Benton considered. "I have built my life around his lordship's needs." Then he waved a hand. "That is not a fair answer. Moment, let me see how to explain." He found himself wanting to give her more than the quick answer.

Cassie nodded, and settled herself in her chair, cautiously.

Benton took a sip of his tea, then set it down. "When I entered service, I was a young man, not sure what I wanted to do in the world. That house taught me the practical skills I could excel at. I am very good at what I do, Cassie, but there are not so many places I might do it. And fewer every year. Head man at one of the clubs, perhaps, but those positions turn over only rarely."

"You want a position with some scope, then."

He nodded. "It isn't just that. I was a farm boy, rough and raw. I didn't know what I didn't know. But that household, they also taught me to speak well, present myself well, and understand how to read a room or someone's body language to provide appropriate service. To enjoy reading, and learning, see the point of it."

"Body language?"

"If someone is tired, one might murmur that there is a message for them, did they wish to see to it now? A chance to excuse themselves for the evening or at least for a few minutes. If they are unsettled, one might bring a soothing drink, or prepare for the evening differently. If a gathering was likely to be unpleasant, one could provide a grounding secure presence. A certainty that they would be as well-presented as possible."

"And that matters." Cassie pauses. "Most people mock dressing well as a tool. Even here."

"They dismiss it as fashion or frippery. Which is ridiculous. Even if it were not for some of the protective elements of clothing, even the finest of sheer veils protecting skin from dangerous enchantments, clothing makes a statement. You helped Miss Penhallow with that, before."

Cassie grinned back at him, for a moment, that flashing smile. "I did. I do wish I could have seen his face with that deep red dress. It suited her beautifully, and knowing her now, it is not something she would ever have picked out for herself."

"I regret I cannot tell you. She did not remove her cloak until they arrived at the party." Benton paused, then leaned forward. "He did bring her back to the townhouse in Trellech that night. I did not expect that of him. It had been some time since he had brought anyone back."

She laughed. "He had a reputation for enjoying pleasures."

Benton frowned, considering how to reply. "Ah. Well.

He changed." He coughed, then continued. "That is a later part of the story."

Cassie gestured. "Please, whatever you are willing to share. I would like to understand better."

If he were going to repay her honesty, that would mean talking of those things he would rather forget.

TWENTY-THREE

FRIDAY EVENING

Cassie looked at him, and then made a decision. "Look, if this is going to be a longer conversation, do you object to coming through into my flat? It's in the adjoining building, through that door." Benton frowned, and she added immediately, "More comfortable chairs, more privacy, and I can lock up here properly."

He hesitated, she could see him weighing a dozen things against each other. "If it is not a difficulty."

"If it were difficult, I would not invite you. Do you mind waiting here while I lock up and turn the lights off. I have sandwiches in the cold box, more than enough to share. Unless you are expected somewhere else?"

He shook his head, looking more than a little baffled.

"Sit there, please, I will be just a few minutes." She stood, going downstairs to turn off the lights and check the locks as she always did. There were plenty of valuable items here, and things that could be easily damaged by fire or smoke or flood all too easily, never mind theft.

She ran her hand along the doors and the spot on the

window frame, worn smooth by her nightly rounds, that set the protections. All humming along correctly, that chord of music the firm she'd employed to see to the warding had trained her to listen for. Solid and unyielding, and yet flexible enough to respond if needed.

Cassie tested the back door the same way, and made her way upstairs. "There. All locked up. This way, oh - could you bring the tray?" It would give him something to do, and she thought that would be a help to him. He nodded, and waited until she led the way to the back door to her flat.

There was a door on the back wall of her workroom, a tiny hallway, barely three feet long, and a door on the other side that opened to the press of her palm against the wood. She felt more than heard the tiny click of the locks shifting, and the door opened onto her private quarters. They were in muted shades, heathered blues and greens and cool greys, making it feel like resting near a pool of still water.

She glanced around, making sure it was tidy. She occasionally had the apprentices up here, and she was not the sort of woman to leave intimate garments strewn around her sitting room, but still. One wanted to check.

Benton was waiting patiently behind her, and she moved through, into the room. "If you'd set the tray there, that table. Let me go get the sandwiches. Do you drink beer or cider?"

"Cider." He sounded quite startled.

She nodded, and went to check the lavatory was tidy, and then stuck her head into the bedroom. Her bed, with its deep garnet bedspread, had a small ball of black fur. "Evening, Chalice." It got her a small meow in response, before the cat twisted into a different position and went back to sleep.

That done, she nudged the door closed with a foot. She unpinned her hair from the formal arrangement she preferred for work, shaking it loose, before tucking it up with a single sturdy hair comb in a much looser style. She gathered up a shawl of woven silk in a deep blue she particularly loved. The fog was rolling in, she could feel the chill in the air.

All of that done, it was a matter of moments to stop in the small kitchen and bring the sandwiches out of the cold box and gather up two plates. She hoped he wasn't picky, the cafe downstairs ran to simple things. Cress and cream cheese, salmon spread, and cheddar and chutney in this batch. Finally, she picked up two bottles of cider, and returned to the living room.

He had set the tray down as instructed, and then had settled on one of the chairs next to the sofa. He looked stiff and uncertain.

"Nothing will bite you. Even the cat, she's curled up on the bed."

He blinked. "I thought cats were difficult around fabric?"

"Less difficult than roosters." She grinned at him. "But no, that is why there is a door, a hall, and another door. I do not open one until I am sure she is safely contained."

"And yet you have a cat?" He shifted uncomfortably at the mention of the rooster.

"Does his lordship not care for cats?" Goodness, now she was doing it, rather than sensibly calling the man Lord Carillon.

Benton did not appear to notice. "His lordship is exceedingly fond of horses, and appreciates a good working hound. We have not had the sort of life that lends itself to

cats previously. Barn cats, but they aren't the same at all."
He considers. "And his lordship had devoted himself to the
study of falconry in his youth, but raptors are not house
pets."

"You were going to tell me about some of that. Here,
you can figure out what those are, I'm sure. Eat as much as
you like, I can go by the cafe in the morning if I need to.
And here, let me get that." She tapped her fingers on the
cap of the cider, the little twist of magic she'd painstakingly
mastered to avoid wrenching her fingers opening bottles.

He took a long drink from his, visibly bracing. "I was
moving up steadily in service. Second footman, though I
would not have been in a household more focused on formal
presentation. But then came the War."

Formal presentation would not have cared for that
broken nose, Cassie supposed, so he likely had that well
before the War. "And you were called up? Or did you
volunteer?"

"I volunteered." His voice was quiet. "But I would have
been called up, I am quite sure. The cook read my cards.
The outcome was poor, if I delayed."

"Do you believe in them?"

"When our cook read them, yes. She had a gift for it.
She rarely read, but when she did, everyone paid attention."

Cassie nodded. "And then the trenches, you said?"

Benton nodded, taking a breath. "I was assigned to the
same unit as his lordship. And see, that is a reason not to
delay. If I'd waited until I was called up, I'd have ended up
somewhere entirely different."

"You'd mentioned that. And he was without someone to
keep his boots polished?" She realised immediately from the
way he went stiff and unyielding that she'd said something

insulting, and held up a hand. "Please, explain better? I clearly don't understand."

Benton paused, letting the awkwardness settle into the room. He reached for one of the sandwiches and a plate, took a bite, then another, setting it down precisely on the plate, and the plate down. Then he took an equally precise sip of the cider, and set that down on a coaster. "Providing service, excellent service, as a valet or a lady's maid, is a matter of being prescient. Of knowing what one's master or mistress will need before they know themselves, so it can be provided. Of finding the loose threads, as you said, before they become visible."

She nodded, silently.

"I am currently training Miss Stone, Mally, to be Miss Penhallow's lady's maid. Some of this I have expressed to her. What I struggle to explain to you, however, is why one does so. She does not need that explanation, she understands, intuitively. Those we serve, they are not better people than we are. Regrettably, many of the aristocracy have entirely undesirable habits."

"Not his lordship?" She offered it cautiously.

"His lordship is exceptional in a number of ways." That at least brought her a slight softening of his expression. "His lordship has responsibilities that I do not. When we were at War, he was responsible for conveying critical information about his men and our circumstances, and for seeing the orders he received were carried out properly."

She inclined her head, gave him space, before asking, "His men looked up to him, then?"

Benton nodded. "We were lucky. He was not asked to give any of the awful orders, to go over the top with no hope of success. At least while we were there. After - his lordship was seconded to other duties, and took me with him. The others were not so lucky." He paused, swallowed, and there was something complex there, an abyss she didn't know how to measure. "He continues to support the survivors." He added, after a complex sort of pause, "Anghus and Roy, they knew one of those who didn't."

There were deep snarls there, and she wanted to get her hands in there, the skills she'd built at easing tangled threads, and she couldn't, not like this. Instead, she offered, "A good officer, then. They were more rare than they should be."

He nodded, more at the gesture than the specifics, then set down his bottle, focusing on what he said next. "Since the War, he has been engaged in acts of unprecedented exploration and scientific discovery and analysis. That involves bringing back plants that might be cultivated and prepared for medicinal or magical purposes. There may be a cure for tuberculosis in his work, or the damage from poison gases."

Cassie considered that. "That is indeed valuable. But most lords and ladies don't go off on that kind of expedition."

"No. And his lordship cannot, not without an heir." Benton was clear about this. "His lordship has responsibilities to the local magics at Ytene. Maintaining the portal, for immediate access in case of war or plague or danger. Seeing that the people on his lands have justice, when required."

He frowned, pausing again. "There are seasonal rites, for the planting and the harvest, and at certain other points. I do not know all of those details, necessarily, but his lordship must fulfil them, or the land will suffer, and the people will suffer. And so he stays closer to home, and must find new pursuits, such as his investigations here and his ponies."

"And what does that mean for you? You had, you travelled with him so freely. It must be rather different to come back to the limitations of society."

That was a hit, she could tell. Benton looked away, and then nodded. "It has been challenging. I have had more than enough to keep me busy, with the various needs of the estate and now his increased social calendar. I admit I preferred the expeditions. His lordship insists on recognising my skills, others overlook them."

"If you could not serve where you are, would you leave service?"

She glanced over to see Benton look at her, his eyes widening, and then down and away. She could read the small shift that meant he was thinking about something he'd been trying to avoid considering. He might be an excellent valet, but he would make a poor card player when it came to betting. She leaned forward to take a sandwich for herself, giving him space and the pretence of not being stared at.

"I do not think I could serve someone else, now, no. But I have not thought of leaving service. My skills are, I do not know what I would do."

Cassie said, as gently as she could. "Many of your skills would be quite valuable. Import and export firms, coordinating magical crafting supplies, even work maintaining the necessary resources for the Healing Temple. Beside the clubs." She'd been thinking about it quite a bit, the range of things a man of his intelligence and competence might do instead. "A number of other things, I'm sure. I am glad you are so well suited to your work, though."

Benton nodded, and then said, changing the subject entirely, "I find the craftsmanship in the woven hangings here quite interesting. Could you tell me more about them?"

She recognised it for what it was, a chance for him to regroup and recover. She leaned back and began to explain where they came from, how they were the result of her basic training in dyework, so she could understand how to work with colour in a way that lived and breathed.

TWENTY-FOUR

TUESDAY THE 14TH OF JULY, AT YTENE.

Benton finished pouring a drink, and brought it over, presenting it on the small silver tray. The library was sorted for the evening, and in a few minutes, Benton could see to the things for the morning and let the evening unroll as his lordship preferred.

"Benton?" His lordship had that note in his voice, the one that suggested that there were plots in the works.

"Your lordship?"

"How complicated, precisely, would it be to arrange to have Hawk's Breath cleaned and sorted out for a gathering?" The Cumbria estate, then. "Lizzie and I were thinking a masked ball would be appropriate."

Benton blinked. This was not at all like his lordship. "When did you have in mind, sir? And how many staying overnight?"

"A fortnight?" It was half a question. "And under twenty overnight. We'd only need to open up the east wing. A hundred or a hundred fifty for the evening."

"It would be a stretch to have it ready that quickly and

prepare the cooking. And people do like time to plan their fancy dress, sir."

"I was thinking we might ask Mistress Castalia to be on hand, for last minute creations. Possibly her delightful apprentices? An illusion-worker, as well, I thought."

"They are not currently in favour in the higher levels of society, sir. That problem, last year, with the impersonation of Lady Summerton, and that situation with the eldest son of the Fitzroys."

"The Cumbria Fitzroys, I suppose. If it were the Essex ones, that would not be such a problem."

"The Cumbria side of the family, sir, yes."

There was a long pause, deliberate, before his lordship allowed, "Three weeks from Thursday."

Benton permitted himself the faintest of sighs. "Sir. If I may begin the arrangements first thing tomorrow?"

"Of course. I can manage without you for a few days. And I'll talk to Mrs Mudthon myself, I'd like her to have a hand with the pastries. Tomorrow morning, if she's available."

"Mrs Callypher needs to be handled carefully, sir." She was the cook up in Cumbria.

"Do you feel she's up to the main event? Buffet, small finger foods, for a hundred and fifty or so. If Mrs Mudthon does the pastries and sweets. I know Mrs Callypher's getting on a bit, but she does that grand range of historical dishes, easy to eat."

Quite complicated to make. "Is there a theme to the ball?"

"Our Illustrious Ancestors." His lordship looked up, eyes gleaming, the expression that meant he was playing out half a dozen plots at once, and had come up with the perfect ribbon to tie them together.

Benton took a step back, blinking, and then said, his voice sharply precise, "If your lordship would lay out the entirety of the fishing expedition up front, I could provide far more efficient service."

His lordship laughed, and gestured at the seat across from him. Benton frowned, disliking the implications of sitting in his lordship's presence, but they had had that argument exactly twice, early on, and Benton had lost both times. Dignity would not permit a third. He settled cautiously on the chair, well forward. He might be obliged to sit, but he would not take his ease. That would not do at all.

"Lizzie was at that meeting of the Albion Inheritance yesterday, and we agreed, talking about it over supper at her club, that something odd was going on. We are not in agreement about the nature or scope of the oddity. More information is clearly called for."

Benton frowned slightly, thinking through. "A particular segment of the group, sir, or more general?"

"Lizzie said the membership falls into a few distinct cliques. There are some, mostly the eldest women, now in their eighties and older, who enjoy a pleasant chance to gather and gossip about children, grandchildren, and great grandchildren. They have their own plots, of course, they have had plots their entire lives, but those run along rather predictable lines. Family matters, status and position."

"Nothing unfamiliar to Miss Penhallow, then." Benton agreed. "But perhaps nothing of particular interest or concern."

"Exactly. There is a group of young women, who came of age after the War." Quite young, then, Benton thought. "And their concerns are their apprenticeships if they have one, finding a suitable gentleman to marry, and their familial obligations. Again, nothing startling, and quite within the expected sort of thing. If with a bit more in the way of giggles and cocktails."

Benton smiled at that. "And scandalously bobbed hair?"

His lordship considered that, tapping his fingers on his glass. "Actually, no. That's an interesting point. Lizzie mentioned specifically they kept the magical traditions. Long hair, and shawls or a translucent layer."

Benton frowned. "Even at a daytime luncheon?" The hair was understandable, many people felt it held one's magic, one's history. An institution focused on history would be even more so. The shawls, however, implied that the ladies had some concerns about enchantments through the brush of liquid or powder against bare skin, or at least adhered to the tradition of appearing to have such concerns. Shoulders and arms made a most tempting target, even as hemlines continued upwards.

His lordship nodded. "Even there." He tapped his glass again. "That leaves three other groups. One mostly of women about Lizzie's age, and of somewhat similar position, women of good families, some betrothed or married, others unmarried due to the War."

Benton frowned. "Some of that generation do take up causes, sir." He offered it cautiously. There was nothing wrong with a well-planned cause. Many of them, however, were not planned, never mind well.

Lord Carillon laughed. "Rather, yes. Lizzie gathered two of them are active in some of the labour movement issues, among our non-magical cousins. Several are agitating for effective medical care, and half a dozen miss the opportunities the War brought to engage actively with the world. They were not the problem. She rather liked several of those, actually."

Benton inclined his head. "So the problem would be?"

"The last two groups. There are a dozen women, of good breeding, but impoverished families, married to those who did well out of the War, financially."

"Precisely the sorts you do not care for, sir."

"Exactly. The Willacys are excellent examples of the type, and relevant to our concerns in several directions."

"Do you have a particular worry, sir?"

Lord Carillon waved the hand not holding his brandy. "Several. They're distasteful people, bigoted, and not at all intelligent. Unfortunately, they are not intelligent in the manner that is most likely to lead to trouble."

"Ah." Benton considered. That was one of the things his lordship most enjoyed resolving, but the road there could be full of the unexpected challenge. "And the last group, sir?"

"They would be something of a mystery. There were a cluster of women, twelve or so, who sat together, talked, did not include the newer guests, and who were paying close attention to how specific people behaved. Lizzie did not have sufficient perspective to catch all of what they were focusing on, but she thought it might be women of independent means, but living in some isolation."

Benton contemplated this for a moment. "Jewel thieves? Seeking targets for some other plot, perhaps the helpful companion?" He rather thought someone with an eye for more subtle sorts of crime could do far worse than manipulate the women's groups.

His lordship threw back his head and laughed. "Exactly. One or the other, we suspect, but we would need more information to determine which, and who should take action on it."

Benton nodded. "Will you be inviting any of that set, sir?"

"Some, yes. I will think on the specifics of the invitation, and what information we might get by singling a few out."

"Council families, sir?"

His lordship shook his head. "Professor Fortier, but not his brother. Not the highest society, I think, in general. We'll come up with something closer to the wedding for them."

Benton considered. "You might consult with Madam Porter, perhaps, about the women? She had that bit of bother that had some similar elements, last year?"

It earned him an approving nod. "I don't pay you enough. Is there anything you wist for, Benton?"

Benton knew what this tone meant. Half an hour of his lordship's increasing bonhomie with a touch of the maudlin. And it would likely end with his lordship having a nightmare at three in the morning requiring cocoa. Neither of them needed that.

And besides, what he rather wanted was a bit more time to sit and talk. He was struck with the realisation that he would like was to sit down with Cassie and talk out what he could see of his lordship's plots. She knew things he did not, and she saw things differently. And unlike the staff here, who were diligent and kind, she had a sharpness and curiosity to her he was beginning to find reassuring rather than disturbing. There would be little time for a lingering conversation with her though, certainly not until after the ball. "You had some thoughts about the party, sir?"

"Ah, yes, quite." His lordship nearly drained his glass. "A hundred and fifty, finger foods and subtleties, some sort of historical timeline effect from oh, Troy to the turn of the century. The challenge is what one can come up with on short notice, of course. We'd provide some bare masks, lengths of muslin and linen and such, and allow people to apply what magics they will."

"So, both withdrawing rooms, with staff. May I borrow staff from here, then?"

"Certainly. Even a couple of the grooms, if you need. Most will come by portal, of course, not carriage or automobile." His lordship paused. "Actually, I'd be surprised if there were any by automobile, but I suppose you'd better have them clear space just in case."

Benton nodded. "Party from seven to midnight? The usual other arrangements?"

"Yes. I'll have the note so you can draw on the bank in the morning, and I'll talk to Mistress Castalia about our costumes. Lizzie has something that just needs altering and perhaps recolouring, and I have something that will match quite well."

Benton glanced up to see his lordship grinning broadly. It was that kind of plan, then, that he would smirk about until it was revealed. Benton had neither time nor inclination to pry it out of him. He took a breath, and murmured. "I will see to setting things in motion, sir, and let you know what else is needed from you."

"Right you are. Off you go, then. I can see myself to bed."

There was nothing to it but to go and begin to make the necessary lists and pack his suitcase for a few days in the north.

"**M**r Benton! I didn't expect to see you." It was the end of the day, ten minutes before closing, and Cassie had just finished showing what was likely the last client.

Benton nodded, a precise movement that made her realise he must be exhausted.

"Come in. Actually. Let me give you some things, go up to the flat, make yourself tea. I'll be up as soon as I close."

He blinked at her. "I didn't mean. I just had a question." His voice trailed off.

"You need some tea before you go on to your next thing. It's perfectly safe up there, and I know you won't pry. Well, safe unless Chalice lures you into rubbing her stomach. The door's open, the apprentices were helping with something this afternoon."

That completely undid him, and he actually gaped. "Chalice?" Goodness, he must be rather tired indeed, to have that be the thing that cracked his shell. It was perhaps odd to name one's cat after a magical tool, but surely not that startling.

"The cat. It's fine to pet the rest of her if she lets you. Go on. This basket. Upstairs. I'll be up in fifteen minutes or less."

There was something to be said for a man who knew how to recognise sensible orders, and more for one who did not get all recalcitrant about not taking them from anyone other than Lord Carillon. He closed his jaw with a soft snap. "Mistress." It was him agreeing, but better than that, he took the basket from her. She could hear his steps on the staircase, then the sound of the workshop door.

It took her twelve minutes in the end. She flipped the sign on the door precisely on time, locked her desk, and checked all of the windows and doors. She was listening closely as she came through the workroom and opened the door. No screams, so Chalice was behaving herself, at least.

When she closed the door behind her, she found that Benton was settled on the sofa, carefully and slowly petting her cat. He looked up briefly, and said, "No customers?"

"Thankfully, no. Oh, thank you for putting things out." The scones were arranged neatly on a plate, and she could see the teapot was right there, steeping. "So. How are the preparations going?"

"Exhaustingly. But Ytene isn't set up for the sort of party his lordship has in mind."

"He explained a little of it. The idea being to encourage people to improvise. My apprentices have been working on lengths of fabric that can be folded or sewn or arranged or charmed in all sorts of different ways. It's rather clever, actually, I've been using some ideas from a book from Venice, for their Carnival."

"I am glad you have it in hand." Benton sounded suddenly tired. Exhausted. "Getting the house ready has been rather more of a challenge."

She considered, and then came to settle on the other side of the cat, who was taking up the middle of the sofa. Chalice moved to settle one paw on her thigh as a reward. That was all right then. "Do you want to talk about it?"

He blinked at her, as if he wasn't sure what to do with that. She would almost have called it startled.

"You must have friends. In service? Somehow?" She suddenly wasn't sure. If being in service meant people not only lived their lives according to someone else's whims, but you couldn't even have friends, that was unfathomably evil.

Benton took a long breath. "I get on quite well with the senior staff at Ytene. The senior staff at Hawk's Breath, I know only in passing. Normally, we'd see each other only if his lordship were in residence there. He has not chosen to be for more than a few nights at a time since I came into his service."

Cassie filed that away. She suspected there was some specific reason. It was not as if Cumbria were in the mountains of the Scottish highlands, or on some remote island battered by sea and waves. "So you have been coordinating a number of things in a place you don't know well, with staff you don't have much rapport with."

His head bobbed. "Exactly. And they do not know his lordship well either. They were largely hired by his elder brother, who was a rather different sort of man."

"Not being an explorer." Cassie began to consider the variation possible.

"Lord Temple Carillon was the elder by eight years. Already in tutoring by the time his lordship remembers much from his childhood, and away from home. I was in his home on a few occasions, between our expeditions. He had been raised to hold the landmagic, but he preferred

managing the active estates in Cumbria over the rather
more ancient magics in the New Forest."

Cassie nodded. "And Cumbria is rather different than
the New Forest."

"Quite." Benton's voice was dry. "His lordship is the
opposite. He would rather leave the Cumbria estates and
the others in the hands of a competent steward and turn his
attentions to the magics of Hampshire."

"Something happened to him, didn't it? Lord Temple, I
mean."

"He died suddenly. We were in Kenya, on our way back
from another expedition, when his lordship - well. Magic
has a long arm. He woke up, shouting, different than his
dreams of the War, and it took me a g—" He stopped
abruptly. "We got the telegram a few days later, and knew
for certain."

"You should have someone you can talk to about that
kind of thing. I won't tell anyone. Certainly not him."

"Even if he asked you?" Benton looked at her quickly,
then away, focusing on the cat stretched out between them.
Convenient, that.

She said, very softly, "I am your friend before I am his
dressmaker." Then, as carefully as she could, she reached
out to touch the back of his hand with her fingers, ready to
move if he jerked away. She felt the shudder, he suppressed
it almost immediately. She said again, more firmly. "I am
your friend."

Benton let out a long breath. "I don't - I am very out of
practice with such things."

"I'm sure you are, but you learn quickly. Anyway. He
felt the magic come to him? Did he know what had
happened to his brother?"

Benton shook his head. "No. Even when we got back,

no one had any real idea. He died suddenly, of an illness that came on very quickly, a few days after his wife."

"That seems very odd." She didn't want to say half the things she was thinking. She read too many mystery novels.

"His lordship wondered about whether someone had done it intentionally. Poison. Certain magics that drain someone's life. A precisely honed curse. But his brother was the sort to have many friends and few enemies. Plenty of competition, at shooting or hunting, pavo or bohort. But nothing out of the ordinary. Nothing personal."

She was not at all sure what she thought of her mystery novels possibly being somewhat accurate. Or that Benton had, apparently, picked up on her ruminations about it. It made her feel as if things had suddenly become too real and solid. "So this is the first time since sorting that out you've been there?" Cassie was trying to put things together in her head, and failing miserably.

Benton frowned, and then nodded. "Bar a few days here or there, not opening up much of the house."

"And his lordship didn't think about that?"

"He kept most of the staff on. Pensioned properly, of course, but not needing to do much other than keep the place up."

"Ben... Thomas." She dared the first name. "I have never been in service, and I have certainly never had a manor to call my own. But even I know that there is a vast difference between the state of cleaning to avoid mice and leaves in the corridors and damage to a beautiful ancient building and the kind of upkeep needed to house a few dozen guests."

He blinked at her, open mouthed, and then had to swallow hard several times, before he managed, "That is not how I would have put it, Ca... Cassie. But it is quite true."

"Well, then." She waved a hand. "So. I have the clothing well in hand. What else can I do to help besides feed you tea and scones and let you think out loud about what else you need?"

He closed his eyes, his finger stopping on the cat's back for a moment. "Would you sew a small pocket into his lordship's outfit?"

"Just his, not Miss Penhallow's?"

He frowned. "I only have one vial of—" He stopped short.

She waited, patiently, shifting her hand slightly so she could let her thumb run along Chalice's black fur.

"Did you get anything from Greer? About that dye you were trying to remember?" His voice was suddenly more intense.

Cassie frowned, not sure where the conversation had gone. "I did." she said, carefully. "I'm not sure what to make of it, honestly." She considered. "It was monkshood. Aconite. Some magical variant. Not a common dye plant, but use by healers in some cases, though it can be quite dangerous to work with."

"Dangerous?"

"Poisonous." She stopped, taking a sip of tea while she gathered her thoughts. "Greer said you have to boil it, quite thoroughly, to make it safe to use. In a way that's rather a bother. It takes certain kinds of charms well, she considered it for Miss Penhallow's wedding cloak, but decided against it, because of the risk."

Benton considered that. "Did she say anything else?"

"It came up because she was talking about a shipment going missing. There was a lot of gossip about it at the pub, and I asked her. Two crates of dried roots, I gather you need rather a lot to make the dye.

"I, that feeling. The nagging one."

She nodded. "Quite, yes. I should have told you sooner."

He shook his head. "We do have protections, to keep people from bringing such things in. Or putting them in the food." He said it like he was reassuring himself, as much as reassuring her. That was an uncomfortable realisation.

She wasn't sure what to say, so she shifted her hand, feeling Chalice purr undisturbed. After a moment, Benton spoke again, as if he needed to explain to someone. "I was in one of the marketplaces in Cairo, in the magical part of the city. I got to talking to a woman who dealt in spices and other natural materia. About my age, someone called her Mariam, but she never told me her full name. I gather the public story was that she ran the stall for her husband who had been injured in the War, but she was the one seeing to all the business."

Cassie nodded. "Quite common here, and honestly, I'm sure the show is more common there."

"She had a cousin who made potions. Unique potions. After we'd talked for some time, I was interested in her wares, the quality of them, the unusual things she carried. She went into the back, and gave me a vial. And she said I'd know when to use it." He shrugged. It had reminded him of Cook, back in his early service, there had been that tone in her voice, the kind to be ignored at his peril.

"A vial?"

"A golden yellow liquid, like distilled sunlight. I had it tested, a year ago, when his lordship had need for other work to be done. He has a consulting alchemist he prefers for such things. He could not name it, it was not a recipe he knew? But he said it would do no harm, and possibly a great deal of good."

"That is rather like something from a fable."

"And yet, though his lordship is not be a third son, rather a second, he is full of virtues and may yet win out over the challenges before him." He paused. "His lordship has not said, but I believe he has suspicions about his brother's death. And he himself has made enemies. A little precaution can't do any harm."

Cassie nodded. "Tell me how big the vial is, and I will find a way to hide it away safely."

TWENTY-SIX

Benton found himself thrown into long days. By the second day, he was keeping extensive lists, something he hadn't had to do since his lordship's expedition in the depths of the Amazon. Lists had been the only way to manage enough supplies to last six months. He'd needed to anticipate everything from snakes to poisons, blisters to insect bites, and all the other dangers of the rainforest.

This was a different sort of dance. Harold Bigford, steward at Hawk's Breath for twenty years, was not ageing well. Worse, the death of his only son had left him grasping to hold onto what he had.

In a kinder world, without the War, he would have been in gentle retirement now. His lordship had kept the man on, out of compassion, rather than pensioning him off into a cottage and idleness. And at any other time, Benton would applaud that. Loyal service should be rewarded, after all.

At the moment, however, it made Benton want to stomp out of the room and yell. It had been frustration piled on frustration. The problem was not just the long list of tasks, but the fact that the staff were so resistant. It was proof that his lordship had been right to set up at Ytene, rather than somewhere so hidebound. And while that had clearly been the best decision, the resulting lack of relationships with the staff here beyond the barest minimum was making things difficult.

He felt, on the whole, that negotiating matters with Cassie had been far simpler, even when they had been a great deal more antagonistic than they were now. She at least had wanted to make sure everything was perfect, and she was willing to set aside her own ego in the process. Not, mind, that she was often wrong, he'd found. Even about that shade of so-called Nile green; it had in fact looked stunning on Miss Penhallow, and quite in the proper mode, he gathered. It was hardly Cassie's fault that the common name for the colour was so terribly chosen.

In this case, his lordship's past choices now meant Benton had to spend three times as much effort to get everything done. He had to sweet-talk not only Mrs Doncaster, the housekeeper, but the two regular housemaids. They felt bringing in women from the village was beneath all involved. Benton, for his part, wanted things clean. Not just clean, but sparkling and shimmering, mind.

In the end, it was girls from the village to help with the food preparation. Benton had prevailed on Madam Porter's connections for a referral to a private service for the rest. Two specialists in magical approaches to cleaning turned up two days later. Of course, someone - Benton - had to escort them from place to place. Someone had to indicate what was to be cleaned, what was not to be touched, and what they should advise on.

That part was actually rather pleasant, as they were skilled at their work and glad enough to explain what they were doing in detail. As one said, it was not as if he were competition. When they left, the art was thoroughly dusted in the public spaces and the wing that would be in use. The silver was gleaming and would stay that way for a month, and the crystal was casting prisms at the briefest touch of light. It had been worth the coin to do that, to uphold the proper standards.

Three days before the party, Benton finally had time to catch up with the necessary items in the paper. A week behind, and that was no good to anyone. He knew the importance of reading everything, at least scanning it. It was the only way to advise on seating adjustments, who should be placed in which room, and whether there was nasty gossip in play. Excellent service was at least four fifths preparation.

As he read, holed up in the small room by his lordship's suite, he frowned, and then began to work backwards. There was a blind item in one of the gossip columns that suggested Miss Penhallow had entirely upset a wasp's nest at one of the many meetings of genteel ladies.

He could not tell the cause or the effect, but he could tell the scope, once he had spotted it. He could see it ripple out in comments about invitations declined, snubs given, and cold shoulders much in evidence.

Not to Miss Penhallow, though. Because of something she'd said or done. There was nothing for it, he would have to directly consult his lordship. Another item for the notes.

There were other curiosities, of course, there always were. A mass of dead fish washing up down a stream down near Shrewsbury. Five shimmering stones, like something from before the Pact, embedded in a tree near Coventry that no one dared touch.

There was some discussion about a series of stories,

passed on by unnamed sources, about certain ladies not wearing their usual jewels. That could be a thief, that could be people pawning off their ornaments to raise funds for something. He couldn't tell, but he was sure his lordship would be intrigued. He noted the obituary of a minor singer, an operatic tenor who had once been in his lordship's regard, a heart attack. He would have to mention that in particular. There was also a notable lack of gossip about prospective proposals and betrothals.

Benton sighed, and decided it was time to discuss with his lordship. He had been at Ytene on the Saturday night and through most of Sunday, for the early harvest rituals, but his lordship had had no time to talk, being much taken up with his land obligations.

He arrived at Ytene in good time to check on the gossip in the servant's hall and bring the tea tray up for his lord-ship himself. Miss Penhallow was not in residence, he gath-ered, she was visiting a schoolmate with her younger sister until the party. That was well and good, and meant his lord-ship would be inclined to talk.

Benton opened the door to the library silently, and made his way in, the tray a reassuring weight in his hands. This was a thing he had done hundreds of times, rather than the fuss and bustle of a party unlike any the house had seen in years.

He set the tray down, pouring a cup exactly as his lord-ship preferred this blend, a small splash of cream. That done, Benton took a precise half-step back, letting the click of one heel against the wooden floor be the only sound he made. His lordship glanced up, then blinked. Benton was pleased to realise his lordship had not startled, but neither had he allowed the tea to interrupt him.

"Oh, bless you, Benton. The new housemaid has a steady hand but she will wait. Noisily."

Benton half-bowed. "Sir."

His lordship took a moment to sip his tea, reach for one of the biscuits, and then he looked up. "I've missed you here, but I gather you have been very busy. Bigford has been sending along regular reports."

Benton inclined his head. "Naturally, your lordship. I trust there have been no difficulties here?"

Lord Carillon waved a hand. "Sit, sit. We may be a bit, and you will wish to take notes. There are a few final concerns."

"The house is in good order now, sir. Though I would recommend sending around a bottle of something appropriately grateful to Madam Porter for her referral."

"How grateful are we being? A good vintage - oh, say a 1921 Bordeaux from one of the better vineyards, the 1900 Chateau Margaux, or are we looking for something more like the 1811 Château d'Yquem?"

Benton inclined his head. "I think she would owe you a favour for the last, your lordship, but there are still a dozen bottles laid down by your great-grandfather. Last I inquired, it was still aging impeccably."

He considered. The middle bottle was an exceedingly fine vintage, and would suit either drinking now or keeping for some later date. "The people she recommended were superb. I would recommend them for a longer engagement here, for the artwork and perhaps some restoration of the mosaic work."

"The 1811, then. She does like ancient things. Something in her blood, I'm sure. And the comet vintages are really quite spectacular. That one in particular." His lordship brushed something off his sleeve. "We have a dozen bottles, still? Bring one up for the bridal suite after the wedding, when you get one for her. I'll take it over myself, after the party."

"And not save them, sir?"

"Exquisite wine is no use if it turns to vinegar. Or if it is not drunk at some point. No matter how well it ages." He waved a hand. "Besides, I would prefer Vivian owe me a favour rather than the other way around."

"Certainly, sir." That was easily enough done. He added a note to his list to bring up the bottles and put them in the wine safe in his lordship's rooms here.

His lordship leaned back, tapping his fingers, watching Benton thoughtfully. "You have questions." It was a simple statement.

Benton took a breath. "Hawk's Breath is ready for your guests, sir, and the kitchen is working hard on preparing the food. Mrs Mudthon will be going up tomorrow to see to the pastry work to be done on site. If you could let Mrs Grieves know which meals you wish to take here at your earliest convenience, that would be a help."

Lord Carillon waved a hand. "I expect to be in Trellech much of the next three days, I can eat at one of my clubs. I know I am being most demanding, and more to the point, disruptive to the household. I do have my reasons."

"We are at your service, your lordship." Benton was amused, mind. "And I, if I am not speaking out of turn, am certain you have excellent reason for it."

That got a laugh, and a "You saying such things is never out of turn in private, you know that, Benton. I could use your help, however."

Benton nodded. "Of course, sir."

"How much have you seen in the papers?"

He paused. "Sir, did you see the obituary for Malcolm Rowland?"

His lordship sobered. "I did. He had wanted to speak to me about something a fortnight ago, and I put him off. I'd thought he was trying to persuade me into one last fling, only...." His voice trailed off.

"Sir." Benton nodded, acknowledging the complexity. "My condolences, sir."

"Thank you."

There was a longer silence, before Benton decided that moving the conversation along was both necessary and kind. "I gather that there was some matter involving Miss Penhallow, related to the Albion Inheritance? And I had thought that there would likely be several betrothal announcements that have not yet appeared."

Lord Carillon laughed. "Oh, quite. Lizzie turned up, in research on entirely other matters, several documents that make the familial relationships of several parties - well, not what they had thought to be true. It has, I gather, lead to several sets of renegotiations."

"Wrong side of the blanket, sir, or something else?"

"One magical adoption incorrectly completed, one case of adultery leading to a child, one grandchild being passed off as a child. You can see the effects rippling out, yes?"

"From the sort of families making matches for -" He considered the evidence. "The latter two would affect families seeking to make matches to build particular magical affinities, wouldn't they."

"Especially the second, yes." Lord Carillon waved a hand. "Distasteful. Breeding horses is one thing, I've never approved of doing the same for people. Never mind the fact that horses and hounds and cats teach us that in-breeding rarely works out well in the long-run."

Benton blinked at the addition of the cats, that was entirely new. It struck him oddly. Mind, he had been thinking more about cats, because of Cassie's, and how soothing it was to have something soft and warm curled up against you. Working dogs were not the same, and horses did not fit on a sofa. Then he tucked the thought away and nodded. "Does that affect the invitations, sir?"

"No, though we'll want to be taking a few additional precautions with the meal."

"And your other project?"

"Oh, the Willacys will be coming. They don't want to, but they will." His lordship was in fact quite smug about it.

"Sir?"

"I am fairly sure they would like to entrap me in something. I am not certain why, yet, and of course, they will not succeed, but I do wish to give them the opportunity to show their hand."

"Any additions to the schedule?"

"Arrival on Friday, falconry during the day on Saturday and some light amusements for those who do not wish to participate. The costume ball in the evening. A quiet day on Sunday, with the Fortescues singing on Sunday night with two others, and everyone off home on Monday. The falcons are ready?"

That had been easy, at least, as easy as dealing with touchy raptors would ever be. "The mews are all in order, sir."

His lordship nodded, then waved a hand. "If you could be back here the night before, pack me up properly, that would be most helpful."

"As if I'd let anyone else pack for you, sir. The idea."

TWENTY-SEVEN

P acking everything that might be needed for a weekend house party complete with a masked ball was no simple task. It took Cassie, Amelia, and Joselyn the better part of five days to make the lists and then pack it all neatly up. Cassie did at least have spacious trunks, even if they were looking dated and battered, since her mistress had left her everything in the shop when she retired.

Now it was a matter of figuring out how to set things up, now they were at Hawk's Breath. The portal had come out on the manor property itself, but perhaps a quarter mile from the house. A cart was waiting to meet them with two sturdy young men who seemed to be stable hands by the smell. Cassie nodded at them, and pressed a suitable coin on each once they had pulled around to the side of the house and turned the cases over to two footmen.

Not only above and below stairs, then, but indoor and outdoor. Right. Cassie was not at all sure where she fit into this. She would feel able to ask Benton, to admit she was now entirely out of her depth, but Benton was nowhere to be seen. Instead, she was met by an older woman, who introduced herself as Mrs Doncaster.

"Now, I'm not sure what you young women know about a great house like this." It came out a bit sharply.

"I've been to a number, for fittings, but only for brief periods of time. Never for a gathering like this, where I would be expected to provide services to multiple guests. And my apprentices have only been briefly to various manors to assist with fittings. I know this is an unusual arrangement, Mrs Doncaster, so please, I would like to know how to help make sure things go smoothly for you and the other staff."

The housekeeper sniffed, before peering over her metal-rimmed glasses, and nodding. "A fair start. This way. Gregory and Conor, bring the cases." She walked along, quite briskly, leaving Cassie, Amelia, and Joselyn scurrying to keep up. Quite deliberately, she thought.

"You'll have use of a side room for fittings. Now, I gather his lordship was quite specific in his requirements?"

"Yes, that we were to have ready and alter as needed various accoutrements to enhance the historical theme of the gathering. Between us, we can alter a number of gowns easily, add ruffs or collars or other fabric to form a fashionable silhouette for the period. Largely in white, but Lord Carillon said that there would be someone to provide temporary colouration enchantments."

"Frederick von Tolman." Mrs Doncaster snorted. "Quite the artiste, he is, but he's reliable at his work. They won't fade until the next morning."

Cassie nodded, and took the opportunity to mention to her apprentices, "You've heard me talk about the colour charms, and how unpredictable they can be. That's why we brought only the muslin and silk, to simplify."

Joselyn was concentrating hard. "And why we had to have the right threads. No wool, no linen, because those will, will react differently to the magic."

Cassie nodded. "Just so." To the housekeeper, she said, pleasantly. "I've met Master von Tolman briefly once or twice, collaborating on parties. He is indeed quite reliable, and unlike some can be trusted to keep his hands away from the housemaids."

She had wondered about what he was like with footmen, but she gathered he was quite polite, as a rule. Subtle, anyway, about his preferences. And the footmen were quite busy during a party, in and out refiling glasses and trays and buffets.

That earned her another nod, and a thoughtful glance. "Here, his lordship wished to know if you need furniture moved, or different lighting, or whatever else." She waved a hand. "He is very thorough in his arrangements."

Cassie couldn't resist. "I am fairly sure, from modest acquaintance, that he said 'Make sure Mistress Castalia has what she needs' to Benton. And Benton thought to ask about the furniture or the lighting." She was delighted to see the housekeeper stop dead for just a moment, and then a flash of some complex emotion.

"Mr Benton is not familiar with the details of this household, he has never served here for more than the briefest of visits. But I will admit he keeps his lordship most well-maintained."

Cassie nodded and dropped the subject of Benton as perhaps impolitic. She pivoted slowly in the room. "If we could have a clear space there, and there." She pointed at two spaces, on either side of the massive unlit fireplace. "Ideally some low riser, if that is available. I mentioned it when we were arranging things."

That got a nod. "Gregory, Conor. Bring those out, you know where they are."

The footmen disappeared, and once they were gone, Mrs Doncaster said, "We do not tolerate mixing, here. Minds on our work, that is how a household runs best. We keep to the old customs here, men have one stair to their quarters, women have another, the door between can only be unlocked by myself or Mr. Bigford."

Cassie inclined her head. "My apprentices will be no trouble, of course." And then a "May I ask about the other arrangements, so we know what to expect?" Very polite, and far more deferential than Cassie actually felt.

"One of the housemaids will show you up when we are done here. Supper in the servant's hall for your apprentices. You may dine with the senior staff. That is Mr Bigford, myself, Mr Benton, and Miss Stone, Miss Penhallow's lady's maid."

Cassie nodded. She couldn't make sense of the details, but she was clear that this was to be considered a signal offer. "And the times?"

"The day of the party, we will eat early, at four. There will be sandwiches and such if anyone needs a quick refreshment during the hours of the party. Until then, we break our fast at eight, dinner at noon, and supper at six. Lunch for the household is at one, and the formal meal is served at eight. Other than during your duties, you will be expected to stay out of sight, and out of the way unless his lordship asks for your presence. We chose this room because there is a direct entrance from the back hall."

Cassie considered, and then said, "Please do tell me if we do something - unexpected, or that causes a problem."

It earned her a brief nod. That done, Cassie walked around the room, getting a sense for the light, laying out the space for Amelia and herself to work in her mind, and for Joselyn to fetch and carry and assist with pinning and sewing in place as needed. It would do well enough.

"We will need some time to set everything up, and after things are out, the room must not be disturbed. No fires, not without my permission. Some of the fabrics are very flammable, the smallest spark could cause a problem. And of course, the soot would be quite damaging to the work."

She could see Mrs Doncaster making a mental note. "I will lock and unlock the door myself." It had a final sound.

"And if we need access?"

"I can generally be found downstairs, in my room, or one of the girls will know where I am." She then gave a sharp nod. "Take your time setting things up. Ring that bell pull there when you are done, and one of the housemaids will escort you down. Your personal luggage will have been taken up."

Cassie thought she was about to turn to go, but instead, Mrs Doncaster asked "How do you prefer to be addressed, below stairs? With visiting staff, they are known by the name of their employer. In this case, that naturally does not apply."

Cassie considered. "Mistress Castalia for me. And - would Miss Amelia and Miss Joselyn be appropriate for my apprentices?" In the curious wars of status, they were decidedly more highly ranked than housemaids and footmen who addressed by their bare first name.

That got a small frown. "That will do well enough. We would call children of the household Master or Miss, but I suppose as the young women are unmarried, it is not inappropriate."

Cassie spread her hands. "If you think of something you would prefer, let me know and we can discuss." There. That at least put things on more even ground.

Mrs Doncaster nodded, and said "Ring when you're done" one more time. Then she went to a door almost hidden by the lines of the wallpaper in the back wall, and disappeared through it. The door closed with a soft click.

Amelia snorted, and said, "You did warn us, Mistress." Joselyn was just wide-eyed.

"Not my usual customs at all, but we are guests below-stairs. And being exceedingly well paid for our work in this room, so we will all be polite, as I said. I trust you've seen enough examples of how to ask if you are not sure what is proper?"

Both heads bobbed. "Yes, Mistress."

"Right. Joselyn, you unpack the folded lengths of fabric. Amelia, help me set up the baskets for easy retrieval. We will see if the footmen can move those couches there, a little grouping for anyone who is waiting. A chair there and there, if people need to sit down, and that table," She paused, considering. "There, I think."

Amelia nodded. "Perhaps those small tables here and here, for the items we want most at hand?"

"Oh, quite. Once they set the risers up."

The resulting transformation of the room kept them busy for several hours, until nearly supper time. Cassie felt the work was well done, however, and that they would make a good show of their skill and attention to detail here.

Joselyn kept them occupied with comments about the various people invited. Some, Cassie had done the costume work for, but others were less well known to her. The

Bensons, a few people she knew were part of Lord Carillon's circles, the Leftons, the Edgartons. Joselyn's comments
were almost frustrating, she kept having a sense there was
something she was missing, like a dress without its proper
undergarments.

TWENTY-EIGHT

THURSDAY AFTERNOON

"That dressmaker is here."

Benton looked up from the long counter where he was counting out the forks. "Mistress Castalia? She is precisely on time, then. Does she need anything?" The idea of having her here, for multiple days, had been weighing on him. He had more or less figured out how to deal with her when they were on their own.

But now she was coming into his world, even if this great house was not properly his home. He wasn't sure she'd understand the necessary limitations, the customs, how not to get in everyone's way. Including his.

"They were about to set up those little daises you had built. Ridiculous, aren't they? Imagining all the fine lords and ladies going up and down the little steps." Mrs Doncaster ran her hands over her skirts, smoothing them out.

"It assists with the hemlines. In her fitting rooms, she has ones with two or three steps going up, so that the dress can hang completely free and be hemmed precisely as desired." He felt himself becoming more defensive with each word. And he repressed, quickly, a desire to go and see her right now. "Thank you for seeing her settled."

"Very plainly attired, I thought, for a dressmaker."

"It doesn't do for the creator to outshine the customer, I suspect. Now, do we have the rooms settled?"

"Mistress Castalia and her apprentices up in the rooms on the end, that bigger one for her, on the women's side, and the smaller room for her apprentices. I made it clear there's to be no mingling. She suggested she might properly be Mistress Castalia below stairs, and her apprentices Miss Amelia and Miss Joselyn."

"Amelia is the older, Joselyn the younger. There's another one, over in France, I gather. And her earned title and first name are the common polite form of address among the crafting masters, I believe. Certainly it is how she is known to his lordship."

"What's - well, dresses. I suppose France makes as much sense as any of the apprenticing does."

Benton smiled at that. "All manner of things to learn. And Miss Stone's room is sorted?"

"The little room by Miss Penhallow's dressing room, of course. And she'll be Miss Penhallow below stairs, naturally."

Benton inclined his head. "The old customs, yes. I did warn her." Just as he'd made it clear to Mally that he would be treating her as the lady's maid she almost was prepared to be, here, to set the proper tone.

"Do you think she'll manage? I can't imagine Miss Penhallow is easy to tend to. All that gossip about her." Mrs Doncaster was not sure she approved, then. Benton couldn't tell if it was about Mally herself, or about not choosing a lady's maid from the existing staff, or something else.

"Which bits of gossip had you heard, then?" He kept his

voice even, despite the fact he was becoming quite tired of needing to defend Miss Penhallow's decisions.

"You know I see my sister and two of our cousins every fortnight, our days off."

"Of course. And natural enough, when most of the time you've the routine tasks here, rather than parties to tend to."

Mrs Doncaster inclined her head, and deigned to go and settle in the side chair in the corner, as Benton continued checking on the silver. "There's quite a lot of fuss about her. And naturally, I wouldn't say a thing about a guest of his lordship, and one he's planning to marry. But quite a lot of words about how she wasn't fit to marry him."

"His lordship is indeed quite set on her. And a number of other ladies had their chance to make an impression and did not catch his eye." He said it as pleasantly as he could, hoping to remind her that a firm decision was better for everyone than a continual procession of the unsuitable, high-handed, and unpleasant.

"Hmph." That was good-natured at least. "One could hope for less gossip."

Benton considered, then set down the fork he was polishing. "Mrs Doncaster, did you ever hear much of how his lordship met Miss Penhallow?"

"I can't say that I did." That might well explain her mood, if she'd been feeling left out of things she felt were within her purview. Best to soothe her with some information promptly, then.

Benton paused, wanting to make his words count, without revealing things that were not his to share. "There was a dangerous magical drink, goldwasser, being shared around. His lordship had an eye to stopping it. Miss Penhallow as well, for reasons of her own."

"Rather brash, for a well-bred lady." It was decidedly

not in the mode of the previous Lady Carillon, Lord Temple's wife. She had been fond of decorative pursuits like embroidery and genteel dances, and a variety of charities. Benton had thought she had had a kind heart, and a sensible nature, but she had never been the type to energetically sort out problems with her own hands. Her death still bothered the household, he knew, and not just because they had considered her a compassionate mistress.

"Her sister had taken a liking to it, and like a good older sister - ah, you'd know this better than I would." He'd heard plenty about Mrs Doncaster's younger sister, Ellen. "Miss Penhallow, the elder, cares quite a lot for her sister, for all they've also had different paths in life."

"The younger one's not expected here, isn't she?"

"Not this gathering, I believe. His lordship felt it might be not to her liking." Laura Penhallow had been more entangled with the goldwasser parties, and Benton suspected she still found large parties overwhelming. He entirely sympathised. "I believe they plan a trip sometime later, for her to enjoy the landscape."

"Is she likely to be difficult?" This time, the question was more practical, her voice had less of the earlier sharpness. He supposed that it must be trying, having guests in the house who didn't understand the customs.

"Oh, goodness, no. She's quite sweet tempered as a rule, most pleasant. She spent a lot of her younger years in, well, some in sanitaria, quite recovered now, her lungs. Otherwise in hotels or spas in restful places. Entirely comfortable with a competent staff. More than her elder sister was, I'm sure."

"Ah, that's a relief. You know how some of them get, when they're not used to a housemaid building the fire, or someone drawing a bath for them. The expectations."

"Oh, quite." He felt it was time to get back to the current gathering. "But the guests are all known, I believe. A mix, of course. Some of the locals who live too far to go home overnight, after the party, and the guests here for the Friday to Monday. Besides the party itself, of course."

Mrs Doncaster tsked. "Rather, yes. And it is entirely proper for his lordship to show his face. We do miss being more central to the plans."

Benton looked down, smiling to himself. He would have to make clear to his lordship that additional visits here would be welcomed. "His lordship is so very fond of Ytene, I am afraid no one could convince him to make this the primary residence. But I am sure as their social schedule settles down, he and her ladyship-to-be will be here at times." And, as he had told his lordship, it would give Ytene's staff the opportunity to use the furniture polish with the scent of honey and lemon.

She nodded, gruffly.

He let the silence linger for a minute or so, before he said, as gently as he could, not pressing, "Was there other commentary about Miss Penhallow?"

"Oh, goodness, yes. The usual sort of thing, some people liking her looks, some not. Though really, she's no stunning beauty, but she's pleasant looking." This part was not something she was overly interested in, he realised, and it made him think better of her, for caring about other than the superficial.

"His lordship is quite clear on her suiting him in that regard, yes. Very decorously at the moment, of course." He let his voice take on the amused tone he'd explored when talking to Cassie a few times.

Mrs Doncaster snorted. "It has not slipped my attention

that she is in the room with the passage down to his quarters."

Benton looked up and grinned. "Ah, they are a modern couple, now, aren't they? Not in the awful ways, but in enjoying the life they have."

"Ah, and that's a fair enough thing." Mrs Doncaster said, tutting now. "His lordship had a dreadful War, and you too."

Benton shrugged. "Few had a good one. And it brought me into his lordship's service, and here I am still alive and with all my limbs, so I count myself exceedingly lucky."

Something had shifted, because Mrs Doncaster paused, then ventured, "Has Miss Penhallow done something awful? Not just as society people count it?"

Benton looked up. "I think it more likely the other way around, she has done something properly others would rather she overlooked. May I ask what you've heard then?"

"I heard a tale - third hand at best - about something at one of those women's organisations. More than one. Nothing so sensible as the women's institute in the village, of course. But them as go to that sort of thing aren't needing to fuss over making the food and drink stretch to suit now, are they, or the rotation of feeding the kitchen."

"Entirely not, no. They have other concerns." He smiled slightly, leaning forward, encouraging her into the shared intimacy, and praising her sense at the same time.

"Some of what my cousin heard, it was about the father, something scandalous? But it didn't seem to be him running off with an opera singer or a ballet dancer or whatever the fashion is this year." Benton could hear, in that, all the fads for scandal that Mrs Doncaster had seen pass through the house and the people.

"Not that kind, no." He tapped his fingers on the

counter, then said. "Her father and uncle were explorers, they raised funds for an expedition to the Amazon, to collect plants and possibly items. Fur, claws, scales, that sort of thing, from animals there. Not that different from his lordship's expeditions, in general terms, though the specific goals were a bit different."

"Raised money?"

"The idea was that bringing back items new to us here, there might be all manner of new applications. For potions and healer's salves, and alchemical catalysts, and crafting. Dyes and mordants, perhaps, or to make jewellery, or all manner of other things we haven't thought of yet." Granted, he hadn't really thought about the dyes, until he'd read more about them, after Cassie had mentioned them.

"And there are quite a few of those expeditions?"

"A few a year. Some funded privately. His lordship did that, his own funds and those of a few friends. But others must raise the money more broadly. And then the Penhallows disappeared, and everyone with them."

"Nothing?" Mrs Doncaster looked up. "Oh, those poor girls."

That was quite the proper reaction. "They had a rather awful time of it. Miss Penhallow took a position helping organise an estate auction, that was where she first met his lordship. Miss Laura had a position in an office. As it turns out, with the people making the goldwasser, which is how she got tangled up in the dreadful affair. But his lordship was most taken with the older Miss Penhallow's poise and intelligent approach to problem-solving."

"Some of the gossip is that he wasn't sufficiently lured by a pretty face." Mrs Doncaster had become prim, like she wasn't sure what to make of that. She might well have heard stories of his lordship's broad-minded preferences for men as well as women. This needed a delicate touch, and Benton paused to acknowledge the moment.

Then he allowed himself a smile, again including her and shaping the conversation to include her, and get her on his side. It would be for the best if she were on Miss Penhallow's side in any future gossip. "His lordship does prefer engaging conversation with his artistic appreciation of a partner, and has as long as I have known him, yes."

There was another short pause, in which Mrs Doncaster stood, though she did not turn to the door just yet. "So if another part of the gossip was about Miss Penhallow rather deliberately making things difficult for certain ladies. Would that be true or not?"

That was new to him, and he did not like how it made him feel caught out flat-footed. "May I ask what you've heard? You have quite a different position than I do." Once he'd had a moment to think he realised it must be a matter of the bloodline concerns that had turned up, but it would be good to hear her out regardless.

"Oh, nothing terribly clear. I went in to Trellech the other day, to look at the spices and cooking wines for myself, and there was talk in some of the shops. I don't know who, they were women I didn't recognise. Not quite the family's class, I'm sure." As senior staff took their status from the houses they served, Mrs Doncaster would have listened, but not engaged, of course.

"Did they say anything specific? So I might best advise his lordship, of course, or let him know he might wish to speak to you about it?"

"Me, Mr Benton? Goodness." The idea made her flutter pleasantly. "It was something about finding out a family secret, something that had been buried a good long while, it coming out. One of the women wasn't sure about it at all, thought it quite rude? The other was more, more thought-ful, I suppose the word is. I think she didn't care for the family in question, she wasn't surprised they'd been hiding things."

"Most intriguing." He paused, then offered some of what he knew for himself. "Miss Penhallow would of course not confide in me. But if she had, I am quite certain there was some purpose behind it, and that his lordship is quite aware of her intentions." He considered. "She is quite aware many people do not like her. And quite committed to doing the right thing, despite that, when doing the wrong thing would bring her more friends. I must say I find that commendable in its way."

Mrs Doncaster nodded briskly. "Thank you, Benton, for the information. I'll leave you to your tasks, but perhaps you might join me for tea in my sitting room?"

A particular treat, then. That was good. Things would go much better if she stayed firmly on his side when it came to the plots that would be flying about in the next few days.

He nodded. "It would be a pleasure. I'll just finish this up."

TWENTY-NINE

THURSDAY EVENING

Cassie glanced at the clock on the mantelpiece and realised it was almost six. She'd sent Amelia and Joselyn off an hour ago to settle into their rooms and wash up. They were doing a reasonable job of taking it in stride, but Cassie didn't need their nerves making her own worse.

They had managed to unpack everything, setting various adornments and fripperies into aesthetically pleasing baskets and hat boxes. The goal - as set out by Lord Carillon - was to provide additional touches to improve each person's costume. Decorations for masks, ruffs for dresses, draping lace-edged cravats, feathers for hats or hair. There were a few full costumes, set on the hanger to be gathered up by valets and lady's maids, for those staying here. Most guests were expected to turn up on Saturday night costumed and masked.

The illusionist would be able to tint what they'd brought to match the costumes precisely. The open chest in the corner held a range of additional ribbons, feathers and even a few costume jewellery pieces.

She had no idea how to get to the servants hall, or for that matter even if she should make the attempt herself. Mrs Doncaster, by implication rather than edict, had made it clear that going through the front foyer was not for her, most of the time.

There was nothing for it but the bell pull. Cassie went to the right side of the fireplace, and pulled it, feeling the heavy weight of it. It feel queer to pull and hear nothing - no sense of anyone elsewhere in the house, no idea whether anyone had heard. Or even, at least at the moment, where it rang. She supposed somewhere down in the servants' hall.

She wasn't even sure where someone would come from. Probably it would be that half-hidden back door, not the main door to the room. But perhaps not. She felt like she was in some fantastical labyrinth, entirely foreign to her idea of how the world fit together. Better to see both doors, she thought, sitting in a chair that let her watch the entire room easily.

Not unlike, she supposed, how the Elizabethan clothing would feel to someone who knew only the latest modes. That made her feel better, rather quickly. This house had history, centuries of it, and it was a sturdy history if she could not hear people moving about at all nearby. And the people here had history. The family, of course, even if it was a rather attenuated family now, she gathered, with Lord Carillon as sole survivor of the direct line, for the moment.

Long-serving staff, too. She wondered - Benton hadn't so much as murmured a hint - what they thought about this party. Or about Lord Carillon making his primary home in the New Forest, rather than the larger, more splendid house here. The more recent house here. She thought it must be Georgian, give or take some additions, by the proportions of the rooms.

She almost didn't catch the crack of the door in the back wall opening, it made no sound. She was immensely relieved to see Benton open it, and then nod at her. "Cassie. Mistress Castalia. Do you need to bring anything upstairs?"

"No, thank you, and I'd hate to make you late." She paused. "Was that the right choice, here?"

He paused, waiting for her to come over to him. "It was not a bad one. You are of a curious status, below stairs. Not housekeeper or butler, not valet or lady's maid, but more akin to a governess or companion, who might at times dine with the family. Your last name would also be appropriate, but I reminded Mrs Doncaster that your title and first name are common in the crafting masteries."

Cassie let out a breath of relief. "Yes, quite. It is a delicate balance, at some times, but I have found with those who have staff, using my last name makes them treat me like a lady's maid. But the title and my first name breaks the pattern and assumptions."

"I would have thought a first name might," And then he paused, and grinned. "Most of those you serve would have no idea of most of the maids' names."

"A regrettable number assign names they like to their staff, too. I do, wait, did I just put my foot in my mouth?" She looked up at him, now suddenly worried.

He grinned at her, and waved a hand. "We do not have that custom here, no, though we have occasionally asked someone to consider using a middle name or a variation, if names are similar enough to confuse. When the house was full of staff, it was sometimes quite challenging to remember if it was Edmund or Edward or Edgar who was responsible for which task."

Cassie snorted. "Goodness, yes. Or for the three of them to pay attention when asked to do something."

Benton nodded, then asked, "Do you have any questions, before we go down?"

Cassie frowned. "What should I expect?"

"Senior staff in the housekeeper's room. Saturday night, we'll all be together, a quick meal before the party, but otherwise separate. Your apprentices will be looked after in the main servant's hall. They were getting on quite well already when I came by. The ordinary sort of manners will do, once you are served. Did you find everything in order here?"

She nodded. "I wouldn't mind a look around the grounds tomorrow, if it wouldn't be a problem. Just to get a sense of things. If you might like to show me around?" She had no idea how much of his time was likely to be occupied with his duties, but nonetheless could not resist trying to determine if he might like to spend some of it with her.

"Before ten would be fine - after that, guests are arriving."

He was, of course, entirely too proper to be diverted. Possibly even too proper to be interested. "That will keep you quite busy, yes?"

"Mr Bigford, the butler, has things well in hand, thankfully, for that part of it. But I should be on hand for his lordship's last minute arrangements."

Cassie wasn't sure how to ask the other thing that was nagging at her, about how things worked, who handled what, so she found herself awkwardly silent. Benton gestured at the door. "Come along. You can wash your hands downstairs."

He led her into the back hallway, dimly lit and with a faint smell of lavender. He caught her inhaling, trying to place it. "To keep pests away, a mix of lavender, mint, and a particular charm."

Cassie could only nod. She followed him down a set of stairs, quite narrow, she thought, especially if one were carrying much at all. At the bottom, he paused to allow her to step into the lavatory. She washed her hands, re-pinned her hair, and considered her reflection. Respectable enough, and the new round of dye had mellowed just enough to flatter her properly.

"This way." Benton's posture was suddenly much more rigid. Naturally, they were going somewhere he was not normally, with people whose cooperation he needed to do his work. Cassie realised suddenly how the hierarchy she hated about such places might actually be necessary, to keep things working even if people did not agree on specifics, or perhaps even could not otherwise get along.

The housekeeper's sitting room was pleasant, and thankfully not too heavily strewn with floral fabrics. An oval table had been set, with enough room for five to sit comfortably, Mrs Doncaster already seated at the end.

"Mistress Castalia, this is your place, here, as a guest." It was the seat to the housekeeper's right, and Benton pulled out the chair for her, sliding it in smoothly as she sat. "This is Mr Bigford, the butler, you already know Benton, and Miss Stone, Miss Penhallow's maid. Below stairs she is Penhallow, naturally."

Cassie inclined her head. "Mr Bigford, Mrs Doncaster. My thanks for your hospitality. I hope my apprentices are no trouble?"

There was a brief moment of silence, and then Mr Bigford spoke. He was quite elderly, she could see, with a slight tremor in his hand. "You can be sure we will tell you if they are."

Mrs Doncaster, more easily amused, said, "They were

showing the housemaids a tip for darning, before supper. That's a useful sort of guest."

Cassie smiled. "Amelia has an excellent eye for close work - far better than mine, I admit."

The dinner proceeded evenly enough, with a kitchen maid bringing in dishes and clearing them, in four courses. Only when they had progressed on to a cheese plate did Mrs Doncaster inquire if Cassie had any questions.

"I know there are guests arriving early, and we have costumes for some of them. But I would greatly appreciate guidance on what to expect. And what the expectations are for me, besides the fittings, until Saturday evening?"

"Ah." Mr Bigford took a breath, "Naturally, as you are in an unusual position, you would want to know what is proper."

That was not entirely what Cassie meant, but it would do.

"You are welcome to enjoy the property tomorrow, so long as you stay out of the way of the invited guests."

Benton responded. "Mistress Castalia mentioned she would like to see the grounds. Perhaps there is a map we could lend her?" His comment was impersonal, and it rather implied he would not be joining her, and Cassie had to suppress her disappointment.

Mrs Doncaster said, "Oh, naturally. And your apprentices?"

"They have some additional preparatory sewing to do, but I am sure they would be glad of a walk."

"The guests staying overnight will be arriving between ten and two tomorrow, either before or after luncheon. There will be some activities in the afternoon, lawn sports and likely a pickup bohort match or something of the kind. You would be welcome to observe, but not mingle unless his lordship requests it, though perhaps some of the guests will need fittings?"

Cassie restrained herself from snorting. She managed a mild, "Of course. And yes, some of them will, I'm sure."

"On Saturday, his lordship requested a falconry excursion. The mews are still well-kept, though his lordship has not trained his own bird since returning to Albion." There was some sort of oddness there, she wasn't entirely sure what, something that was touchy and sharp-edged.

Cassie considered that of all the pursuits of aristocrats, falconry was the one that made the least sense. She had always thought that being that close to sharp beaks and talons, having them on your arm, was absolute foolishness. On the other hand, the medieval ballads did make it clear how much the predatory nature of birds and lords might have in common. She could see why Lord Carillon might have a complex relationship with that.

Benton offered, quietly but steadily, "If you'd like to see them flown, I will be going up to the field in case anything is needed. I can explain some of it, when his lordship does not need my service."

Cassie nodded. "I - I think I would appreciate that. It's not a thing I've had a chance to see." His offer, to invite her to something with other guests, felt suddenly overwhelming. She reminded herself, firmly, that she was no schoolgirl. He would have time for her, or he would not. Her heart leaping when he made an offer was not helpful at all.

"And it's something you must have read of, yes, or had read while you were at your sewing?"

Cassie smiled, finding it a little easier that he'd remembered that. "A number of the medieval romances are heavy on the imagery, yes. But one never knows how much they elaborate unduly." She felt a little caught out in her thoughts, but given the opportunity, she felt she owed it to his lordship to see the thing in truth, and not keep making assumptions about it. Or perhaps she owed it to Benton, to take the thing seriously.

Benton smiled, but let Mrs Doncaster finish up. "For tonight and tomorrow, you are welcome to have a book or sewing or some other small task with you in the servant's hall. Or you are welcome to be in the room set for your use, or to retire to your sleeping room, whichever suits you."

Cassie nodded. "If someone could show me where the sleeping room is and how to get back and forth, I will finish a few things in the trunks tonight. Then I may have more leisure tomorrow before the guests are ready for the fittings."

That settled, at least, where she would be and what she would be doing for the foreseeable future.

THIRTY

FRIDAY MORNING

At breakfast, Benton waited until everyone was settled, and then spoke. "Mistress Castalia, I have no obligations this morning. His lordship is already off for his ride. Would you still care to see the gardens?"

Cassie looked up, then nodded. "Oh, yes, certainly. Now, or?" She let her voice trail off.

"Eight o'clock, by the side door, just at the end of the hall here. You might wish sturdy boots if you'd like to see the wilder spaces of the grounds."

She smiled, and as the lower staff cleared the plates, excused herself politely. Mrs Doncaster watched her go, and said, "She's not one bit sure about being in a house with staff, is she?"

"Not what she's used to, no. But she likes his lordship's custom, and she understands we all have our role here. If there's anything that's a bother, just let her know, she takes learning well."

The housekeeper peered at him dubiously. "If you say

so, Benton." She seemed like she was taking his measure, but he couldn't figure out why.

At eight, he made his way to the side door, and Cassie was waiting for him. He nodded, noting she had changed shoes, and he thought to a shorter and sturdier skirt. "This way, Mistress."

They walked down the gravel driveway, around the side of the house. "The stables are over there, including space for automobiles on the end. The portal is just down in the grove of trees, where you came through."

"Ah, so it must be of a period with the house?"

Benton beamed. "Yes. Not many know about the nuances there."

"Oh, I don't know much, just that some eras need the trees for support and anchoring, and some need stone. The Trellech ones rely on flowing water, there's an underground," She paused. "Lake, no, aquifer, isn't that the word?"

Benton nodded. "The one at Ytene is also anchored in wood, though different wood." he said. "There are different fashions, but of course locations have their own requirements."

Cassie nodded. "And the estate - the house is Georgian, but is the estate older than that?"

"Tudor, give or take." Benton replied. "Granted not long after the Pact. Decidedly the junior estate among the family possessions, but with rather more farmland and income." They came to the back of the house, and he paused when she gasped at the gardens and fields laid out below her, sweeping down toward the lake. "Quite impressive, yes."

She bumped his elbow with hers, rather familiarly. "More than a bit. You set me up, didn't you?"

In another person, that would make him uncomfortable, the idea that he would. Only, of course, he had. Even if that unexpected touch were quite distracting. It was the pleasurable equivalent to the rooster leaping into his arms. He ducked his head, and smiled. "Yes. It is - the colours, the greens and golds. Very impressive."

Cassie was almost distracted, he could see, given how her eyes were scanning back and forth across the ground, taking in the shifts of ground. "What is that there?" She was pointing to a stone tower, set in the right corner of the formal garden.

"A folly. Shall we walk down to it? It has a delightful view from the first floor." He thought she might like how you could see the patterns from there, the way the land spread out. And the colours, particularly. He was sure she'd like the colours.

She glanced up at him, but nodded. She had a little curious smile he couldn't figure out how to interpret. "Of course."

The gardens were in splendid form. Cassie pointed out a few flowers, he pointed out others. "Is this a working garden, then?" she asked. "Everything along here has been useful for dyes."

"This is planted to the specifications of his lordship's mother, using a plan from the Elizabethan era adapted for the larger footprint of the house. They felt strongly about their apothecary gardens, especially this far out, and with no portal here yet, and quite a ride from the lake or river or queen's road."

Cassie tilted her head, pausing to pivot in place, looking over the garden beds. "So, laid out formally, but with plants meant for specific purposes." She frowned. "Drawing on the theory of the humours, am I right?"

"That was the supposition for many years, yes. You may have heard about the discovery of the home from the time of the Pact, with a full kitchen garden? Some of what grows there suggests that there is a more complex theory here, a memory of propitiation of the Gentle Folk."

Cassie frowned at that, pivoting on one heel to look out over the gardens and take in the patterns. "And still you plant it this way?"

Benton shrugged. "It is tradition, and it does no harm and possibly much good. Besides, his lordship decides about that sort of thing. Here, this path will take us easily to the folly." They turned to the right, near the bottom of the garden, slanting along a diagonal to the corner.

Cassie turned to look over her shoulder, looking further down the hill. "And that is Lake Windermere?"

"It is." They had come to dark green double doors that led into the ground floor of the folly. He had been enjoying showing her the grounds, and he wondered, not for the first time, what it would be like to show her around Ytene, properly. The way she looked at him, and the way she smiled, he liked that, too, how they were together in this rather than him fighting his way through on his own.

Benton couldn't tell if she had been doing fewer things that startled him, or if he were less overturned by them. He thought her moods had been rather more even, once he had settled into the challenges of arranging the gathering to come. He was so caught up in his thoughts that he almost missed the way the grass to one side had been crushed. It was as if someone had set a box down, something sturdy and heavy.

"Let me go first, please." Something was not as it should be. It was something small, because he could not see anything obviously wrong besides that grass, but he could feel it, that prickle at the back of his neck. The folly was not off-limits to the staff, but it was rare that the current staff would come out this way.

He opened the door. "There are steps up." Benton barely glanced back at Cassie before he started to climb. The room at the top, the main room, looked much as he expected. A sizable daybed, comfortable chairs, a small table and broad stools to go with it. He stopped at the edge of the stairs, looking around more closely. The window was closed, the glass was whole. The bed looked entirely undisturbed.

Cassie came up behind him, he could feel her almost touch him, then pull her hand back.

"Moment, please." He took a deep breath, remembering how his lordship had taught him this. It was not a magic that came naturally to him, it was one he practised diligently every few weeks, so that when he needed it, he could call it back. Like one of Cassie's loose threads. Or perhaps, more so, like a line of embroidery, something snaking through, tying the theme of a whole dress together.

One breath, then syllable after syllable, learned by memory. He closed his eyes for a moment, and then heard the gasp behind him. He finished the chant, then opened his eyes. Ghostly figures moved around the space.

The chant was never enough clarity to identify a face, or even more than a very general sense of size and shape. This time, though, that much at least was informative. It was a man and woman, not children fooling around. Probably a man and woman, at least, he was fairly sure those were skirts.

The figures stood together, doing something on the table, and he could see they had a bottle of something, and distilling containers. They moved around, pouring something from one container into a vial, gathering up something he couldn't identify. They were packing it into a wooden box, some sort of packing crate, perhaps a foot on each side. Then they were gone, with no sense of how. That happened sometimes, that the magic caught the essential moments, not the final ones.

"That..." Cassie almost breathed it out, so softly it barely made a noise.

"A useful tool his lordship taught me." He swallowed. "It should be safe enough, but don't touch anything yet." He went to the table, first, and drew out the small enamel container he kept with him constantly, with the little waxed paper envelopes, and the folded silk, and swabs.

Benton carefully removed most of the items, sticking them into the larger of his jacket pockets. Then he carefully swabbed the faint places he could see rings on the table, once with a dry bit of silk, and once with a bit of silk dampened by a vial of pure water from his kit. He tucked them back into the enamel box, sealed it, before turning back to Cassie.

She was standing only a step or two from the stairs, not touching anything.

"What, what was that?" Her voice was uncertain now, he could see the shock reaching her. She wasn't used to this kind of plotting or subterfuge. For all she'd been helping him all along, it must be startling to see such evidence of a direct plot, and somewhere unexpected. He realised, too, that perhaps his own knowledge unsettled her. It wasn't a common magic, and it rather underlined what he was called to do in his lordship's service.

He came over and almost without thinking about it, set his hands on her shoulders. "Right here. This is quite a good

sign, generally. To have a sense that they were doing something, here."

"But. Why, what." She was on the edge of hysteria, or at
least a proper attack of nerves. He said the only thing he
could think of that would change the subject enough.

"May I kiss you?" The question came out of him before
he could think better of it, but he knew as he spoke that he
was entirely in earnest. And in truth, he'd been wanting to
since, well. Since before she'd arrived in Cumbria.

She blinked at him, once, then again and again. But
there was the small nod, as if all her words had fled. He
knew that moment, how it felt, and how the nod had to
carry everything she meant. He bent, cautiously, trying to
remember how this worked, he had never had much practice at it.

Their noses bumped, then she shifted, angling her head
differently. She was warm, and trembling under his hands.
After a moment he felt her arm around his waist, cautious
and measured, and let one of his own hands shift to her
upper back. Nothing aggressive. He wasn't sure he could be
aggressive at this if he wanted to.

It felt like forever before she pulled back, blinking up at
him and swallowing. "That was not what I expected from
this walk." There was a tiny pause, then a softer, "Either."

He grimaced, and said, "Not unwelcome." It did not
quite come out like a question.

Something in his tone made her laugh, at least he assumed
it was the tone. She said, "I've been fancying you for a bit, but I
was so sure you wouldn't have any of it. You kept not noticing
when I sort of offered things? Beyond sandwiches and conversation. That even bringing it up would go badly. But if you were
willing to kiss me, well, that gives us something to talk about."

Benton had to laugh. "If you put it like that, Cassie." He tilted his head, then asked, baffled. "You were offering?"

Cassie peered at him. "Walking in the garden is an invitation. Asking you to my flat was." She swallowed and asked, "In private, may I stop calling you Benton?"

"Thomas," he agreed. "Please never Tom."

She tilted her head. "What they called you as a hallboy?"

He nodded. "Thomas was at least a footman."

"And Tam to your family?"

"Quite." He took a breath, let it out. "I had thought the wards extended this far, but possibly not. I will have to discuss this with his lordship as soon as possible. I'm afraid we must cut the walk short." He felt that other people would not dive back into the immediacy of the plot after such a kiss, but now that was resolved, he could not ignore the evidence of his eyes and magic.

It did not seem to bother her. "People with nefarious plots involving distilled liquids do come before personal pleasures, yes. Let me know what you can share?"

"Oh, I am quite sure I will need to discuss a number of things with you, when we get the opportunity."

Now was not that time, so all he could do was offer his arm once they were downstairs, and escort her back to the house.

They returned quickly enough to the main house, a matter of ten minutes. At the side entrance, he paused, then said, "Actually. If I might ask a favour?"

"You may." She said it easily, but it came easily because it was true.

"You don't know what it is yet." Benton - no, Thomas - sounded disapproving.

"You are the one asking, so I am quite sure it is reasonable in scope, ethical, and not expected to be dangerous. Otherwise you would have asked me differently."

Thomas paused, blinked, and then his solemnity cracked. "True, thank you. And no, I do not expect it to be dangerous. Or at least, not if you can play the part, and I am quite sure it is within your skills."

Cassie tilted her head. "Yes?" This sounded intriguing.

"You are a guest here, in a particularly unusual position. No one will think overmuch of it if you wander the grounds - the gardens, the stables, the mews, and so on, and see what you see. You don't know country houses, you don't know some of the things that would be out of place, but you have a grand sense of people. You'll likely be able to spot if someone's hiding something. Will you do that? And tell me what you spot that doesn't make sense?"

Cassie laughed. "I thought you were going to ask me something hard."

Thomas blinked at her, then smiled, fully. "Thank you. I - once the guests have settled in, I should have some time. Be back for tea, and we can find a quiet corner when we get a chance."

"I can always shoo Amelia and Joselyn out of the room the clothing's in. That is easy enough. And ask for your help evaluating his lordship's preferences."

"Are you sure you haven't done this kind of thing before?"

"What, kept my ear out for a dozen tiny clues about some piece of gossip? That's an ordinary Wednesday, Thomas." She paused for a moment, then added "Dear."

That, wonder of wonders, brought up a blush on his cheeks. He looked at her wide-eyed before his eyes shifted down and away. "Later." That was firm.

"Later. Ta! Good hunting."

Cassie turned, and then considered her options. The light was good, it was not currently raining, but there were some dubious clouds rolling in. If she were going to thoroughly investigate the gardens, better to do that first. She turned, heading back down the path she'd just climbed. At least she was getting plenty of chances to stretch her legs.

She set off, moving clockwise around the garden, across the top. She walked down to a point where a young gardener had begun working. He was pulling seed pods off some plant she didn't quite recognise into a basket and plucking dead leaves.

"Ma'am." He bobbed his head, and she was sure he'd have tugged a forelock if he had one.

"Good morning!" She kept it bright and cheerful. "I'm helping with something for the party, they told me I could walk around so long as I didn't bother anything. Can you tell me where else I can go, besides the garden here?"

He blinked and ducked his chin. "Ma'am." Then he said "Gardens, here. Formal up here, kitchen there, to the side. Orchard that way. Fine thing, the orchard."

Cassie smiled, and nodded. "Ta, appreciated." She set off, making a large loop around the formal gardens, back up and across to the kitchen garden, then across to the other side and the orchards.

It was in the orchard that she found the next curious thing, a few broken plants near an elder tree, like someone had been clambering around it. Looking more carefully, she discovered a fresh wound on the stem, a branch maybe a finger-width at the base, a bit above her head. Enough that someone was hoping no one would notice, she rather thought.

She frowned, then made a beeline for the kitchen door, waiting for one of the kitchen maids to have a moment. "Pardon, there's - the elder, the one by the orchard gate. It looks like someone broke a branch off. I don't know if there's a custom here. But my mother would have my head if I noticed a thing like that and didn't make the proper apologies."

The kitchen maid's eyes went wide, and she said "Pardon, mistress, I'll be getting Mrs Callypher." Cassie waited patiently, and a minute later, there was a bustling woman, who Cassie had seen only in passing. Plump, as cooks were generally thought best to be.

"What's this then, Mistress? You're sure there's a break?"

"Quite sure. You're the one keeps the orchard?"

"Properly, I suppose it should be Mr Bigford, but he's not much for the outdoors now, more than he has to, it plays up his bad knee something fierce. Don't you be saying I told you, embarrasses him so. No, I do the magics for the gardens now, have done since his lordship's brother was here. Splash of honey wine, few other things."

Cassie led her along, back into the orchard, and gestured at the spot where the limb had been broken off. She was gratified to see that Mrs Callypher's reaction was just as it should be. She reached up to touch the scar of the torn branch, then carefully drizzled the honey wine over it, using a tiny wooden ladle. She murmured a chant that wasn't the one Cassie knew, but some sort of cousin, in a dialect Cassie couldn't quite place.

Something, unmistakably, felt better, after, where it had felt unsettled. Like the ground after a rainstorm, resilient and soaked in potential, rather than hard and unyielding.

"There we are then, and I'm sure his lordship will sleep better tonight for it. Gather he was up last night, sometimes is."

"The War?" It was the safe inquiry.

"Gather so. That Benton makes him cocoa, but he doesn't singe my pots, so I don't mind. There we are. You let me know if you see something like that, and - what do you like for pudding, dear? I was thinking a bit of syllabub for supper tonight?" It came out in a cheerful burble.

"Oh, please, yes, if it's not a bother. I'm sure you have a lovely touch with them."

The cook beamed, and went cheerfully back off toward the kitchen, after saying, "You enjoy the orchard, dearie."

Cassie waited until she was inside, and then went off on a tour of the mews and stables. The mews were more than a little oppressive, with narrowly barred windows, and a smell she couldn't quite describe, but more like death than she was comfortable with. She didn't get too close to any of the birds, especially not after one, well back in the shadows, made a screeching noise. She didn't want to upset anyone. Or any bird, either.

She didn't think it was anything she was wearing. The lightest scent, her mastery pendant, set in silver, with the comforting charm that echoed with her magic. Perhaps it was the ever-present hint of cat hair, no matter how carefully she cleaned.

The stables were easier. There were a couple of people - two men, one woman in breeches, intriguingly - exercising what she thought might be hunters, out in a paddock behind the stables. Another man, younger, was standing by the gate.

"Help you, ma'am?"

"Here to help with the party, they said I could look around if I didn't disturb things. Do these horses live here all the time?"

"Oh, aye. His lordship has a breeding stud down at Ytene. These are - few of the local young gentlemen and ladies keep them here for hunting. Need a bit of training, these three, that's what they're doing."

Cassie watched, and nodded. "The young woman?" She seemed to be, to Cassie's entirely untrained eye, rather better than the men.

"Stableman's daughter. Grew up riding before she could walk, near enough. She'll be taking over, sooner than later, I'm sure."

Cassie could only nod at that, and say, "Pleasure."

He shrugged, and said "'s fine to pet the horses in the stalls, mistress, if you don't press them. Here, here's a few carrots. All well mannered, here, just keep your hand flat."

Cassie was not at all sure about this, but she took the gesture as it was meant, and the half-dozen small carrots he pressed on her from a grubby pocket. She went off to the large open stable, to be met by an equal number of horse heads popping up from their stalls.

She'd been around horses before, but not for a long time, there was no place for them in her life in Trellech. But she went from one to the other, reaching up and offering a carrot to each, and then petting the broad warm nose.

As she was finishing with the horses, she heard foot-steps, and glanced up to see Thomas approaching. "His lordship is welcoming his guests, and the other staff are handling the drinks. I gather you found something?"

Cassie nodded, giving the large brown nose in front of her another pat before stepping back. Thomas took her arm, gently, guiding her out toward a flat wooden bench on the other side of the paddock, where still more horses were turned out in a field.

"I don't know enough about what the mews are supposed to be like. You'll have to check that, I think. I'll admit one of the birds startled me a little. But, did Mrs Callypher explain?"

"No, she just said she approved of you and we were having syllabub. She only makes that for people she especially likes. She doesn't for me." That last had his same dry humour, and she found it immensely reassuring.

"There was a branch broken off the elder tree - the one by the gate in the orchard. And it, is that..." Cassie fumbled for words. "That one is especially important, am I right?"

"It is, it's one of the anchors for the household warding.

A branch from that taken, oh, that would be enough to get into the folly, certainly. Not and do much direct damage, but it's not nothing." He shook his head. "I will have to let his lordship know. You put things right?"

"Mrs Callypher came out with honey wine and poured it over. Not mead, she was clear on that."

"She would be." There was a ghost of a smile. "We'll have to see about the mews later. My evening is going to be more of an intricate dance than I anticipated, his lordship will want to see to the warding himself."

"Is there anything I can do?"

"I don't suppose you have a white silk tablecloth edged in tawny brown?"

"Owl colours? I could put something together in an hour or two. How big?" She paused. "You don't have something here?"

"A yard square, please, border some multiple of three, after the edging." Then, softly, he admitted, "I did not pack his lordship's complete ritual kit, and his brother was Fox house, and his parents. I'd rather not have to go back through the portal." And leave his lordship alone, was the implication.

She didn't press that particular lack of preparation, he could scarcely have predicted that the more ornate ritual formats would be called for. "His lordship prefers the Kentish approach, then?" Putting together cloths for the various ritual magics was something she'd done as an apprentice, to earn a bit of extra cash. They were simple to sew once you had the knack of it, and she knew all the variants.

"He does. Good, you know what's needed. I'll leave it to you." He paused, then leaned to peck her on the cheek, his thoughts visibly dashing off elsewhere as soon as he'd done it. "Later, Cassie. I'll explain, I promise, when I can."

With that, he was up and gone, leaving Cassie blinking out at the horses for half a minute. Then she gathered herself and went in search of the stocks of silk she'd brought to find the right ones.

THIRTY-TWO

FRIDAY

The arrival of the guests after luncheon put everything into chaos. It was chaos driven along channels, like a surging river that had not yet breached its banks, but chaos nonetheless. The staff at Hawk's Breath were suddenly fussing about things Benton had thought about a week ago. Granted, they were out of practice, but the lack of foresight and the edge of panic were decidedly getting on his nerves.

When it came to the guests, some were easier than others. The Davenports, for example, were entirely familiar with the ways of a great house party. Benton was entirely unsure what his lordship was after, inviting them early, but that was no matter. He had brought his valet, she had brought her lady's maid. Both were familiar with the house from visits when Lord Temple was alive, and both of them enjoyed a brisk walk, a good meal, and some open country-side. Not necessarily in that order. They were quickly shown up to their rooms, and sorted out.

Others, though, were rather more of a challenge. The Fortescues were next, trailing boxes and scarves and handkerchiefs behind them. They caught up all of the upstairs in their train for a good twenty minutes. Benton quietly detailed one of the housemaids to follow them and see to what they needed, and show them where things were. Better not one of the footmen, Mr Fortescue was never quite sure what to do with men outside his own art form. With a housemaid, he'd flirt genially but without any real depth, and everyone knew where they stood. It was something of a challenge, still.

It was the Willacys who most puzzled Benton. He knew that his lordship had a professional interest in them, the sort of professional interest that tangled up with Intelligence work. Or at least potentially crossed paths with it. Mr Willacy seemed, frankly, rather dim. He certainly didn't listen. Competent staff had a dozen ways at hand to redirect a guest who wasn't picking up on cues, and Mr Willacy was requiring every trick in the book.

They had arrived by portal, half an hour early, and before the staff were entirely done seeing the Fortescues inside. Then they walked off, with no instructions about which cases went where, and were found arguing that they ought to be able to wander through the kitchens to get to the gardens. They had brought no staff with them, despite saying they would, which would mean having to rearrange the staffing assignments. He didn't envy the staff any of that, given the heavy load from the party itself. They would take rather a lot of tact, and that was likely to be in shorter supply than preferred in the next few days.

Benton started out uncertain whether they were not sure how things were done, or if they were actively trying to be rude. Three minutes in, he was sure they were both rather dim and trying to be difficult. Thankfully, they were not clever enough to be creative with their difficulties. He spent twenty minutes sorting out half a dozen minor things. More towels, no, different towels. Explaining the linens, and offering an additional coverlet, if they'd like, and noting that the room would warm up with the fire going. Inquiring if Mr Willacy wished him to unpack for him, until the footman assigned to him were available?

Mr Willacy did not, and Benton could not tell if the man were simply shy of poorly made underthings being seen, or something else. The man treated him with a rather dubious distance, and it seemed not one made solely of class. Benton wondered if he'd heard any of the recent wave of rumours that Benton and his lordship were scandalously close. Even if it had been appropriate, which it was not, he was not his lordship's type. At all.

He could make no more headway with the problem, so he went down the back stairs to alert Mr Bigford and Mrs Doncaster of the need to assign still more people. That part was simple enough, but the delicacy required to suggest who they might assign had him folding his hands behind his back so he could pinch the skin between thumb and forefinger, as a reminder to keep tight hold of his frustration and temper.

The last two arrivals, the Bronsons and the Conifers, were largely a relief. He had gathered from his lordship that Maud Bronson had become something of an ally to Miss Penhallow in whatever her current goals were in the Albion Inheritance, and that the invitation to stay was seen as something of a coup.

Whatever the reason and the background, she and her husband knew how to attend a house party, had come with their own staff, and were briskly efficient about settling in, once he had pointed out the amenities. Benton rather thought Madam Bronson the more dominant of the pair, but her husband kept up pleasant conversation, rather than sulking or decamping for the men-only sections of the house. It was a pleasant change from some.

Madam Conifer was mousy and entirely cowed by her husband, trailing along after him rather like a neglected puppy. Her husband was far too loud, paid no attention to her whatsoever, and had a tendency to put his foot in his mouth. He inquired after the other guests, and was not at all pleased to find the Willacys on the list. "What did that fool invite them for, that's what I want to know." His wife murmured something conciliatory, and Mr Conifer continued, louder, "No one who'd had them for supper would invite them again, especially not him."

Benton did not dignify that with acknowledgement, never mind a reply. He did, however, make a point of mentioning that he was sure Madam Conifer's costume for the ball would be lovely, he knew the dressmaker and others had been working on the various options.

By tea time, everyone had been shown their rooms, and wrangled tactfully into place. Each had been guided downstairs to the drawing room. The customs would help now. Tea and sherry in the drawing room, a pause for everyone to change for supper, and then the supper party, each person with their prescribed seat. Even the Willacys knew how that went, Benton had seen that when they had come to supper previously.

The later evening amusements ran to tarrochi and some other card games among the women. The men settled into the billiards room, and Benton was glad he had seen to having the table properly cleaned and maintained among his many other tasks. It was not a game his lordship preferred. More to the point, he preferred to save strain on his shoulder for the more active outdoor pursuits, such as riding and falconry, and ideally, a pavo match.

The guests, despite the somewhat awkward invitation list, kept each other talking until rather later than Benton had expected. His lordship did not have time to tend to the reinforcement of the warding or the investigation of its disruption until after all had retired for the night, well after ten.

His lordship had seen everyone upstairs before turning to the family wing, all geniality and no sign of suspicion that there had been a disruption. Then he had changed silently from his formal clothes into a working robe of thick white samite, with the deep silver-gray fabric wound round his waist to hold everything in place.

Benton, for his part, had slipped into his own room and changed into his own working robes for such rituals, made of plain soft wool dyed with an indigo so deep it was almost black, and belted by a plain white silk cord. That done, he attended on his lordship's final preparations. His lordship was delaying, and Benton didn't understand why until the passage from Miss Penhallow's rooms opened.

She joined them, looking charming in a long gown held in place by a beautifully cut dressing gown that echoed some of the Chinoiserie elements. Instead of the sometimes overdone and inaccurate depictions of some foreign land, the embroidered birds swooping from shoulder to waist were falcons, the lower half decorated with fields and forests full of horses, sheep, and a variety of trees.

The style of the embroidery was decidedly English, the effect created mostly by placement and the stylistic elements. It was not Cassie's work, he was certain, though elements echoed aspects of things that he had seen before in her shop. He was caught, for a moment, by what Cassie would look like in something like that, something made to her own tastes.

He was drawn away from his contemplation by his lordship's needs. They made their way down the stone stairs tucked into a hidden passage along the outer wall, into the private family workroom, Benton bringing up the back, carrying the tray with his lordship's personal magical effects and his book of charms.

Benton had prepared the space after supper, when he was not needed to see to anyone's needs. Cassie had done wonders preparing the cloths so quickly, and they made the ritual working look entirely proper, as if this had been planned for weeks, not hours. The oil lamps were lit, and for this working, he had cast the charm that would warm the stones to something comfortable for bare feet.

His lordship took a deep breath, and began. First, he placed the ritual stones that were the symbols of the points of the primary wards. Benton handed tool after tool; tongs, piece of slate, water drawn from the central well of the estate, clay from the riverbed. It went on and on. Part way through, Miss Penhallow began to help, moving symbolic rounded pebbles from one plate to another, then handing his lordship a vial so he could add droplets of distilled water and plants from the gardens.

The end results were unsatisfying to all three of them. There were disturbances in the wards, unspecified. They had already known that. His lordship went smoothly through the ritual magics to smooth the wards, renew the protections.

But there was little new information. They already know there were plots afoot. None of them discussed it, other than the occasional word of clarification. He was sure his lordship was taking the consideration of the elder branch into his calculations, he could see the little gestures and actions to see if that were the cause of the problems. But while nothing disproved the idea, it appeared there might be other influences at work.

Benton suspected, the way they worked together, that it was not the first time his lordship and Miss Penhallow had done the dance of the more formal ritual magics together, but he had no idea what the previous occasions might have been.

When it was done, his lordship and Miss Penhallow climbed the stairs back to the master bedroom ahead of him. Benton took a moment to put the lamps out, picking up the ritual case and bringing it upstairs. He set it in the magically locked armoire, and made sure it was secure, before he turned to bow to his lordship.

They were already sitting on his bed. Miss Penhallow was speaking quietly, so much so he could not make out her words. His lordship dismissed him to his own bed with a wave and a mouthed "Thank you."

Some valets would be offended, but Benton would not fuss, certainly not about this. Miss Penhallow's arrival was a thing he knew must come, as soon as they had had that awful telegram announcing that his lordship was Lord of Ytene. There would be a marriage, there would be children, and he had to trust that his lordship would treat him fairly throughout.

With some other masters, he might have doubted, but here he never did. If he no longer served, his lordship would pension him out, or find him a more suitable place, so long as he were loyal and honest in his service. And his lordship's choice might not be of aristocratic birth, but she had kindness and presence and intelligence. More to the point, his lordship loved her, and she loved him. Benton found it made going to his own bed more lonely, though, tonight.

He wondered, as he turned down his bed, what it was like for Cassie, sleeping in a strange bed, in a great house she was entirely unfamiliar with. And whether she was lonely, or whether she did not permit herself to indulge in that.

W hen Cassie came down for lunch, the mood belowstairs was very different. Yesterday, there had been a sense of anticipation, but no one had been overly hurried. She had had the sense of pieces coming together, in a more or less predictable fashion. It had felt so much like the steady work of piecing a dress, setting everything in place for a final fitting. No rushing, no chaos, just everything laid out properly in order.

Now, even just since breakfast, the mood had shifted. She claimed a seat at the staff table, and she was handed a plate, encouraged to take her food from the bowls on the table or the plates of small sandwiches. She served herself and nodded at Amelia and Joselyn, who were in conversation with a couple of the housemaids.

There were plans within plans, as far as she could tell from the conversation flowing around her, with people talking through the eventualities, anticipating difficulties, and making arrangements for the course of the party. More than one of the guests had been difficult already, someone had been found trying to get below stairs for some reason, and others were demanding all manner of special meals.

Cassie had never had the opportunity to hear people talk about this sort of thing before. She knew that some people had valets and lady's maids, and some people didn't, or made do with assistance from the senior housemaid or butler when required. Here, though, they were working through staffing, who would need assistance, who wouldn't, with Mrs Doncaster making notes in a tight close hand in a notebook.

"If one of the guests tries to come down, Mrs Doncaster?"

"Tell me, and I will see to it." That was Mr Bigford. Cassie supposed he was the proper person, though he was not terribly imposing.

Once she was done eating, someone whisked her plate and cup away before she could even look around. Without looking up, Mrs Doncaster said "Mistress Castalia, we'll be eating supper at five. We'll be busy with arrivals, so if you could let one of the housemaids know if you need anything for your space in the next hour, it would be much appreciated."

Cassie could tell a dismissal to her duties when she heard one, and she stood up. "Of course. Amelia, Joselyn, let us go through our own inventories, and make sure everything is entirely ready before the appointments." She waited for them to bob and start upstairs, and Benton gave her a quick nod as she followed. There was no time to talk now, but she flicked her fingers at him and hoped he understood that she'd like to pass a few things on.

The afternoon was decidedly mixed on her end. Making sure everything was well-organised, that was no bother. This was the part that Cassie liked most, besides the actual design work. Laces and ribbons and beads and buttons could all be very unruly, tangling and snarling or rolling everywhere, and it was satisfying to see everything arranged properly, tucked away into tidy rolls, the beads and buttons in the little travel case that kept them separate.

They had appointments today with those invited to stay over, the Friday to Monday guests, to do the fittings and figure out what fripperies they would add, the little details of lace cuffs or ruffs or ribbons. They'd be providing items for the various hair arrangements, and fans and clutch bags, and whatever else suited.

The Fortescues, being artists, and thus rather lower in the social status department, were the first appointments after the upstairs luncheon. Alice Fortescue turned out to be a delight, chattering away amiably, in the manner of one used to having people fuss around her body and take care of things. She had learned the powerful and much appreciated skill of staying still and not wriggling. They had both picked outfits from Shakespeare's histories, though with a distinctly fantastic air, with Alice as Katherine, the wife of Henry V. Her brother had chosen a romanticised Julius Caesar, for the draping toga.

Considering the summer heat and humidity, Cassie rather thought he'd made a wise decision, as the clothing would be comfortable, graceful, and elegant even in this weather. It helped that she'd made it out of a smooth mid-weight linen, rather than the wool that would have been more historically accurate. Costume parties were a time to gesture at the era, not replicate it exactly.

Their fittings did set the tone well, and the next visit was also smooth and comfortable. The Bronsons were rather higher up the social status, but Maud Bronson admitted that she preferred to get this out of the way so she

could enjoy the afternoon. She had chosen to focus on Eliz-
abeth Gloriana, all broad velvet skirts and high ruff. It
required some conversation to figure out what would be
most comfortable for the lady, and what charms she would
permit that would make the weight of the cloth easier to
manage.

"Nothing that changes how it falls." Maud Bronson was
firm on that. "Though, I suppose, can you manage a cooling
charm on something like this?" She sounded wistful.

"We had planned on that, madam." Cassie gestured at
the metallic thread she'd used for the embroidery. Most of it
had been done with manufactured ribbon, nothing too
ornate, but much faster than doing all the sewing by hand.
Amelia had tacked it on with a metallic thread that would
hold the magic of the charms properly. "I promise you'll be
quite comfortable, we'll do that at the final fitting, tomorrow,
and it will last through the night."

"It is lovely." There was a pleasant note of sentimental-
ity, there, something Cassie had not quite expected from
someone with Maud Bronson's reputation as a battle-axe.
Her husband finished up his simpler robes first, murmured
something inaudible to his wife, and left the room.

There was the kind of thoughtful pause that Cassie
knew would be leading to a question, so she busied herself
with the last adjustments to the bodice to make everything
lie smoothly. "You are the one who's been making sure
Elspeth Penhallow's so well dressed, I gather?"

"Lord Carillon has an excellent eye for suitability, and
for quality. Which I'm pleased to say I provide. And Miss
Penhallow has been a pleasure to work with, a woman with
grace and class."

"There were doubts about her. Her family, her father's
side. Not quite the usual sort."

Cassie didn't reply, just murmured "If you could lift your hands, madam, as high as you might wish, tomorrow, for the dancing?"

Maud Bronson lifted her arms, precisely as they would be to dance with her husband. "You do fine work. Even for something as fleeting as this dance."

"Thank you, madam. We take pride in our workmanship."

"Might you have time for an extended appointment? Myself and my eldest granddaughter. She's due for her debut this winter."

Cassie crowed in her head. That was quite the coup, even if they only wanted a few frocks. "Of course, madam. Shall I write early next week to arrange a visit? We've begun working on some designs for the winter already."

"Do write. We'd want something exclusive, of course. For her debut. And other dresses, we have quite the list of expected invitations already. Appropriate, but singular. Beginning a style she can grow into as she matures."

"Of course, Madam Bronson. We would be delighted. A consultation, looking at fabric and colours that would best suit, and then I will do sketches, and we can go from there."

Maud Bronson nodded once, regally. "Good." Then she considered the effect in the mirror in front of her. "Oh, that is quite fine."

It took a good fifteen minutes to get her out of the dress and the stays, and the various necessary padding, but Cassie considered it time well spent. After making arrangements for the final fitting, when they would add the ruff and some final decorative touches, Cassie was ready for a short break. Joselyn had arranged tea and sandwiches.

"Who else?"

"The Davenports are just tomorrow, there isn't much

detailed fitting for the Byzantine robes they wanted, though I do think they came out well. And the same for the Conifers. He had that suit already, it's just the colouring, and her Regency dress is also simple to fit, just taking in the bodice if we need to, a little."

Amelia nodded. "That leaves the Willacys." She was counting off names in her head, and Cassie nodded, approvingly. "Lord Carillon and the Misses Penhallow, we saw to them earlier this week." And those were easier since they were working off known measurements and the outfits were only being adjusted not made from scratch.

It was then that the door opened, without even the brief courtesy of a knock and the sharp voice of Madam Willacy. "Come along, we have places to be. I do hope you're all ready." She was one of those, then, all edges and unpleasantness. Not someone Cassie wanted or would take as a long-term client, and in fact, she was already trying to decide on how much of this she might report to Benton.

After some consultation by letter, Cassie had prepared Tudor clothing, on their request, using some older costumes they had available. Madam Willacy had provided an older velvet gown, which had turned out to be a bit worn at the hem and needed to be let out a bit in the bodice.

It had taken some notable skill to turn it into something worth wearing. Cassie had had to call in favours with one of her friends most gifted at cleaning and restoring old fabric. Lacing her into the farthingale, the kirtle, and then the heavy French robe took rather a long time. Cassie had already gathered from the gossip below stairs that not only had Madam Willacy not brought a maid, but that no one was looking forward to seeing to her costume.

"It is abominably hot." That was a statement, a declaration of enmity.

"We have included cooling charms, to be activated for the party tomorrow, madam. If you would prefer something lighter weight, we could put together something Roman, or perhaps Regency, quickly, if you wished."

"Wear no proper underthings? Do you think I'm a slattern, then?" She was a woman who still insisted on a corset, even though even the milder S-shaped corsets had largely disappeared before the War. In this case, Cassie had used a rather Victorian model laced to get something that at least gestured at the proper silhouette, since Madam Willacy had not wanted to spare the time to fit another, never mind any cost.

Cassie had little patience for people with that approach to historical clothing. She was no expert in it, but it irked her to do the thing poorly. On the other hand, Lord Carillon had been quite clear she was to follow the Willacys' lead on their costumes, and make it possible.

"Of course not, Madam. But it is a masked ball. If you chose to wear something well outside your usual, it might be a better amusement. But of course, this flatters madam, the long lines of the bodice, and madam has the height to be most impressive."

Madam Willacy nodded once, sharply, then turned her attention to her husband's clothing, with half a dozen suggestions that were barely avoiding being orders. Cassie had the sudden thought that neither of them were particularly clever. Certainly, they were not showing much sign of it with her. It wasn't just how they were treating her, though that was distasteful enough.

By the time they were both done, she'd heard several points where they were being either willfully obtuse, or had not managed to pay any attention to important details. Cassie worked around both of them, until the French hood, the cap that covered Madam Willacy's hair, was properly fitted. Then she coughed. "If we may help Madam change her clothes, we will have these ready for you tomorrow."

Thankfully, there was not much to be done. The kirtle and gown fit well enough that the adjustments could be done through the lacings. Madam Willacy ignored her, throughout, and it was only when they were well gone, at least half a minute after the door closed, that she permitted herself to sit down.

"Sit for a minute or two, both of you," she instructed her apprentices. "In case she comes back. Then we'll get started on the final preparations."

THIRTY-FOUR

SATURDAY MORNING

The next dawn came far too early. Benton had had maybe five hours of sleep, more likely four. He bent to open the compartment in his trunk, bringing out one of the vials he kept for such days, when he needed all his wits about him.

His lordship could not risk this one, it was too close to things that would leave him shaking and lost to the mists of time. But it would make Benton sharper, more observant, from now until well after sunset. He would pay for it later, this kind of magic had its costs, but that was also a problem for later.

Benton downed the vial in one gulp, grimacing at the flavour, all sickly sweet with an edge of sharp metal. Only then did he stand, dress for the day, and go and prepare things for his lordship. There was the morning check with the household staff, to make sure everything was in order, while one of the kitchen maids put together his lordship's tray.

Cassie caught his eye as he was about to take the tray. "A moment, Mr Benton?"

He wanted to take the tray up, promptly, but he also trusted she had some reason to interrupt the flow of the morning. He hadn't seen her last night, she had been busy with the costume pieces when he was free, and free when he was taking care of the ritual matters.

Benton drew her off to the side hallway to the stillroom, where no one would bother them. "Yes?"

"May I ask, is there some reason the Willacys are here? They are rather unlike the other guests." She looked him up and down, as if she'd picked up on the effects of the vial, but she said nothing about it.

"There is, but his lordship has not vouchsafed all of the reasons to me. Did they cause you any difficulty?"

"They were rather unpleasant. I would not wish for them as ongoing clients, certainly, but nothing his lordship might feel the need to take action about." She paused. "On the other hand, Maud Bronson is quite interested in substantial future work, and as far as I'm concerned, that repays any possible annoyance from the Willacys."

Benton considered, weighing that. "I don't suppose you could tell me what they're wearing tonight?"

She reached into a pocket in the small bag she wore over one shoulder, and pulled out a piece of paper. "The complete list of costumes I've worked on. I'll add the ones we're just doing final touches on this evening."

Benton blinked. That was the kind of attention to detail he expected of himself, and rarely found in anyone else. The list had names, and not just the type of clothing, but the colours and millinery. He ducked his chin, firmly repressing the desire to kiss her again. "Queen of dressmakers. When all this is over, I would be glad to reward your attentions."

It made her laugh, freely, though she quickly settled

into a grin. "I'll hold you to that. But not now. You've plenty to keep you busy."

Benton nodded. "His lordship's tray. Are you still interested in the falconry? I'll meet you down here at half-nine." She nodded, and then stepped back to let him go to work, without any sort of visible resentment. He wondered what had changed for her, that she was now respecting the demands of his service, rather than being offended by them. He would ask, when they finally had time to talk properly again.

He checked the tray over quickly. There was the strong tea, and an extra sugar, along with toast. His lordship would break his fast properly downstairs, but this would see him started well. He brought the tray up, to find that Miss Penhallow had only recently fled the bed. The imprint of her head was still on the pillow. She would be in her own room, now, with her own tea tray.

"Your lordship. The falcons will be ready at ten, plenty of time to take them out before a picnic luncheon. All the food preparations are well underway for tonight, and Mrs Mudthon has a particular touch with the subtleties. More than her usual."

"Right, right." His lordship rubbed his eyes, then caught a movement. "You've taken one of your vials, haven't you?"

"Of course, sir. We can't risk missing something today."

"Good. I'm glad one of us is on top of things. You let me know what you spot."

"I had thought, sir, with your permission, to invite Mistress Castalia to accompany me. She has no duties this morning, and I believe her eye would be of some use."

"With the staff?" His lordship looked up, blinking, looking every bit the dissolute lordling he pretended to be in public. "Oh, fine, of course. Whatever you think best."

"You might manage an hour's nap this afternoon, sir. Your costume will not take long to put on."

"Oh, I expect I'll need it, yes." He waved a hand. "Falcons, Benton."

"Helena is ready for you, sir, and you know she flies well for you." That was his current bird, a gorgeous merlin.

"Only because Ruskin is one of the best falconers who ever lived. But I will not embarrass myself, no. Nor that lovely lady." His lordship looked up at Benton for a moment, then out the window. The shoulder wound might be paining him physically, as well, the way he shifted.

Benton inclined his head, quietly.

There was a silence, then his lordship said, "No use fussing over spilled milk. And Helena's a fine bird."

"Sir. Shall I come back to dress you?"

"Half an hour. Make sure Mally - Miss Stone - has everything she needs, please?"

"Already done, your lordship." He bowed slightly, and withdrew, closing the door quietly behind him.

The morning routines went smoothly from there, which meant that at ten, everyone had a pleasant walk to the top of a nearby hill. The birds were brought up on a smooth-rolling cart, separate from the dozen people who'd be flying them today. Miss Penhallow was there, naturally. She had a strong stomach, she'd grown up in the country. There were Willacys, the Fortescues, the Davenports, all not quite sure how this would go.

Benton withdrew to the back, where Cassie was standing. "Have you seen falcons flown before?" He kept his voice quiet.

Cassie shook her head. "Never. Oh, they're different kinds of birds, aren't they?"

"Rather, yes. His lordship's current bird is a merlin,

quite small. Traditionally a lady's bird." He let that be, without defending the choice further.

"If his lordship is aware of some of the gossip about him." Cassie's voice was barely audible even to Benton. "He does like thumbing his nose at it, doesn't he?"

Benton smiled. "He used to fly a Eurasian eagle-owl. His lordship trained her from a fledgling, during his apprenticeship." Long before Benton had come into his life. "He took an injury in the War that means he can't take her weight comfortably for long enough now. That bird, there, that Ruskin is bringing out now, that's Theodora."

"Named for the empr.... Magic's sake, she's enormous!"

"Named for the Byzantine empress, yes. She's not as cranky about being flown during the day as some owls are." Though still a bit out of sorts, as they watched her mantle and cry out before she settled more steadily on Ruskin's forearm. She twisted her head towards his lordship and made a softer sound, then, as if she were disappointed that he was not offering her his own arm.

The initial part of the outing went smoothly enough. They flew the birds once, then again. There were no successful kills but there was a rustle in the grass, likely a rabbit, that suggested a near miss.

The party strolled along the hill, to a new spot. People were moving around, as often happened on this kind of outing. It was difficult for Benton to keep track of precisely who was where, he caught a glimpse of someone going down over the ridge, but not which man it was. Of course his attention was partly on his lordship. And some on Cassie, who was being careful not to distract him unduly, but who kept asking thoughtful questions, far beyond the usual squeaks of excitement common to ladies, in his previous observations.

This time, when they loosed the birds, one after another, there was a scuffle. Ruskin went swiftly off to the edge of the woods to figure out what had happened. Benton and Cassie followed, a yard or two behind the main group, so Benton was close enough to hear a quick, "Benton, you gloved?"

"Sir."

"Take Theodora."

Benton braced himself, and then Ruskin transferred her to his arm. He could feel the weight immediately, and more to the point, how restless she was. It was not the first time he had held her. She was decidedly of the opinion that if someone other than Ruskin was carrying her, it ought to be his lordship, and only settled for him as a distant, barely tolerable third choice.

This seemed to be somewhat more than that, though, and he frowned as he tried to figure out what was annoying her. There was a small scrap of something - cloth, he thought - wrapped around one of her talons. He took several careful steps backwards, angling away from the fuss and noise of the group, working to calm the bird. He had no hood for her, he could only hold the jesses securely, and feed her a scrap of meat from the bag on his hip.

Once he was back closer to Cassie, he said, "She has a scrap of fabric tangled in her talons. Do you think you could..."

It was an immense thing to ask anyone, to get that near dangerous talons on an unsettled bird. But Cassie took a breath, moving slowly. Her art, at least, had given her skill in small precise movements, and taking the time that was needed without rushing.

Theodora cried out, in a way that seemed oddly deliberate, with a repeated and insistent note, but neither Ruskin nor his lordship seemed to make much of it. Benton cooed to the bird, the gentle cluckings that reassured her she was being respected, and fed her another piece of meat, doing his best to divert her attention.

Cassie reached her hand out, working to free the fabric. She drew back, and said, "Later. You take care of that fine empress."

In the end it was a quarter of an hour before he could hand her back to Ruskin. The falconer loosed her one more time, to settle her, give her the routine she expected. She came back proudly with her tawny feathers glowing in the sun and a small rabbit in her talons, but tried to fly to his lordship, instead, and there was a bit of confusion. Eventually, Ruskin praised her, lured her onto his arm, and hooded her. And of course, he completely ignored the way Mrs Willacy and two of the other women were audibly disgusted by the reality of the hunt.

"Benton, see to things back at the house, would you?" His lordship's tone was brisk, clear, and expecting that Benton would resolve half a dozen issues without anyone noticing.

Benton nodded at his lordship, glad of the excuse to retreat, and figure out what Cassie had found. They were halfway back to the house before she giggled. "What did Mrs Willacy expect, of falcons?"

"No idea. But you see, Theodora is a fine bird."

"Oh, far better than you think. That's a scrap torn from someone's sleeve. And see here?" She pulled it out, and there was a dark line of deep red-brown along the edge of the fine-woven linen. "She, I believe she got the edge of someone's arm. That is a man's shirt, almost certainly. See the smooth weave here?"

"That is easy to hide." Oh, it was something of a clue.

"There's a test, that can match blood to the person it came from, but it is not simple. Not something his lordship could do, certainly not with sufficient decorum."

Cassie glanced at him, and said "Goodness. You - and he - have limits. I was beginning to wonder."

"We can, however, bring it to the Guard, when we have someone to match it to. I wonder what they were at." Benton frowned. This was perhaps a critical clue, but he could not think what would provoke people with plots to be that public about it. And it was not like Theodora to strike out at someone, certainly not without provocation.

Cassie frowned and looked up at him, uncertain. "I didn't see all of it, but there were three of the men, near that line of the trees, wandering around in the brush, when we were coming up to the second spot. It seemed curious at the time, but with this," her voice trailed off. "Willacy, Bronson, and that short man with the eyebrows." She considered. "I don't think Mr Bronson and the other man like Mr Willacy much. Though I gather they're in a large company in that."

"Conifer. Mr Adelphus Conifer. If there were something someone needed, that they did not want to bring through the portal." Benton frowned. "His lordship renewed the wards, but there were signs something was still unsettled. Nothing specific."

"What would that mean?"

"The elder branch that was cut, someone could bring in otherwise banned items through the wards. If it were touching the banned item."

"Banned?"

"Poisons, the sorts of potions that take another's will. Particularly nasty classes of illegal things." They were almost back at the house. "As long as the branch still is wick enough that it has a little spark of magic to it, it would work. Even with the repairs his lordship did last night."

"So nothing good."

"We can scarcely search all their rooms, and most of the guests brought their own valets and maids. The Willacys didn't, but they have been - limited."

"I will keep my ears open this afternoon, while we're doing fittings. And tonight."

"And I will see if I can find excuses to leave things in their rooms." Back at the kitchen door now, all he could do was smile at her. "I'm quite grateful for your sharp eyes. I'm sure his lordship will be more so."

For the moment, he had to get back into the fray of managing half a dozen tasks. Added to that, he needed to find time to slip away and take a better look at the woods, where Theodora had taken that scrap, and see if there was anything there.

THIRTY-FIVE

SATURDAY AFTERNOON

Cassie found herself back in the parlour, organising the final fittings, before she had time to think through the implications of the morning. On one hand, it seemed like something out of a bad novel, plots and poisons and falcons, for magic's sake. Well, and an owl.

She did not think a gigantic eagle-owl named for an empress of complex reputation improved anything. Even if she were terrifyingly beautiful. Something kept nagging her about the owl, as if there was something Benton was missing. She had no idea what, though, she didn't know how Theodora usually behaved. Besides, clearly, being quite fond of his lordship. Being raised from a fledgeling seemed likely to do that to a bird.

What startled her more than the rest of it was how much Benton took this in stride. She had thought he was in a menial position, dancing attendance on Lord Carillon, at his whim and fancy.

And she admitted she liked Lord Carillon, more than many of the noble families she had done work for. He paid well, on time, and ungrudgingly, which was rare enough to be worth keeping, but he also had a good eye and an appreciation for her art. She had been pleased when he brought Lizzie Penhallow to her, and more pleased when that relationship flowered. She'd even rather envied them finding that kind of love with each other.

That did not solve the challenge of Thomas Benton, who was no menial at all. Seeing him here, in service, made her more and more sure she could not ask him to leave. Not for her. Not for anyone who would ask it of him. He deserved better than that. Like it or not, want it or not, that service was bone-deep in him. Not in a menial way, not in a grudging way, not in a way that made him less of a man.

He handled gigantic eagle-owls with ease and obvious comfort. He could debate the precise nuances of fashionable shades of colour - and hex him - be right most of the time. He thought broadly, about what was needed. You could drop him into a cock fighting ring and he would come home battered but victorious.

The eagle-owl did put the cock fighting somewhat in perspective, now she thought about it. If he had reached to catch the cock the way he expected to catch a falcon or owl, that could well explain the injuries.

While Thomas Benton had not attended one of the magical schools, that bit of magic he'd done that morning made it clear he could hold his own. And then some. She knew plenty of her own peers who could muster one or two closely aligned forms of magic, for a precise purpose, and nothing else. That might well lead to a profitable workshop, but there was no denying it was limited. Even those who had the capacity to study more broadly rarely did, when there was no particular professional reason for it. Like it or not, the mastery of magic for itself was largely the provenance of the idle rich, who did not have to spend their days in actual labour.

Thomas had none of those preconceptions or focus upon a trade fencing his ability. He was a man of great range and solidity. He'd been made better by his service, the way it gave him access to the sort of wealth and potential that made his breadth of knowledge and experience possible. She wondered, now, if he'd particularly liked the explorations to mountains that he'd made, because he was rather like a mountain. Stubborn, long-enduring, patient, and relentless when he needed to be.

She was quite certain that by this evening, he would be circulating around the edges of the party. He would be making sure all was in order, a second pair of eyes for his lordship. Benton had been busy before the falconry outing that morning and had a brightness and sharpness to him that made it clear it had already been a full day by luncheon.

Cassie had thought herself too good for him, when they'd met. Or rather, that he was no sort of man she would consider worthy. It was upsetting to discover it was the other way around. He was a man of great skill, remarkable subtlety, and far-reaching awareness, and she had utterly dismissed all of that. Despite her sharpness, he had never treated her with anything less than courtesy, if occasionally a rather brusque and mulish sort of courtesy. Oh, he'd argued with her, and disagreed, and he'd done her the favour of telling the truth. Of trusting that she had integrity and intelligence.

She shook her head. The only thing for it was to repay that trust was to do what she could to gather information he could use, and share her skills with him. And to share them as unstintingly as he did. Nothing like a challenge, then.

"Mistress?" That was Joselyn. "Master von Tolman is here."

Cassie turned around, letting out a breath as she did. Before her was a sharp-featured man of middle age, going slightly bald. He clicked his heels together and bowed in a most precise fashion, peering at her over small pince-nez. "Mistress Castalia, I am honoured to work at your side again."

She inclined her head, holding out her hand, palm to the ground, so he could kiss the air above it. He was fussy and particular, but he was also good at his work. And in her experience, pleasant and easy enough to work with as long as he was treated with respect. The combination was invaluable.

"Master Frederick, a pleasure, as always. You may remember my apprentice, Amelia. This is our newest addition, Joselyn. Ladies, this is Master von Tolman. We have the space set aside for you here, with the curtains the way you prefer." He required a small white canvas tent, magically enchanted to seem larger inside. There was a charmed light set in the peak, so he could set the colours precisely as he wanted.

"You do remember!" He beamed at her. "A pleasure, Miss Amelia, Miss Joselyn. Ah, yes, this will do quite well, quite quite well. His lordship is most attentive to my requests, I see. Such a relief. One cannot always count on that. Do you have a final list of the guests?"

Cassie waved a hand behind her back, and Joselyn promptly brought over the copies of the list they had made. "Here, with the costumes waiting for them. Two pair Tudor, one Elizabethan, one Byzantine - a request for proper Tyrian purple. Two pair Regency." She paused. "And one pair who seem to be assuming all of Shakespeare is historical." Not that she grudged the Fortescues their amusements at all, really, they were pleasant enough people, but the right humour would put Master von Tolman in a fine mood.

He snorted. "We will do what we can, then. Good. And the others, they bring their own costumes, little colouring?"

Cassie nodded. "Those are the ones we are providing. Smaller pieces, and many, like the ruffs and so on, can be left uncoloured."

"Right, yes, yes. Tea in thirty minutes, please." He disappeared into the little tent, muttering pleasantly if inaudibly to himself.

Cassie drew the apprentices away. "He will let us know if he needs something, but this is a small party by his standards. Ten minutes at most to set the colours, likely fifteen for a couple. The illusion will last until morning, but that is why we were using neutral fabrics."

They looked at her, then nodded, visibly a bit nervous.

"Now, we'll manage this just wonderfully. Amelia will take the gentlemen, remember, I'll take the ladies, and Joselyn, you will help bring things, and help them choose accessories if needed. A shawl or a fan or a mask if they did not bring one."

"Yes'm." Joselyn did not often fall into that habit.

"And you let me know if any of them cause you problems. You remember the code words, yes?"

"Mistress, your expertise, if you have a moment?" They said it in chorus, and she beamed at them.

"Exactly so. And likely I'll hear, since I'll be right at hand."

They looked only modestly reassured, but the distraction of the final touches and preparations kept them busy enough not to dwell on it. Tea, then a steady progression of visitors, at intervals that were managed with the help of the housemaids and footmen directing each couple into their parlour.

"Good afternoon! Everything is entirely ready for the final fitting. Madam Bronson, this way, and Joselyn will help you into your dress. And we're ready with the cooling charms, of course. And then we can see to all the little details that will make it perfect."

Once they were in the midst, things went smoothly enough. They came, they were helped into dresses and coats and costumes, fussed over and made much of. She and her apprentices fitted lace cuffs and ruffs and draping stoles, ready to be coloured. She had been taught by more than one of her teachers that the fussing was as much their mastery as the sewing, of giving people the confidence to suit their clothes.

Some took to it better than others, however. Amelia struggled with this, for all her comfort chattering along, she was still learning the knack of putting a client at ease and making them feel pleased with their choices. Joselyn was less practiced, but some of her reading was paying off, enabling her to ask an occasional question about the more pleasant or engaging bits of gossip during the pauses.

Madam Conifer was a mousy thing, clearly used to never getting a word in edge-wise with her husband, and not sharp enough to keep up with the wives of his colleagues and chosen conversation partners. Cassie felt rather sorry for her, and pleased when the costume - one of the Regency outfits - came out a gorgeous soft forest green, with a cream shawl over the top. The shades brought out honey highlights in her hair, and a spark in her eyes.

When she left the room and they had a short pause, she nodded. "There, that is a fine tribute to our art, and to

Master von Tolman's," to her apprentices. "You think about how to do that for more people, if you want to sharpen your wits."

It was not until the Willacys, the last of their appointments, that there was much difficulty.

"This is not at all what I requested. I saw Maud Bronson, and she had full Elizabethan regalia. I cannot have that, that woman outdo me."

"Madam Willacy, here are the notes. Of course, we can make adjustments." Cassie drew out the folder of material. "You had asked for something properly regal, and you quite rightly suggested something to suit your figure, not force it into the narrow confines of the Elizabethan figure. The Tudor lines are much more flattering to you, echoing your natural shape and enhancing it. And don't forget how impressive the sleeves will look, the linings."

"Hmph." Madam Willacy sniffed, but submitted to being dressed. Then she agreed to be adorned with various baubles, costume jewellery, and yes, the extravagant and ridiculous fur sleeves that turned up to cover most of the elbow and crook of the arm.

Halfway through, she began talking to her husband, as if no one else was in the room. "I still can't believe the Conifers dared come, he must have known you'd be here. After how things went at the Sibleys. And I must say, the standard of service is abysmal. Not at all what it was when his parents were alive. You can almost smell the mustiness. I suppose if he will hide away in that awful crumbling Ytene."

Her husband coughed and said, "We have our reasons, dear. And you look very fine." He was not quite broad enough in the chest to make an impressive showing in his own costume. But he did make a decent match to her, at least, and their costumes would be a coordinated rich blue.

"I'm sure that Lizzie Penhallow will be in something not at all suited. And there were those stories about Laura, being far more free with her favour than she should be. An entirely unsuitable family. Did we have to..."

Her husband cut her off, with a sharp, "Enough, Dorinda. Enough. We are here, we will be pleasant, we will see things through."

It was something in the last phrase that made her certain it was more than a weekend's social outing. It wasn't even the words, though the last phrase was worrisome. It was his tone. She had heard it often enough in the War. Usually from men about to be sent to the Front, who had some premonition that it was a turning point for them, and they were destroying any chance of the lives they could have had.

It made her certain she needed to tell Thomas as soon as she could.

THIRTY-SIX

SATURDAY EVENING

The ball had begun an hour ago, and Benton was increasingly ill at ease. Everything seemed to be going normally, but that little sense would not settle, the one that raised the hair on the back of his neck. It was the feeling minutes before an attack in the trenches, before the sounds of explosions and screams.

Given the situation, Benton had taken particular precautions to avoid anyone interfering with the food. When one of the punch bowls responded oddly to the charm he used to check on any additives, he directed the staff to discard the entire thing, after he had taken samples in case they were needed later.

He did not think it was anything more than perhaps one of the potions people used to enhance a good time, the way the charms reacted. Still, that would not do. Just to be certain, he sent two of the footmen to either end of the buffet table with the strictest instructions to report anything unusual. He set himself to making sure his lordship and Miss Penhallow had food that came straight up from the kitchens.

Having a sense of the angle of difficulty was not much help. Cassie had found him during the last preparation of the ballroom, overseeing the placement of the flowers and the food being set out. He had passed the list of costumes on to his lordship while dressing him, and received a nod and a brief murmured thanks, but no additional information. He could not provide his best service under these conditions. He would simply have to keep a close eye on the Willacys and some of the others.

The room itself looked well. There were seasonable flowers from the gardens in vases and garlands, filled out with greenery, ribbons, and decorative charms. The musicians in the gallery above were playing splendidly.

Thirty people were dancing in the middle of the hall, another forty or so around the edges talking and laughing, and more spilling out onto the terrace at the end. Certainly a fair number at the buffet tables, as well. The night was pleasantly cool for the middle of the summer, especially for those with heavier costumes.

Almost all those invited were here, and the exceptions were largely people who were close to his lordship but had familial obligations elsewhere, like Professors Fortier and Wain. A few others were missing, and for reasons that were less clearly expressed, like the FitzDonalds. It was a larger mix than some of his lordship's other parties, including a handful of women in their thirties, apparently unattached to men.

He was positioned near the door that lead to the passages to the kitchen, in case anything was needed. There was a nook in the wall, excellent for lurking just out of sight, and meant for that purpose. From his spot, he could see almost all of those gathered except the ones further out on the terrace.

His lordship looked superb, and Miss Penhallow. They were in theatrical clothing of seventeenth century France, full of gathers and flourishes. His lordship was attired as Moliére, complete with wig. The waistcoat and breeches were of a bold blue, the long jacket a bit darker, decked out with layers of drooping lace. The effect made his lordship appear like some sort of blue jay, sharp and attentive.

The era's dress suited Miss Penhallow particularly well, her eyes were gleaming as she moved in the steps of one of the more active dances. He thought that was not one of Cassie's pieces and the fabric looked older, but he could see her touches in the decorations, in the swoop of the lace and the bows. The brighter green, almost on the edge of turquoise, brought out her eyes and the shine of her hair. His lordship certainly could not keep his eyes off her.

Near them, he could see Captain Lefton dancing with her husband, Major Lefton. She was wearing full skirts in a dress from the early eighteenth, far more encompassing than her usual Guard uniform, but in the same deep blue. It suited her auburn hair particularly well, though it was quite odd to see it set in curls on top of her head rather than pinned back in a bun. Her husband's hair was even more abundant than hers, a wig of powdered ringlets.

Their movements were smaller, more controlled, and he could see her mouth move in a quiet murmur, alerting her husband to where they were in the room. They were masked, of course, as everyone here was, but their body language was something he could read easily, having seen them together at such gatherings before. There was no way to completely hide that Major Lefton was blind, not when they were in the swift movements of a dance that she was deftly leading.

Half the people here truly wished his lordship well.

Benton was certain of that. The other half, however, were far more complex. Some of them looked angrily at Miss Penhallow. A good dozen had thrown their daughters at his lordship, and even if the daughters had moved on without resentment, the mothers were still upset and frustrated. And there were clusters of women who were watching and pointing fan or chin at one person or another, whose purpose remained entirely obscure.

And then there were men, some uncomfortable in the fancy dress, as if they rarely attended balls of this sort. Likely they didn't, he suspected they were the set on the guest list who were parvenus who had made their money in the War or just before it.

There was a shift in the music, and the dancers came to the end of their patterns and made their bows and curtsies. His lordship offered Miss Penhallow his arm, and they moved to get a glass of refreshment.

Benton was pleased to see that the footmen were right there, ready to be of proper service. He let his gaze wander for a moment, checking in on a dozen different figures as they spread to different areas of the room. The Leftons had moved to sit down and talk to someone she clearly knew and trusted, the way she was laughing and smiling.

He felt rather than heard someone come up behind him. It was only when he said, "No staff this side, please," that he realised it wasn't one of the below stairs staff.

"Even me?" Cassie grinned at him, moving to one side to keep out of the way.

"You are an exception." He smiled. "Come to see your work in motion?"

"Oh, I was doing that from the gallery. They were very kind, shared around their cider."

Benton snorted, glancing up at the gallery. "They're

professionals, quite reliable. As well as being friendly." He shifted, enough to brush her fingers with his. Improper, but so very tempting, and he could allow himself that much, he thought. She slipped her hand into his, so she must agree.

"Friendly, but not you. I found I would rather lurk and enjoy the party from your vantage point. Have you seen them?"

She had told him what the Willacys were wearing, of course, she had given him the complete list, though some of her notes were mysteries to him. He had no idea what a *robe battante* was meant to look like.

"Out on the terrace, a few minutes ago. Do you know the others?"

Cassie shook her head. "Just the ones whose clothing I did."

Benton nodded. "That's Captain Katherine Lefton and her husband, Major Giles Lefton. I think they're talking to her superior officer in the Guard, Lord Richard Edgarton, and his wife Lady Alysoun Edgarton." Something in him felt a little better, for both those pairs being here. Captain Lefton and Lord Edgarton were both well-respected officers in the Guard and good friends of his lordship.

Cassie nodded slightly. "How do you know?" she asked, curious.

"Lady Edgarton has a preference for that shade of blue, and Captain Lefton likes them both, see how she's smiling? And that, over there, those two women, his lordship mentioned he'd met them at a party when he and Miss Penhallow first met. They were wearing quite extraordinary costumes then, he said, symbolically echoing a serpent and ... something else, I forget what." He was distracted. "I'm not sure who they're meant to be, but decidedly together."

The two women were both wearing flowing Greek

tunics, with a gauzy shawl fluttering behind one. Sappho, perhaps, but that seemed perhaps a little too obvious. Cassie laughed, near his ear. "Oh, yes. They're most certainly a couple. I like that about his lordship, that it doesn't bother him."

It visibly bothered some of the guests, Benton could see the stiff shoulders, the awkward way some of them moved aside. The women didn't let it deter them, one of them drawing the other out as the musicians began tuning up again after their short break.

Someone in a broad Elizabethan ruff went by him, obscuring his line of sight. He could see some movement behind, but it wasn't until the woman passed that he could see someone had dashed his lordship in the face with something. Miss Penhallow was right beside him, too close if there were more danger.

"Good grief, man." That was his lordship. Benton was moving before he could think, dropping Cassie's hand. His lordship took a step back, then another, and trying to clear the liquid, whatever it was, off his face.

"Your lordship?" He immediately proffered a handkerchief, spotlessly clean, from the inside pocket of his coat. Lord Carillon cleaned off his face, patting it dry, then frowning, as if there were an awful taste or smell. It didn't carry far, but then Benton got a whiff of it, something sickly sweet, but also full of decay. He wheeled, and said, "Basin of water, Hector, for his lordship, and clean cloths."

The mask had caught much of it, but there was a sudden brightness in his lordship's eyes when he pulled the mask away. He stood, blinking, as if confused. Benton glanced around, not able to make demands of guests on his own account.

He was suddenly reassured to see Captain Lefton and

Lord Edgarton move behind the man in the Tudor doublet, the one who had thrown the glass. It had to be Willacy. The perfectionist in him appreciated the way they had suddenly dropped into sync with each other, like two wolves about to pen their prey in.

"None of that. Curious thing to do to someone, don't you agree, Kate?"

"Oh, quite, sir. That wasn't an accident. He didn't even do a good job making it look like one." She was sharper than Lord Edgarton, because she promptly said, "Lord Carillon, have a seat, and let your man see to you."

Lord Edgarton shook his head. "Most rude. Madam Bronson, Master Bronson, perhaps you might be a help in keeping this area clear?"

One of the footmen immediately caught on. "There are plenty of seats in the dining room, ladies and gentlemen. We'll bring refreshments around in just a moment." Benton couldn't place the voice entirely, he was too busy with his lordship. He could just sense people moving away, directed into other places, and a couple of his lordship's better friends taking up the call to gather people up.

Someone moved a padded bench closer. Benton realised that his lordship was wavering on his feet, swaying front to back, and there was a sheen of sweat on his face, not just the remains of the drink.

"Sir, sit. Take a deep breath. As we do." He kept his voice even and calm.

"Benton." Then a "Lizzie? Lizzie? Where are you?"

She moved to settle next to him in a rustle of fabric. Benton said immediately, "Don't touch anywhere that drink was, Miss Penhallow. Let me see to it." He took a long look, taking in the places he could see the glistening liquid, a pale green.

It was then he made the connection. "Sir. Your inner pocket. There is a vial. Drink the vial."

Lord Carillon just blinked at him. Benton was driven to curse, under his breath, a forceful "Nine hells". Hector had come back with dry napkins, and he wrapped one around each hand, moving to undo the costume, and rummage for the vial.

It was awkward from this position, damnably so, an intimacy his lordship would hate having revealed in public like this, even if the staff had been diligently encouraging the guests to withdraw from the area. But Benton reached, and altered the angle of his wrist, feeling the glass of the vial slip into his fingers. He eased it out, willing himself not to move too quickly, not to drop it.

Then it was in his hand, and he could uncork it, and say, "Your lordship." His tone was sharp enough to get those clear blue eyes fastened on him. "Take your dose now."

A tip of the vial, at an angle he had repeated hundreds of times. Even if it was years ago, the hands remembered. His lordship swallowed once, then twice, and then took a longer, easier breath.

Benton glanced up, to see Lady Edgarton escorting Major Lefton out the door, wig discarded on the table as they went by. That was all right, then. Between the two of them, Lefton had rank with the Guard as a consultant, and Lady Edgarton could describe what she'd seen. They had plenty of information to summon a Healer and whatever other necessary reinforcements would be required.

Benton rummaged for his lordship's wrist, and looked up to find Cassie. "Follow Lady Edgarton and Major Lefton, please. Let them know it's some sort of distillation that quickens the pulse to an uneven beat, causes confusion and disorientation, profuse sweating. A plant-based poison,

I suspect the one we discussed, pale green." He didn't wish to say the name and frighten the listeners or his lordship. "Tell the Healer on call he's had a remedy, but will need additional care."

His lordship made a murmuring sound, and Benton said firmly, "Sir, it builds a better case."

As it had before, that worked well, and the mumbling resolved into silence again. Cassie said promptly, "Of course. I'll come back once I've done that." He could feel her retreat.

Now it was a question of seeing how well that mysterious potion worked, and what the culprit might confess to.

Cassie hurried, nearly running, and caught up with Lady Edgarton and Major Lefton just before they got to the portal. "Pardon, Benton sent me after you with some additional information. There is a good chance it's aconite, monk's hood." She repeated what she'd been told, as precisely as she could, and watched Major Lefton repeat it to himself.

"Monk's hood?" Major Lefton frowned, then said "Benton has his reasons."

"Thank you." That was Lady Edgarton, looking her up and down. "Let them know we're going to go through the portal and speak to the Guard and the Healer on duty, and we'll be back promptly." They'd be an interesting sight, in costume, but Cassie supposed there was no helping that. Certainly, Lady Edgarton wasn't going to let it bother her.

"Of course."

"And - do make sure Geoffrey listens to Benton? He'll want to get up and fuss, the dear man."

"I am quite sure Benton knows how to handle him." Which was entirely true.

It made Major Lefton snort, and then say "Portal." It was abrupt, but cordial enough.

Cassie ducked her head. "I'll ask one of the staff to come out to the portal with a light for your trip back." It got her a sharp and pleased nod, and then they were gone, Lady Edgarton taking quite large strides toward the grove around the portal. Cassie turned back to the hall, catching one of the stable boys to send him off with a charm lamp to wait.

By the time she got back to the hall, someone had herded most of the attendees out on the terrace, or into the dining room. It left only a small group in the dancing hall. Benton was on a bench, facing Lord Carillon, making sure he drank a glass of water, a second one, judging by the empty glass on the nearest table. Lord Edgarton was gingerly putting the glass, the assorted cloths used to clean up, and various other items into a large enamelware pot, clearly brought up from the kitchen.

Cassie took a deep breath, and came over. "Lord Edgarton, Lord Carillon, Captain Lefton..." She thought that was the proper order for etiquette. Did one address the officer in charge or the host first? "Lady Edgarton asked me to let you know they would be seeking out the Guard and the Healer on duty, as soon as they went through the portal."

"Oh, Alysoun will find the right person. Thank you." He sounded supremely confident in his wife.

Cassie wasn't sure what to do with herself. Benton was so utterly focused on his task that interrupting them would be something like sacrilege. She ducked her head, and then, generally, to the three of them, said "Can I be of help?"

It was Captain Lefton who tilted her head, and said. "Come explain some things to me, why don't you? You saw a lot of the people here for the party. I'd like to know more about some of them." She had a considering note to her voice, the kind that made Cassie sure she did not want this woman angry with her.

Cassie let out a slow breath, and Benton said, without looking at her. "Tell her everything, Cassie, please."

Well, if he was going to be like that, she would tell. "Of course, Captain Lefton, perhaps somewhere private?"

"The workroom you were using? That's the back parlour."

"The blue room, yes." That was Benton again, still without turning around.

Captain Lefton nodded sharply. "This way." She strode off, in the manner of someone who had utterly forgotten she was wearing an eighteenth century frock that came down to the floor and had panniers. Even if they were very modest panniers for the time. Cassie's mind was racketing around, trying to find any kind of normalcy she could, and so she would contemplate panniers.

Three minutes later, they were back in the blue room. Somehow, along the way, Captain Lefton had liberated a tray and some food and drink, brought it with them, and bustled Cassie into a chair. Cassie found herself holding a glass of brandy and a plate with an arrangement of small finger foods, not at all sure how that had happened.

"Drink a bit of that. Then tell me what you know." Despite the words, it wasn't threatening at all, but eager, like a hound who was picking up a scent.

Cassie took a sip of the brandy, which did help the queer feeling of butterflies dancing a jig in her stomach. "Pardon, Captain, but - may I ask, why..."

"Why you're talking to me? I lead a group who solve interesting puzzles, is how my husband puts it. I helped Lord Carillon with a matter a year or so ago, and I tidied up for him on other cases before that. Lord Edgarton oversees our division of the Guard, and he gives me a fair amount of free rein. You're talking to me and not him because he's able to make sure Lord Carillon sits still and lets himself be tended to. I can't pull that one off, being junior in age, rank, and not Benton."

That made Cassie laugh. "Oh, so like that. You do know them."

"My husband has known them longer, but yes. How long have you known Benton, that he calls you by your first name?"

Cassie coughed. "Some years, but only professionally, I've been dressmaking for his lordship's companions for some time. Um, a few months, the way you mean. He's..." She blushed, despite herself.

"Oh, like that, then? Good. I was beginning to think he had only the one passion in life. Not that his lordship's not an interesting challenge."

Cassie had no clue what to say to that, and just blinked.

"So. Start at the beginning. Including whatever bits you are sure will sound too silly to me. I live for that. It's often the key."

"If you're sure." She began with the gossip, back when, and about deciding to tell Benton about it, and all that had unfolded. Captain Lefton listened intently, other than asking if she could borrow some paper for notes.

"Aconite, was it? And you say the crate was never found?"

"Two crates, ma'am, but no." She took a breath, and then continued to the gathering, and the events of that morning. It felt like that had been weeks ago.

"This thing with the eagle-owl?"

"Theodora." The name was somehow soothing. "She was behaving rather oddly, I thought, but Benton didn't seem to think so, and he surely knows more about birds of prey than I do. She was restless and made a noise I thought rather peculiar, but maybe that's the sound they make? I heard it in the mews when I had been in there earlier."

Captain Lefton tapped her hand with one finger briefly, as if counting something mentally. "Do you know if someone tested the scrap?"

"It went off to whoever does his lordship's testing, not long after. I'm afraid I don't know where."

"Oh, that's easy enough to get out of Benton. Or I can take a guess and likely be correct. His lordship does prefer to keep competent people around him." Captain Lefton tapped the pencil on the pad of paper. "What about the costumes you made? Did anyone say anything that caught your ear?"

Cassie waved a hand. "I told you, the Willacys. What he said about seeing things through."

"It was the tone, you said, not just the words."

"Yes. They were - neither of them were very pleasant, but there was something. I can't get the tone out of my head. He sounded almost tired."

"Do you know much about the family? You must hear things, that it would take us time to track down."

"Not much, no. There was," she paused to gather her thoughts. "There was an older son, killed in the War. And at least one other, I don't know what happened there. The eldest, it was early on, before - when everyone said they'd be home by Christmas. Before the Christmas Truce."

Captain Lefton clucked her tongue. "What else would you like us to know?"

"Is Lord Carillon going to be all right? Aconite. I didn't think, I didn't think it would be like that. Miss Penhallow is interesting, and clever, and - is he?"

"We think so, but it was a nasty dose of something made to be especially lethal. Do you know what was in the vial?"

"Benton told me about it when he had me sew in the pocket for it. It was a peculiar story. But you should ask him. I don't want to miss something important."

Captain Lefton nodded. "Anything else?"

Cassie shook her head. "I'll let you know if I think of anything."

There was a tiny pause, as if Captain Lefton was weighing something. "Look, this dress is lovely, but rather ridiculous. Can you do anything to make it easier to move around?"

Cassie blinked, but then she nodded. "I - yes. Quickly, of course. If we take the panniers off, and I tack the extra fabric up, it should hold for the evening, or until someone can get a change for you."

"Oh, good. Giles liked other people complimenting me in it, but the, the things on the side, I keep wanting pockets and hitting my hands."

It made her very human, suddenly, and Cassie smiled. "If you'd stand there, and hold up the outer skirts so I can get at the panniers." Freeing her from those didn't take very long, and sewing a bit of ribbon into the side seams of the skirt to lift and pull back the extra fabric only took a minute or two.

"Turn around, make sure that's comfortable?"

Captain Lefton obliged, turning around, then bending over and reaching up. "Not as good as the uniform, but much better, thank you. I could run if I had to." The rearrangement had revealed she was wearing tidy black ankle boots under the dress, not the slippers Cassie had assumed.

Cassie ducked her head. "I'd be glad to make you something your husband would appreciate, ma'am. And that would be easier to move in. If you - if that's not inappropriate." She flushed, but that would be a grand challenge, and making something with the right sort of tactile detail would be an interesting puzzle. Velvet and silk and maybe something else, a soft wool. Her mind was running away with her again. "Of course. Um. What's next?"

"Come back with me, and we'll find out."

Cassie nodded. They went out into the main foyer, only to find it now crawling with a good two dozen of the Guard. Captain Lefton clearly knew all of them on sight, and she whistled sharply, three particular pitches. Six of them snapped to attention. She made a few gestures with her fingers, wordlessly sending them off on different tasks, before she strode back into the music room, Cassie trailing behind her.

The other people had all been cleared out, presumably talking to some of those Guards. Lord Carillon and Benton and Miss Penhallow weren't there, just Major Lefton and Lady Alysoun, chatting as if they had all the time in the world.

Major Lefton tilted his head as she approached, as if he was sure who it was, and said "Kate, they're upstairs, healer's with him, he should be fine for questioning. Your suspect is in the side room here, locked in with a guard. Suspect's wife in her bedroom upstairs, also under guard. Your Adria's on her."

"Ah, giving Adria a chance to be properly fierce." Cassie could see the Captain's shoulders relaxing. "Anything left for me, then?"

"Evidence to be labelled, there." He waved a hand at the correct table. "Richard would be pleased for you to join him upstairs when you're able."

"And you?"

"I've been promised a comfortable bit of sofa. Or Alysoun says she'll see me home if you think you'll be all night."

"All night and into tomorrow, I suspect. There's something more at work here than personal differences."

"With our Lord Geoffrey, there often is. He's such a pleasant man, of course." That was clearly a shared joke of theirs, because Captain Lefton's face broke into a broad grin for just a moment.

"Go on home. Fuss with your current metaphysical equation. I'll send word one way or the other."

Major Lefton nodded, offered a bow, and said "Mistress Castalia, good evening. Alysoun, best to see ourselves home." Lady Edgarton shifted to let him take her elbow again, and led him off. Cassie couldn't help staring.

"My husband delights in identifying people by the way they walk. And logic. He's right far more often than he ought to be because of the logic."

"Logic, ma'am?"

"In this case, he knew I'd taken you off with me, so if two sets of steps came in, and only one were boots, the other was likely you. And he'd have heard my whistle, of course."

"That's…" Cassie blinked, uncertain how to take this confidence. "He's very sharp, ma'am."

"You should see us play bohort. No, seriously, you'd enjoy it." There was the grin again. Cassie had no idea what to do with it. Captain Lefton shrugged, then said, "You know the upstairs, yes? Can you show me to his lordship's room? We need you to stay here tonight, at least, but you can change and go to sleep. And your apprentices can as well."

Cassie let out a breath. "Oh, they…"

"They've already been sent up to rest, no worries. Show me where, and then you can take your rest as well. There'll be the Guard here all night, you'll be quite safe."

It hit Cassie then, that she might not have been. Throwing a liquid on someone, that was a dreadful imprecise way to kill someone. What if they'd put something in the punch, or - honestly, she had no idea.

Captain Lefton must have seen something in her face. "We're making sure any refreshments are entirely safe. We brought in a specialist to test everything in the kitchens."

Cassie nodded, and then felt her knees half-buckle. She suddenly remembered the conversation from earlier. "There was someone who had tried to get downstairs. One of the guests. Friday afternoon." Just yesterday.

"Thank you. Keep telling me things like that. Here we go, come on. Upstairs." There was a strong arm under her elbow guiding her to the stairs. Five minutes later she had been deposited in her bedroom, given Captain Lefton directions to the family rooms, and been told to ring if she needed anything.

She sat on her bed, unsure what to do for long minutes, before making the bare minimum effort needed to remove her party frock. She pulled on a nightgown and dressing gown in case some new emergency struck in the middle of the night, and curled up in bed.

THIRTY-EIGHT

MIDDLE OF THE NIGHT

B enton rubbed his face with his hands. It was well past midnight, nearer two in the morning, and he didn't know what to do.

For a little while there had been plenty to occupy him, occupy his mind. The specialist the Guard had sent around to mind the food had tested the tainted punch and determined that it had merely had some of the pest-repelling lavender fall into it, somewhere along the way, which was a great relief all around.

The scattered droplets of sickly green had been cleaned off the floor and added to the evidence. The Willacys' rooms had been searched, and turned up the elder wand, stripped of greenery, tucked into, of all daft places, his socks. He kept track of it all, as his lordship certainly did not have his wits enough about him to take in the information. Eventually the immediate investigation was over, and there was nothing to do but fret.

The Healers had sent him off to get some rest, but he couldn't manage to settle. He could still hear them talking, in his little room off his lordship's dressing room. Talking quietly to each other, moving about. It made him jerk every time he heard a tiny sound.

Orders were orders. Even if they weren't his lordship's orders.

He had been reassured - three times, because he couldn't let it drop - that his lordship would be fine. They had confirmed the antidote worked, and were keeping an eye on him to make sure there were no further bad reactions. His lordship would need to take it easy for a day or two, but he'd be fine. He had looked up aconite poisoning, of course, when Cassie had mentioned it, and he kept having visions of his lordship's face, the sweating, the confusion, like it was a sight his mind could not release.

And of course, Miss Penhallow had wanted to stay. He had known there would be some moment in the future, where his lordship would turn to her, and not to him. For all his lordship had promised Benton the security he needed and wanted, he'd known that from the first time he'd seen them in the Trellech library. She'd broken his lordship's heart and sent him back into the distant skies he'd lived in after the War. Benton had forgiven her that, when she won back his lordship's trust and his warmth. He was duty-bound to forgive her this, too.

Now, though, everything had changed, and not when he had expected. They were still two months out from the wedding, he didn't think he'd have to cede his place so fast, so suddenly. She had done everything right, and that was worse, he didn't have a reason to complain about her care. It was only proper that his lordship should turn to her now, in this moment of sudden awareness of mortality, and not to him.

The deaths produced by aconite looked, he had read, like a natural heart attack. Like Lord Temple Carillon's

death had been, only that thought was too wild, too implau-
sible to be worthy of consideration. Only, there might be
some link there. His ruminations turned, with a dread
inevitability, towards the minor singer who had reached out
to his lordship recently. The one who had died, abruptly, of
a heart attack.

All of a sudden, his room felt too small, too cramped,
and he rolled off his bed, still dressed, and slipped on his
shoes. He didn't grab his suit jacket, there'd be no one
around at this hour who would care and he was taking the
back stairs. Something about that felt suddenly scandalous,
but the right sort of thing for his mood, the way his thoughts
were churning, wanting to do something different.
Anything different.

Up he went, to the servants quarters, thinking at first he
might find a spare room. Maybe something with a window,
where at least he could look out at the night. He walked
across, slowly, not wanting to wake anyone, but realised all
the spare rooms on the men's side were full.

He crossed over to the women's side, using a charm to
unlock the door, a thing highly forbidden, to get to an empty
guest room on that side of the house. He was almost to the
end when a door opened, and there was Cassie, robe tugged
around her. She blinked at him, and then gestured.
"Come in."

Benton was so startled he obeyed, even though every
rule he'd ever grown up with about proper behaviour
screamed otherwise. She held the door, and he found
himself in a perfectly pleasant small room, window to the
front of the house.

She considered, and then made a few odd gestures with
her hands, and pressed them to the wood of the door. He

could hear the little noises of the house fade away, the creaks and shivers of an old building.

"It quiets the sounds. Ours as well as outside." Cassie turned around and tsked at him. "Sit, Thomas, please. Sit. You must be run off your feet. How's his lordship? Do you need to go back down?"

The rush of questions made him blink again, and again, and suddenly he found himself speechless, not sure where to begin.

Cassie moved toward him, and the next thing he knew, she had nudged him to sit on the bed somehow. She just said, "Let me." She took a breath then asked, "When do you need to be back in your room?"

Finding even just the one word was like trying to catch fish barehanded. "Six."

She reached over, for what must be an alarm clock, twisting to set it, before she put it back on the bedside table. "Set it for quarter to six," she said. "Can I fetch you anything? Snack? Cocoa?"

The mention of the cocoa made him shiver again, and suddenly he was clinging to her. It was completely undignified, unmanly, and he couldn't stop himself. She was very still for a dreadful awful moment, then her hand came up, and he could feel her patting, then stroking his back, not pulling away.

He clung like that for what must have been minutes, not quite crying, but not at all in his right mind. He'd seen this before, from the outside, helping his lordship when he needed a shoulder after a particularly bad nightmare. It had been years since he'd felt like this, though. Not since that trip, five years ago, where he'd slipped in a river and hit his head, and the disorientation had overwhelmed him.

He'd felt lost then, like he couldn't get his feet under him, couldn't even remember what feet were for. Thought had trailed thought in no useful order, he'd barely remembered his own name, or his lordship's, or anything except that he had failed, was failing, would continue to fail, in a relentless aching bombardment. This time was better only in that his head did not actually ache like it had been rattled to pieces.

As he began to come back to himself, he shuddered, realising exactly how close she was, and how much he'd let her see. He half-jerked away, and she immediately shifted, until just her hand was on his shoulder. "Is that too much?"

He let out a long breath. "I'm not used to..." Then he couldn't figure out how to finish that sentence.

She let the silence be. It startled him. He was used to the women he knew filling it. Starting with his mother, every housekeeper he had ever worked with, and the house-maids and lady's maids and cooks. She just sat there, hand resting on his shoulder, with the steady pressure of her arm across his back.

Finally he said, "Would you mind making cocoa? Is that?" He had no idea how to end the question and left it there instead, rather awkwardly.

"I can make you cocoa. Though I'm afraid if you want a shot of brandy in it, you'll have to tell me where."

"Just - be quiet, Mrs Doncaster sleeps downstairs. And one of the footmen. I don't," He stopped, not sure how to explain.

"I won't say you're tucked up in my bedroom. Make yourself as comfortable as you like. I don't know your reading preferences, but there's books on the side table, feel free." There was a small pause. "The first one might or might not be to your taste, it's about a duke getting accused of murder."

She shifted, moving to stand, and tucking the dressing gown around her, twisting her hair up and stabbing a hair pin or two into it automatically. A moment later, she was gone, closing the door quietly behind her.

With nothing else to do, he removed his shoes, and then cautiously, as if they might bite him, reached for the books. One was a novel. He flicked through it, realising after a few moments that it must be from the non-magical community. The bookmark was well toward the end, around the point where the mystery was presumably getting wrapped up. Much more tidily than in real life, he was sure.

He set it aside after reading the first few pages. It was well-written, by someone with a good sense for a country house and the duties and difficulties of the aristocracy, but not good reading tonight.

He glanced at the other, which was a far more sedate work on the history of the Spitalfields weavers. Not his usual line of thing at all, but that just meant it was unlikely to have sentences that would jar his equilibrium further. By the time Cassie reappeared, with a pot of cocoa and a mug, he was through the first chapter.

She closed the door carefully behind her. "Sorry it's only the one mug, Hector was watching, and I couldn't very well say I had a valet in my bedroom."

Benton snorted. "Hector has very strong opinions about the proper way things are done. Which is as it should be. We should find him a place he can learn more, really." Saying that helped settle him, too. Remembering that the world would go on. It always did, somehow. Perhaps they could bring Hector to Ytene, see how he did.

Cassie settled on the bed, after pouring the cocoa and handing the mug over. Benton shifted, and said, "I should let you sleep."

"As if I'd be sleeping now. No, you - look, just be as comfortable as you can."

He looked away, then said, quietly. "I don't know what to do."

Other people might have dismissed that, or judged him. She leaned back, watching him, considering. "About what?"

"His lordship." He stopped. "The healers say he'll recover, that the vial was just the right thing. They're keeping an eye on him. And Miss Penhallow stayed."

"Should I let her know to write me when they need you?"

He flinched, realising in a rush he hadn't left any note of where he'd be. He'd abandoned the post that had been his for a decade now. He hadn't even taken his journal with him, there was no way for anyone to know where he was. He was lost again, in the tumult inside his head, all the noise and chaos, when he felt a hand on his cheek.

"Hey. I have a journal. I know she does, and I'm sure she's got it by now. Let me write her, tell her you're with me, and to let me know if his lordship needs you."

Benton swallowed hard, tasting bile, still roiling. There was nothing for it, though. He could not bear to face that dark small room alone, not now. Someone had to say something. It was a sensible plan. Efficient. Finally, he nodded, not able to speak.

Cassie stood, going to the dressing table and gathering her journal, writing a brief note, then showing it to him for his approval. "Miss Penhallow, Benton could not sleep. If Lord Carillon needs his services, could you write and let me know, and I'll make sure he gets the message promptly. He intends to be ready for service again at six. Castalia".

It was a simple note. She wrote the sigil that sent the message along to Miss Penhallow's journal. Before he could speak again, there was a most prompt response. Cassie turned her book so he could read the simple reply, "Thank you, of course. I do hope he can get some rest."

"There. All accounted for."

He swallowed again, then looked down at the cocoa, and took a sip, though he wished she'd been able to get at the brandy. "What do I do now?"

"You let me take care of you. You had a nasty shock tonight."

The idea that he needed taking care of seemed ridiculous, and yet he could not argue with it. "A shock?"

"You've wrapped your life up with his lordship for years, seeing to his every need. And then not only is he hurt - not badly, thanks to your excellent foresight - but there is not much you can do for him now. And it is true Miss Penhallow has some right to be there, and that's a change you're still figuring out. All three of you."

He wanted to argue with it, but he did not have the strength or the coherence. "What do you advise?" It came out stilted and sharp, but she just patted his knee. "You drink the cocoa, and if you want to lie down and rest, you do that. I could read to you?"

Benton considered, then just nodded. He knew he was being managed, he had done almost the exact same things hundreds of times for his lordship. Warm drink, comforting sounds, being present without expectation. "Not the mystery novel. Not tonight."

"Rather, no. You might like it eventually, though." She considered, then stood, leaving him alone on the bed, before she went to her trunk and pulled out a different book. "Lie back, at least, your shoulders must be aching." He did as she said, and she perched on the end of the bed, facing him, opened the book to the beginning, and began to read. Her voice was even, clear, and pleasant.

"What Herodotus the Halicarnassian has learnt by inquiry is here set forth: in order that so the memory of the past may not be blotted out from among men by time, and that great and marvellous deeds done by Greeks and foreigners and especially the reason why they warred against each other may not lack renown." She paused there, and said, "I'll be reading his travels, not the battles, mind."

Benton nodded, and after a moment, ventured closing his eyes. The last thing he remembered was something about the Oracle at Delphi and Croesus.

Cassie was not at all sure what she was doing at Ytene.

The morning after the chaos of the party, she'd woken when the alarm went off to find an empty spot on the bed still warm from Thomas's body. The morning had been taken up with a more formal testimony. They were tightlipped and cautious. She had at least been told that Lord Carillon, Miss Penhallow, Benton, and several others had decamped for Ytene first thing, at the healer's advice.

Captain Lefton had explained in a moment of greater privacy. "Something something, lord of the land, something, ancient magical theory, something, also there's a well with healing properties nearby that made the healers happy."

There was more going on there, Cassie was quite certain that the captain was precise and measured about everything. But in the stark light of morning, when Cassie felt turned upside down, the fact Captain Lefton hadn't overcomplicated the explanation felt like a gift. It made Cassie entirely determined to design dresses that the

Captain would enjoy wearing much more than her costume for the ball.

That had been the only brighter spot in the morning. Her apprentices had packed most of the things up by the time she was let free from the questioning. But it took the better part of the afternoon to get the trunks through the portal and back to the shop.

She had been too busy to think the next few days, with a number of people drawn by the scandal. Almost all of them wanted her time without spending much money. She made arrangements for a certain number of decorated shawls and scarves - projects Amelia was developing quite a style in - but that was it.

By the time the note arrived by messenger on Thursday inviting her to Ytene on Saturday, the gawkers had disappeared, and she had been alone with her thoughts far too much for any good to come of it. She could not refuse to go, even though it would likely be quite awkward. Thomas - she could not quite insist that he was Benton again - had not come by, he had not written, he had not anything.

So, she had come to Ytene. To face the music, or whatever the proper word was. She had barely been able to eat any lunch, and she had worried about being delayed at the portal, so by the time she walked through at one, she felt entirely out of sequence with herself.

She was met at Ytene by an amiable woman in her twenties, who introduced herself briefly as Ferry Pride, and led her into the house. She wore an emerald green dress with a broad skirt of good quality linen, nothing fancy, but well-made, and clearly not a uniform. She didn't carry herself like one of the staff, even like Benton, but she also did not explain her role. She knocked on the door of what

Cassie knew was the library, and said, "Geoffrey? Here is Mistress Castalia."

"Thank you, Ferry. Tea at four?"

"As if I'd miss it." It was easy, relaxed, and a moment later the woman was gone.

"Do come in." Lord Carillon was standing, moving from behind a large wood desk. "Please, do sit down. May I pour you tea? Something stronger?"

It was baffling, and Cassie had no idea what to do with it.

Lord Carillon glanced off at the door. "Did Ferry mention? Her husband is head of my stables, a fine local man. She's from the Cumbria Wrights, good family, finishing an apprenticeship in weaving with a focus on tapestries. I do hope you can stay for tea, you'll have a lot to talk about."

Cassie blinked, and said, "You asked me for tea, your lordship." She recognised the family as impoverished but well-bred, which explained why Ferry had called him Geoffrey. Possibly.

"Grand!" He was clearly largely recovered, because in that moment he was near shining with vitality and joy.

"Now, I'm sure you're wondering what happened since the party." He handed her a saucer of tea, prepared as she preferred it with a single lump of sugar, and she wondered how he knew. Surely it wasn't something Benton would have mentioned.

She nodded, not trusting herself to say anything.

"Benton was exceedingly confessional, once I had my wits about me." Lord Carillon's tone was easy and conversational, but Cassie couldn't help straightening up.

"Your lordship, I don't, I didn't mean..."

He held his hand up, that single gesture illustrating

generations of aristocratic certainty and power. "Let me say my bit. I am not upset, let me start there. With either Benton or with you."

She nodded and subsided, managing to sip the tea.

"Benton confessed to me that he had spent more time with you, in private, than I had realised. And that during that time, he had begun to understand that he would like to spend more time with you than his duties allowed. The day after the party, he did not tell me much, only that you made sure he was all right. Thank you for that. He has saved my life more than once, and I wish only the best for him."

It was utterly sincere and earnest, Cassie could see that, hear that, feel that. He was leaning forward, eagerly.

"But Benton is in my service, and no matter how I think of him, that complicates things. In talking with him and a few others over the past few days, I believe we have a solution that should suit on several fronts. You are not obligated to anything, by this. If it turns out you and he do not suit, it will still be a better position for him, long-term, that uses the fullness of his skills."

Cassie blinked at him, and she was certainly not following.

Lord Carillon smiled at her, and said, "Let me lay it out. Benton has been a superb valet and companion in my adventures since the War. He has been essential in establishing our home here, hiring staff, overseeing repairs and necessary renovations. Now that most of them are done, I realise that asking him to return to being my valet would not use his skills at all appropriately. Asking him to focus just on the state of my clothes and my person."

She opened her mouth, concerned at where this was going. He lifted his hand again.

"I asked him, two days ago, if he would become my

steward, overseeing the household as a whole. In houses such as this, it is common for the steward to be treated as a trusted professional, like one's Healer or solicitor. Invited to supper at times, and more personal social events, such as tea this afternoon. Stewards most often live on a small home on the estate. We would need to build something suitable, something like the cottage I built for Ferry and Rufus. More independent."

Cassie let out a breath she had been holding since this conversation started, it felt like. "Oh." Then, she asked. "Would he - immediately?"

Lord Carillon chuckled. "Oh, we'd need a bit of time. My thought is to make sure he has two evenings a week he could spend with you, an occasional night off where I do not expect him until the next morning. I am in fact capable of dressing myself, as he well knows. I would ask for him to come on the honeymoon, and that will be six weeks or so, November and December. It seems right to do one last trip. But after that..." He waved a hand. "He could find and train a new valet, and settle into his own role."

She considered, turning the pieces over in her mind. "That seems possible, your lordship."

"As I said, you are not obligated. If you decide you do not fancy him, I do hope you'll be gentle, though." Lord Carillon's voice grew softer. "He is very taken with you. Despite his sense of duty."

It was that comment that won her over. "I find myself quite fond of him, too, your lordship."

"Right then. He's in the music room, crawling out of his skin. Go along and have a chat, will you? That door. Take your tea if you like. I asked Ferry and Rufus to come and join us at four, along with you and Benton, and Lizzie and Laura. Might as well begin as we mean to go on."

Cassie had to laugh. "You do realise he's never going to stop looking out for you, don't you?"

Lord Carillon had stood, but he stopped, the expression on his face a glorious combination of amazement and blatant need. "Oh, I hope I'm that lucky." Then he straightened, and waved a hand. "Go on. You've been patient enough with my rambling."

She ducked her head, and went through the door, hearing him go out a door behind her as she opened the door to the music room. As soon as the door opened, she heard a voice, uncertain. "Cassie. Uh, may I?"

The room was wallpapered in a pale blue with a white pattern. She could not place the blue for a moment until Benton took a step towards her and then another, and she realised it almost precisely matched his eyes.

"Lord Carillon," She began the sentence, and then she wasn't sure how to continue it.

Thomas stepped forward, and then one hand was on her waist, the other on her shoulder. He had barely breathed "May I?" and had time to see her nod before he was kissing her. It was not the most skilled kiss, not that she had a wide range of experience. But what it lacked in refined skill it more than made up for in desire.

When he finally pulled back, he was breathless, and so was she. She opened her eyes to find him blinking at her, looking completely overset.

"I didn't mean to start like that." He began talking, then stopped, and she patted his arm.

"Can we sit down? Or go somewhere, I don't know." She didn't even know what to ask for. She suspected there was nowhere truly private in this house.

"His lordship has permitted me the night off. If, after tea, I might escort you home?" The phrases came out prim and proper. But she looked at him and she could see all his composure crumble like an ancient wall that had stood through war and plague and celebration, and could finally yield to gravity.

"That would do very well, yes." She slipped her hand into his, meeting his eyes. "There's a lot we should talk about, but later, when we can do it without rushing. For now, his - his lordship is most thoughtful and generous. And if you like the idea of seeing me more often, and learning if we suit, I, well, I like that idea very much too."

It felt ridiculous saying it, like she was in some school-girl fantasy. She had never gone in for that kind of thing when she'd been that age, starting now was ridiculous.

"Oh. Oh. Well, then." He drew himself up, and then said. "I should bring down my overnight bag. Then may I show you the gardens here?"

"The gardens?"

"It is about as private as we may find, for the moment. His lordship promised he would find other places to be until tea."

Cassie laughed. "Well, we should make the most of the opportunity, then."

FORTY

SATURDAY EVENING IN CASSIE'S FLAT

Benton had felt terribly wrong, sitting down to tea, but his lordship had been insistent. Gleefully and broadly insistent. Benton knew it was no use arguing. And besides, one couldn't disobey and argue that one was obeying at the same time.

Once they had settled in, plates and cups and seats, his lordship had been his most charming self. Benton suspected there was some edge of the manic in there, a mix of the magical healing and the bathing in water from the well.

But once the conversation got going, it was more comfortable. The others kept conversation on topics Benton knew well, without feeling stupid or ill at ease, sharing tidbits of information about Ytene and the surrounding lands with Cassie. At the end of the meal, the Prides took their leave, and his lordship had shooed Benton and Cassie away.

Which is how he had come to sit on the sofa in Cassie's flat, feeling awkward and out of place. She had gone to fetch bottles of cider. When she came back, he saw she had unpinned her hair in the process, letting it fall loosely in waves across her shoulders. It made his breath catch, and then he looked away.

"Hey." She sat next to him, her voice quiet. "Too much?"

He blinked at her, unable to make his eyes focus, and then just nodded.

"He rather rushed us into this." Cassie didn't sound upset. He wasn't sure what he would do if she was upset at his lordship. Instead, she sounded thoughtful and relaxed. "Where do we start talking?"

Benton swallowed, then decided best to tell her quick and fast. If she turned away, well. He could slink off, tail between his legs, his shame for anyone to see. Something of it must have shown, because she immediately moved to put a hand on his.

"I've near enough no experience. With women." He hated admitting it. Then, feeling he'd been insufficiently clear, he said "In private."

"That's no problem. Unless it's one for you."

That got him looking up, managing to meet her eyes for a moment. There was no judgement there.

"I'd like to know more about that. What you have done. Why you haven't. Because, well, that might help us figure out how to go about things better." She glanced away. "I've some, but not for years. I'd much rather go at it together." Then she blushed at the implied innuendo, and he found it a great relief.

Benton took a breath. "When I was in service, before the War, we weren't encouraged." Then, softer, he added. "During the War, men took me off to places. Several times. And I just couldn't. It wasn't..."

He didn't have the language to explain how he'd felt. How bodies could spark something for him, but he had no real interest with someone he didn't know. Didn't like. And there had been precious few of those in his life where it'd been at all proper to think of them like that. "Not with a stranger."

It wasn't just that, but it was a place to start. He'd been overwhelmed at how fast things seemed to go for most people, how many places they touched, how many things were going on all at once. He didn't think he could manage that, and it had made him feel ashamed. Now, he glanced sideways, wondering if she'd want that. The rushing.

"Fair enough." Cassie patted his hand again. "And me?"

That made him blush, he could feel it burning on his cheek. "You're no stranger. Not now."

It made her grin. "So. Do you have objections to doing more things? Kissing, and then - see how it goes?"

He hesitated. "I don't, I don't want to rush things." And then, he realised he hadn't heard her history. "Can you, I don't know what you like."

Cassie laughed. "Oh, I will do my best to make that clear." Then she shifted, moving to settle next to him on the couch. She did it in such a way that it was entirely natural for him to slip his arm over her shoulder and let her nestle against him. She let out a sigh, like she was coming home. "I walked out with three men at different times. The last one, before he knew he was going to War, we had a handful of nights together."

She paused, as if trying to figure out how to put it. "He and I were lovers, but we didn't have time to explore. It was rushed. Awkward. I had to sneak him into my room, or there was a hayloft, once, at a summer dance." Cassie scrunched up her face. "That was itchy, on top of everything else."

Her tone made Benton laugh, then squeeze her closer. Words chased around in his head until he managed to sort them out. "So you know some things you'd rather not. But not enough about what you like."

"Yes. And, well. Doing things is the only way to solve that. Eventually."

He shifted, to kiss the top of her hair. "His lordship has a number of pillow books. A renowned collection, actually. I have glanced through them, when he has asked me to put them away. Illustrations of things people get up to in bed."

Cassie laughed. "So you have more ideas than I. Though I have a few, I suppose."

"I mostly found the books puzzling, honestly. But there was one that talked about what the point is. That being in bed with someone you love, or at least value, should be something unfurling, in its own time. That all the positions, all the toys, all the magics and charms to increase sensation, are nothing without observation and care and patience."

He let out his breath all in a rush. "And you are observant and patient and delightful." Saying it out loud, that bluntly, made his heart slip. Feeling her against his side, warm and soft and focused on him, that made him suddenly harden in his trousers, in a way he hadn't felt since before the War.

If she noticed it, she didn't say so, but she let her hand move to rest on his knee. "And you are so attentive and diligent and loyal." Her voice had a purr in it all of a sudden, and it made him shudder, to have that kind of interest aimed directly at him. He had to close his eyes, and swallow. When he opened them again, she asked, again, "Too much?"

He shook his head. "You had an idea?"

Cassie nodded. "For tonight." She paused, watching him closely. "My bed has a trundle bed, that pulls out, underneath. Sleeping with someone else, I'm not very good at it. But I could pull that out, and we could both be comfortable, and touch, but not be too much? And before that, I would very much like more kissing. And curling up against you. Maybe in your lap, if you liked the idea."

He let out a long breath. "That would do very well. How did, how did you know?"

Cassie blushed again. "I might have a few thoughts about what I'd like to do with you, after the last time you were here. Before the rest of my head caught up and started wondering how we could make it work."

Benton blinked at her. "You did?"

"You are a quite attractive man, Thomas. And more than that, you're thoughtful. You plan ahead. You think about other people's comfort. Perhaps too much, but we can work on that." She then paused. "What do you think about his lordship's proposals?"

"Nervous." It came out before he could say anything else. "But his lordship is right, that I am already doing much of it, and taking the role on properly will mean it is done well. And he will make sure I get the training I need for the rest." He glanced away. "And it, I wouldn't ever make you give up the shop." It seemed suddenly essential to say that.

A moment later, Cassie had positioned herself in his lap, sitting sideways. This was entirely too fast, all of a sudden, but it also felt like something slotting into place, something he'd been ready for without realising it.

He was quite sure she could feel how his body was reacting, earnestly wanting more of that, now. How his hips were trying to rock up to rub against her, and he wouldn't permit that. She kissed him then, stopping all thought, her mouth warm against his. Then her tongue, and the way her head tilted as her hand came up to steady herself against his shoulder.

He lost control enough to moan, the sound swallowed up between them. It made her arch in his arms, and he brought a hand up to the back of her shoulder. She pressed against it, like a cat eager for more attention.

When she finally pulled back, she looked like a cat proud of its work, her hair framing her face, the broadest smile lighting up her eyes. "Does that give you some more ideas?"

He grunted, rocking again, and she laughed, throwing her head back. He tried for words, and then managed to get out. "You like this?"

It made her laugh again, softer and longer, and then she asked, taking a step into something he couldn't figure out fast enough, "May I do something very daring?"

Some small part of him wanted to say no, that this was too new. The rest of him, almost all of him, was shouting to find out what she wanted. Knowing that she wouldn't lead him wrong, she'd had so many chances to mock or hurt him, and she had taken none of them. That she'd take him to the edge of what he could manage, and notice when she was about to tip over the edge. She had before. He sucked a breath in between his teeth, and whispered. "Dare."

There was the flashing grin again, and then she was watching him, intently, like Theodora the eagle-owl waited for a rabbit. He almost didn't see her shift, but then he felt her hand, down between them, before it cupped against his hard cock, where it pressed against her leg.

All dignity fled, and he threw back his head and groaned with it. It was an intimate touch, even through his clothes, and it was so deliberate. Making it clear she liked this part of him, too, wasn't shying away from it. And he, oh, he wanted her right there. Every part of him. Not like in the maison close, in France.

His reaction pleased her, he knew that as soon as he could breathe again, by the way she worked her hand further down. She was rolling her wrist to shift the pressure and explore. "Mmm, yes. Shall I, more?"

He could not refuse, and he certainly did not want to. He managed a weak. "Please." It sounded feeble to him, but it made her purr, her fingers working at the buttons of his fly without a pause. Some small part of him supposed she must have a lot of practise undressing people smoothly.

"Let me move." A moment later, she was wriggling to straddle him, pulling up her skirts to let her get a knee on either side of his legs. Then she settled herself down to rock against him, urgently enough the couch let out an undignified creak. It just made her laugh, and lean forward to kiss him, suddenly urgent with it.

Something in it, the whole tumble into something he had never expected to have, had him whimpering, feeling as if he was in the midst of an amazing wonderful explosion. Even with that, he was not sure of her complete intentions until she pulled from the kiss long enough to purr, "You know how to clean up after. I'm most sure."

Something in the tone, in the certainty, had him groaning again, his hand coming down to keep her close against him. He let his hips press up into her again and again, three times, until he felt himself explode in heat and need against her stomach, crying out with it.

When he came to, she was nestled with her head on one shoulder, her hand on the other, quiet and steady. He must have been out of his senses for some time, since his breath had slowed, and she was barely trembling against him. He swallowed, took a breath, and threw himself into the challenge. "Show me something you like." He could feel the mess and the cooling stickiness, and it was new and strange. Pleasing her would settle him, he knew that, bone-deep.

It earned him a kiss on his cheek. "You. I like you." Only then did she begin to remove herself from his lap, letting them both stretch limbs that desperately needed it. "Come to my bed? Where we have more space?"

The offer was a little uncertain, but he smiled back at her. "Of course." The rest of the evening was full of discovery after joyful discovery.

"The court is ended, go forth and spread the word."
The traditional phrase freed the enchantment on the courtroom, the layered magics that had compelled truth-telling. Cassie let out a slow breath, feeling the tension finally ease as the Guard led Mr and Mrs Willacy away separately.

There was so much in the trial she hadn't understood, that Thomas hadn't told her about. Perhaps hadn't known about, though she had long since learned not make assumptions about what he did and didn't know.

She had been seated in the long row along the side of the courtroom, with the other secondary witnesses, and the court room had been full. Choosing an outfit to appear in the witness box was not something she'd had to consider before. Yesterday, when she'd actually testified, she'd worn a deep forest green suit, with cream. Today, she had wanted to fade into the background, and had on a day dress of heathered purple, which felt somehow comforting.

She could see Lord and Lady Carillon across the room. She could not think of them without their titles at the moment. They were very proper, somber and reserved, nodding at people who offered their comments and respects. Benton - also very much in formal mode, she could barely think of him as Thomas looking like that - was right behind his lordship, scanning the crowd, and occasionally murmuring a comment in his lordship's ear.

He caught her eye and gestured for her to join them, and she nodded. But people were moving slowly, gossiping about how long it had taken for the case to come to trial, when a month would be far more usual. Once people had finally moved along and the crowd around the Carillons had thinned out, she made her way over.

"I've a private room at my club. I do hope you can join us, please, there are a few things to discuss." Lord Carillon was as polite and respectful as ever, but extremely formal and worried. Cassie was suddenly sure she'd missed more than a few things that had come out.

Cassie nodded. "Of course."

They made small talk as they waited for the courtroom to clear, and Cassie kept her comments to the usual pleasantries. Clothing, the current break in the weather, the upcoming bohort season for the apprentice guild. The last was not precisely a safe topic in some circles, but agreeable enough here, where no one had unpleasantly strong opinions.

Ten minutes later, they were gathered in one of the small rooms of the Explorer's Club, his lordship's preference for privacy and good food. Once the staff had brought their drinks and some light refreshments, Lord Carillon gestured, and the staff disappeared.

"That was not as helpful as I hoped." He leaned back in his chair.

Lady Carillon raised an eyebrow. When Cassie looked

puzzled, she said, "We know who was responsible for the direct action, but we still have no real idea what to do about what came out in the questioning. And how many other people might have been involved."

Cassie nodded slightly. "May I ask - I feel like there are things I missed."

For a newlywed couple, they thought surprisingly in sync, and Cassie found both of them peering at her, and saying "Do, please." nearly in unison.

Thomas settled next to her, less formal now, and took her hand. "Your questions might help us sort through things better. Being not so enmeshed." She glanced over at him, smiled, and squeezed his hand, momentarily delighted that he was being that outspoken. Given the way Lord Carillon looked at him, she thought he felt much the same.

She took a breath. "So. The Willacys were convicted of the act itself, attempting to poison you. One of you, that was the part I hadn't quite expected?"

Lady Carillon nodded. "A poison made of aconite, in an alchemical base designed to allow it to be absorbed by the skin much more easily than the usual run of things. The Guard would very much like to stop that kind of invention."

Cassie shivered. It was one thing to wear the light protective layers common in the highest social circles to bar against the sort of potions that made someone too drunk or silly, indiscreet or rude. But outright poisons, at that strength, she thought those were a thing no one had much done since the Romans. Or perhaps the court of the French Sun King.

"And there is no way that is the work of the Willacys. They wouldn't have a clue where to begin."

Lord Carillon snorted. "No. Someone else made the vial, and Willacy was supposed to get it into something I ate or drank, by preference, or Lizzie. It did not matter which of us, apparently. Or barring that, against my skin, or hers. And he was foiled at getting anything into the food, and a good thing, too. That would likely have been too quickly fatal for any aid."

Cassie shivered, and Benton took the unexpected step of an arm around her. There was a long pause, before Lady Carillon said, "It is all very upsetting. We'd expected to smoke something out, but I certainly wasn't expecting layers of conspiracy."

"That was the bit this morning, yes? The FitzDonalds?"

Lord Carillon nodded. "That came out in questioning. Oh, you were being prepared as a witness, I think, when they went through it in court. They will be tried shortly. I was allowed to listen in to some of it, and they, specifically Mrs FitzDonald, were supervising the Willacys in the plot."

"For Madam A." Cassie spoke hesitantly. It sounded like something out of the sillier sort of mystery novel, now.

"Who does seem to be a real person. Madam Aylett, we strongly suspect, given the alchemy skill required."

"Madam Aylett." Cassie frowned. "I don't know much about her. Not one of my customers."

Thomas murmured. "Not a nice sort of person, you'd not want her." It made Cassie glance at him, and smile, and she knew Lord Carillon caught it.

"I gather Kate - Captain Lefton - mentioned she'd helped me with a problem last year. I am sure you also heard about the goldwasser parties."

She had, but Cassie had not put two and two together. "That is how you met." She nodded at the Carillons. "That's what she helped with? I think it's fair to say I've heard a fair bit of gossip, but I don't know how much of it is right or real."

"Ah, yes. Well. Madam Aylett was not at the goldwasser parties, but she was addicted to the stuff. And it is quite addictive, more so than a number of other things I've had occasion to try. It made you dream of foreign places, times things were better. A potent drug, in the aftermath of the War to end all Wars."

Cassie felt, not for the first time, that she was glad the War had, in honesty, passed her by as lightly as it had, and also guilty for her luck. "And so she was not pleased when you brought an end to her supply?" If that was how one put it.

"Not at all." Lord Carillon's voice was light, but in a measured tone that felt quite separate from his actual emotions. "Miss Stone, Lizzie's lady's maid, served in one of the households that made it. She recognised that the Fitz-Donalds were providing Madam Aylett's supply."

Cassie frowned. "Miss Stone has unexpected depths."

It made Lady Carillon grin. "Oh, quite. It's why we lured her away." Then she added an additional piece of information. "We have gathered that Madam Aylett and her husband were very much in love, and that his death lead her to the goldwasser. I have some sympathy for that, upper society is rather unkind to the idea of honest affection, I have found."

"With a few notable exceptions." Lord Carillon waved a hand. "There are reasons we see the Edgartons and Leftons frequently. And a few others."

Cassie nodded. "So she - particularly disliked you, your lordship, because you destroyed the goldwasser. It meant she couldn't remember how things were the same way."

"Exactly. We're not sure when she left precisely, but she is not in Albion, the Guard made a, well, a particularly urgent search of her home near Shrewsbury, with all the means at their disposal." Cassie didn't know much, but she knew the Extraordinary Magics were only used in rare cases, being both exceedingly difficult and costly to do, and naturally, a particular invasion of privacy. "Her laboratory, however, was still largely intact. We think she had not time to destroy it before she fled."

"Madam Aylett? I thought it was her husband who was the alchemist."

"He seems, on investigation, to have not been seen by anyone for nearly two years. The Guard has confirmed he is dead, but not yet how or where his body might be."

Cassie winced. That suggested that Madam Aylett was able to play the long game, and quite ruthless. If not ruthless, able to adjust in some ways to her husband's death. And entirely unable to in others, clearly.

Lord Carillon continued, "And she placed some kind of geas, or some other similar magic, on the Willacys and Fitz-Donalds, allowing her to slip away. Mind, she'd have had warning. There are strong suggestions she had a network of, what does one call them, minions? Very pulp novel. Collaborators. What have you." Lord Carillon waved a hand. "More than the Willacys, certainly someone else at the party seeing how their plans worked."

Cassie nodded, piecing it together like she'd make a dress. "So if she had someone else there, they'd have told her, immediately, somehow." She considered. "Is - is this part of the reason Theodora attacked him? Mr Willacy?"

Thomas looked suddenly abashed, flushing. Lord Carillon coughed. "I was not paying sufficient attention, that morning. I trained my lovely empress to alert me, if she caught something magical. She's particularly attuned to it, anyway, and she does like hunting the star hare." A magical subspecies, Cassie knew that, much prized for their fur, among other reasons.

She considered, then said, "And so she - she went at him, because he had something magical?" Her fingers twitched towards her Guild mastery pendant. That must be what Theodora had reacted to in the mews. It must have been.

Lord Carillon looked positively embarrassed. "As far as we can tell, Madam Aylett and someone else came to the folly to distill the poison, from those crates of roots that were stolen. We're not sure who the other person was. The roots themselves wouldn't have alerted anyone, but the distilled poison would have, so they had to make it within the property wards."

Cassie thought that was logical, if really exceedingly risky, and said as much. "And they didn't think anyone would catch them?"

"We think it was during the solstice festival, when near everyone was out of the house, or certainly not wandering around in the garden. It would only take a few hours, and it would be easy enough to hide what they were doing unless someone actually went upstairs in the folly. Someone that skilled - well, she would certainly know half a dozen ways to discourage curiosity."

Cassie was not at all sure she liked the kinds of plots that her customers seemed to get up to. "And then they hid the vial?"

Lady Carillon nodded. "With the stick of elder, so that Mr Willacy could bring it through the house wards. There are all sorts of things permitted on the grounds, but not under the roof, as it were."

That made some sense. "And then he was in charge of - doing something with it. Surely, I mean, had she met them?

If I were picking someone for a plot, that's not who'd I pick. Especially if they might have to think quickly on their feet." Her indignation had finally caught up with her tongue, it seemed.

Lord Carillon laughed, and said, "Quite, quite. No, I agree. It may have been a matter of which of her - let's go with minions - could get an invitation. And Willacy was a tempting target for me to find out more about. He really isn't a very pleasant man."

Lady Carillon said, quietly, "Madam A, Madam Aylett, had a hold over them. Their only surviving son, who needs a particular potion for his War injuries. One her husband invented, and that she controlled."

"Oh." It was hard to entirely hate someone in that sort of bind. "Do we know why she wanted to target you, your lordship? Or was it simply because of the goldwasser?" Not that that was simple at all.

"Geoffrey, please, in private." He was insistent. "That is why it took so long for the trial. They were hoping to find her. Or at least untangle more of the plot. She seems, from what they could find, to have had desires to improve the strength and the - " He stopped, searching for a word.

"The apocalyptic nature of the weapons." Lady Carillon's voice was crisp and sharp.

"That. I can't tell why, I certainly can't read minds. But I have heard a thread of discussion, the idea that the ultimate weapons might deter a future war bogged down in the trenches, tens of thousands of men drowning in blood."

There was a long silence, no one speaking. Thomas cleared his throat, after nearly a minute. "Sir. The other matter?"

"Indeed." Lord Carillon added, "If we find out more, we

will let you know. And do keep your ears out? But that is the summary of what we know now."

She nodded, glancing at Thomas, and then back at the newlyweds.

"The reason the trial was now - even with so many unsatisfyingly loose threads - was of course, our honeymoon. We'll be gone for six weeks, and they were already getting complaints about the delays, even murderers have a right to a prompt trial."

Thomas leaned over and added, "Right to a prompt trial aside, it is most inconvenient when your key witnesses are out of the country."

Lord Carillon snorted. "Quite. So, do you have any questions, before we turn our attention to more pleasant things?"

"Should - should I be worried? Or anyone?"

"Oh, I expect I should be." Lord Carillon sounded blithe about it. "We'll muddle along somehow. Though I do hope you'll accept the provision of a warding specialist to look at your shop and flat thoroughly. Just to make sure all's set as well as it might be?"

There was, really, no polite way to decline. "Of course not, your lordship. Um. Geoffrey."

"And I do hope you can bear without Benton while we're gone, but at least you've a journal, and so does he."

"That will be some help, yes." Not that it would help her nights, occasional as they were at this point, but they had managed before and they would manage now. And it was only for two months or so. Through the winter festivities, some of which she was invited to, and then they'd be looking at something new themselves.

"The new house is coming along nicely. Let's see, we're leaving next Thursday. Could you come out on Monday, and we'll give you the tour? The builders have a few questions."

Cassie nodded. "Thank you, of course, I'll make that work. Three, again?"

"Plenty of time for the discussion, and some tea. And now, I am quite sure you'd like some time while you can get it. Benton, I believe I can do without you tonight and tomorrow night, and also Monday, if you can see to the packing otherwise? Hector is not you, no one could be, but he is certainly capable right now of doing up my cufflinks."

Thomas smiled a little. "His training will take a little time yet, your lordship, but he is indeed most promising." Then he nudged her, gently. "I would like to retreat, Cassie, if we may, and make the most of the evening."

Thomas asking for a thing, that direct, that was a glorious change in him. And of course, she wanted the same. "Mmmmm." She let her pleasure at the promise of a leisurely evening show. "I got your favourite cider in. And," She grinned at him. "A rooster at the market, thought I might make coq au vin tomorrow."

She was sure, then, that Thomas had not told his lordship quite everything about his part of the investigation. She was certain because when Thomas snorted and then broke into laughter, Lord Carillon looked entirely baffled, before he made a shooing gesture with his hand. "I'll see you tomorrow. No sooner than ten."

"Yes, your lordship." Thomas took her hand, and they went out together, down the street and back to her flat as the sun set.

IF YOU ENJOYED *On The Bias* and would like to read more of this series, please sign up for my mailing list to get all the latest news and fun extras. Your reviews (on whatever review site you use) are much appreciated, too!

Find out more about Lizzie and Carillon's meeting in *Goblin Fruit*.

Read on for more historical details about this book and an excerpt from *Seven Sisters* .

AUTHOR'S NOTE

I do hope you've enjoyed *On The Bias*! As always, I owe my editor (Kiya Nicoll) and my early readers a great deal of thanks for making this a much better book. Particular thanks to Kiya for a discussion with a friend that led to my difficult rooster encounter. (Read on for more about that.)

As the copyright page mentions, the version you are currently reading has small revisions from the original, to reconcile the timeline of this book with *Eclipse*, which deals with Professor Fortier. It involved removing a few sentences in chapters 4 and 8 and half a sentence in chapter 36. There are also some small edits for clarity and smoothness.

I knew once I wrote *Goblin Fruit* (the story of how Lord Geoffrey Carillon tripped over Lizzie Penhallow, and they found themselves investigating the mysterious goldwasser drink) that I wanted to know more about Thomas Benton. I was intrigued by his loyalty, his attention to detail, and the fact that he made everything look easy.

Once I started writing, I was fascinated by how informative Benton could be in the right circumstances, compared to Carillon's marked tendency to hold things at a distance. It was a pleasure to figure out more about their adventures and travels, and about how they'd come back to Albion.

And of course, one of the great delights of the 1920s is the clothing, and I'd known for a while I wanted a character who would give me lots of excuses to look at gorgeous dresses. (Check out my blog under the *On The Bias* category for links to more.)

I also had tremendous fun figuring out how magic would enhance or change the process for dressmaking. Cassie uses charms for everything from cutting a pattern and the fabric for the dress to decorative enhancements, to things like cooling charms for people who will insist on wearing Elizabethan gowns on a summer night.

The **apprenticeship** system in Albion gets explored more in this book, since Cassie both served an apprenticeship herself, and has three apprentices. I've based this part of things on an expansion of the mediaeval guild systems.

Nile green was a very popular colour in the 1920s, and it was also a great excuse for an argument, since the Nile really isn't that colour. And of course, Benton knows, he's been to Egypt. He also believes in things being properly labelled. (Arsenic was in fact used to make a variety of green pigments until people discovered it was quite dangerous to the health.) The other colours mentioned are also popular shades around the time of the book.

Life below stairs is a culture all of its own, and now that Ytene has an almost complete staff, it was time to explore a bit more of that. I found *Servants: A Downstairs History of Britain from the Nineteenth Century to Modern Times* by Lucy Lethbridge very helpful reading. (And I admit to having imprinted on the original *Upstairs, Downstairs* as a child...)

The story of how Mally Stone came to be a lady's maid is in *Goblin Fruit,* and it was fun figuring out all the things she needed to learn to keep up with Lizzie and Carillon and their plots (and imminent wedding).

One of the pleasures of writing and editing books the way I do is that I get to introduce characters and ideas for future books while I'm editing. You'll be seeing more of Professors Fortier in *Eclipse,* the third book of the Mysterious Power series, and also more about the mysterious Council (and a lot more about how Schola works). As I write this, I'm writing the first book in that series, so there will be a little bit of a wait.

Cock fights were officially made illegal in England and Wales in 1835, but of course, that didn't actually stop it happening. It's an ancient and rather bloody sport.

My editor, Kiya, was talking to a friend who had been reading machine-translated versions of romance novels, and the technology had decided to translate a particular explicit phrase as "He suddenly had a difficult rooster". Kiya inquired if I might perhaps work that into a book. I'd actually already been looking for what kind of illegal setting Benton might find himself in, searching for more information, so I said "Sure! Cock fight it is!"

More relevant to the plot, while roosters sometimes had metal spurs put on them for cock fighting, they have sharp natural spurs on their legs that can do quite a lot of damage. And since those feet are around quite a lot of farmyard material, the chances for infection are quite high.

I am, as you might have noticed, fond of picking a thematic unity in my books, usually something that occurs three times. (I blame a classical education.) Here, it is a thematic unity of dangerous birds. Which brings us to **swans**.

In 1482 (so, for those of us in Albion, right around the time of the Pact, just before the death of Richard III), the crown decreed that only people who owned land and had a certain income could own swans. Who owned which swan was recorded with a mark on the beak. Over time, it came to be that only the crown and two guilds (the Vintners and Dyers) could own swans, and that for anyone else to do nearly anything with them was treason.

Of course, swans are not easy to manage, and rather dangerous in their own right. Which leads to the sensible question, "Why would you want to do anything with a swan except admire it from a safe distance?" The answer, of course, is the luxury aspect.

Chalice, the cat, is a nod to my own Astra, who is also black and likes to sit in the middle of the bed and take up space. (There are few photos of her I can share, because taking photos of a black cat is tricky.)

Comet vintages (like the 1811 Château d'Yquem) are a particularly interesting bit of wine lore, and I hope to explore this one in more depth at some point in the future. Basically, that's "Wine bottled when there's a comet".

Chinoiserie is the term for a European interpretation and imitation (often rather exoticising) of Chinese and East Asian elements in clothing, furniture, art, and so on. Mostly fashionable in earlier centuries, it still showed up in the 1920s from time to time.

Falconry is an ancient sport of noble households, with a complex history I don't do nearly enough justice to here. It does however get us our third dangerous bird. You might be familiar with eagle-owls (at least as a reference) from the Harry Potter books, since Draco's owl is an eagle-owl. They're quite large birds, and were being used for hunting through the 1920s.

Theodora, for whom the bird is named, was the wife of Justinian I, and empress of the Byzantine empire. Her parents were a bear trainer and a dancer and actress, and various histories (both of her time and later) have all sorts of comments on how someone from that background rose to be empress. They all generally agree she was exceedingly clever, strategically sharp, and very clear about what she thought needed to happen. She also did a great deal to improve rights and opportunities for women.

The bird, of course, is also quite clever and has her own ideas about what should be happening.

At the masked ball, Molière was a famous play-wright, actor, and poet, and generally considered one of the greatest writers in the French language. Carillon and Lizzie pick him and one of his leading ladies because he did a great deal to publicise the Commedia dell'Arte form of drama. (Their meeting in *Goblin Fruit* explains why.)

Giles Lefton is costumed as Nicholas Saunderson, a famous 18th century blind mathematician. He was good friends with Isaac Newton, Edmond Halley, and others. I admit, though, this costume choice was largely so I could put Kate in a dress she'd find difficult to deal with. 18th century panniers are a feat of complex engineering, and entirely change the way you have to walk.

The potion that Benton has obtained comes from Mariam, who is mentioned very briefly in *Magician's Hoard*

- she and Ibis knew each other in Cairo. (Perhaps sometime I'll write more about her. She clearly is mistress of some complex magics.)

The books in chapter 38 reflect the range of reading available. I had originally intended the mystery novel to be *Clouds of Witness*, but after reconciling a couple of time-lines, this book is in 1925, not 1926 (when the Sayers book came out).

The translation of Herodotus quoted here is from the Loeb Classical Library edition by A.D. Godley (Harvard University Press, 1920-1925, now all in the public domain) and available in various places online if you're curious about most of it.

When I was taking Greek, we spent a semester on Herodotus, where I discovered that if he is talking about people's customs, and you don't know a vocabulary word, it probably is a kind of food. If it is a battle, that verb you don't know probably means "to attack". He's been a favourite ever since.

One final note about **Benton**. As I wrote this book (and especially in editing) it became clear to me (and Kiya, as my editor) that he is autistic. Autism presents in a wide variety of ways, but Benton is someone for whom the sometimes rigid structure of service has been reassuring, much more than limiting. Learning to navigate the kinds of changes Cassie presents is rather more of a challenge. He would not self-identify that way, of course, since the naming of autism is some years in the future, but he certainly knows how he works best and lives most happily.

Ancient Trust, a prequel novella available when you sign up for my mailing list (https://www.celialake.com/newsletter/) tells the story of Lord Geoffrey Carillon inheriting the land magic. It alternates between Carillon and Benton's points of view, and introduces a number of their more intimate social circle.

You can read more about Lord Geoffrey Carillon further adventures (with an appearance by both Benton and Cassie) in *Best Foot Forward*, which takes place in 1935.

As always, if you have any questions about my books, please feel free to contact me through my website at http://celialake.com or any of the social media connections you find there. You can also find more about upcoming books and other tidbits there.

www.ingramcontent.com/pod-product-compliance
Lightning Source LLC
Chambersburg PA
CBHW022005050726
47499CB00002BA/364